I0702417

HANGTOWN

BY MICHAEL BAILEY

HANGTOWN © 2023 by Michael Bailey

Cover design by Ben Baldwin
Illustrations by Mar Garcia
Interior design by Michael Bailey

"The Elephant" first appeared as a short story in *Blood in the Soil, Terror on the Wind* by Brigids Gate Press, edited by Kenneth W. Cain and Chad Lutzke, © 2022.

"Diggin Ghosts" (poem, a few stanzas used herein) first appeared in *Softing the Ashes* by Crystal Lake Publishing, © 2022.

"Bleeding Cowboys" font created by Guillaume Séguin and Roger S. Nelsson, used with permission.

No part of this work may be reproduced or transmitted in any form or by any means, electronic or mechanical, including photocopying, scanning, recording, broadcast or live performance, or duplication by any information storage or retrieval system without permission, except for the inclusion of brief quotations with attribution in a review or report. Requests for reproductions or related information should be addressed to written@nettirw.com.

The following is fiction based on historical events, with some of the names and locations factual. All original characters, products, corporations, institutions, and/or entities of any kind in this book are either products of the author's twisted imagination or, if real, used fictitiously without intent to describe actual characteristics.

Published by Written Backwards
www.nettirw.com

ISBN: 979-8-9867488-8-7 / Hardback Edition
ISBN: 979-8-9867488-9-4 / Paperback Edition

For Janice, my mother, who brought me to life in Hangtown.

The following is based on a true story.

HANGTOWN

Bury me 'neath a tree,
When I am dead:
Let birds chirp merrily
O'er my head.
No monumental stone
Raise o'er my tomb—
Let it be marked alone
By the sweet bloom
Of flowers, bright and fair,
By Love's dear hand
In memory planted there,
By soft winds fann'd.
And let no willow weep
Above my tomb;
I could not sweetly sleep
Beneath its gloom;—
And let no tear be shed
When I am gone,
Nor breathe for her that's dead
One sorrowing tone.

No somber weeds be worn
By those I love—
I would not have them mourne,
But look above,
Where 'mid a seraph throng—
Celestial—bright:
My soul shall dwell among
Angels of light.
And man—exalted man:
Image of God,
Seek wisdom whilst thou can,
E'en from the sod
That covers my poor clay—
The Chrysalis—
From which the spirit may
Ascend to bliss.
Think kindly too of me,
When I am gone;
And let sweet charity
Judge me alone.

– Olivia

AUTUMN
1848

THE DREAMING TREE

A canopy of near-bare branches from the great oak shades Huata's body under moonlight, a Miwok girl no older than thirteen; under its open arms she rests, having finished her autumn acorn-gathering, her wide-pupil eyes reflecting starlight death.

Aside the girl lies her woven basket, toppled. She made it herself, a tradition passed on from one generation to the next, the weave tight enough to hold water. The collected food, spilled and forgotten, will feed the nocturnal in the late hours and the crepuscular as the sun ascends to replace night with day. Her body will cool, even under its warmth.

The girl's mother, praying words in a Penutian dialect, waits patiently in their kotcha a half-days' walk away if directly following the crooked dry creek behind the tree. Through the gap in a hide covering, she peeks out their tule- and bark-covered abode. The shelter will not last the winter, she realizes, but it's a home for now—her home, at least, for the conical structure points skyward like the toes and face of her daughter unbeknownst.

The girl's father is on the hunt and will not return until days after she is discovered. As one life expires, so does another. Instead of final words to his first-born, he offers gratitude to an expiring buck. He thanks the creature for its sacrifice, which will provide both nourishment and clothing for his family and tribe. He smiles, thinking of his daughter at the mortar and pestle grinding acorns into flour, for she's prone to make a mess—as he had with the deer. A single arrow brought the animal to the ground, but its death had taken longer than any creature should have to suffer. He'd tracked its blood in the tallgrass for hours to find its panting body.

Two men pull blades simultaneously from the dead.

The dreaming tree drops leaves over the girl's body with each wind sigh. If the oak can no longer feed the girl, it can at least hide her from future harm. Soundlessly, an owl glides through the air, lands on its largest branch where ropes will eventually dangle, and scowls curiously at the aftermath; the same owl had watched over the deer.

And the man who took the girl's life, and so much more, he stares upon the young Miwok. A hand shakes, covered in blood, the other curled as though mimicking the smaller hands of the oak. Ghost fingers splay around the young girl's neck, which haunt him now, and will continue in his dreams until his dying day. The miner's hands are heavily callused from pickaxe and spade, from pushing 'barrows full of rock. Hands strong enough to roll barrel-sized chunks of earth from the ground have crushed her windpipe, yet are unable to muffle her final cries, hence the knife. He wipes the blade on the grass and openly weeps.

What have you done? he wonders.

But he knows what he's done; this is the fifth time he's taken innocence from a child, although the first at taking a life. He helps the tree by raking its fallen brown-yellow leaves over the body, covers her whole. Even so, the night breathes heavy to uncover what he's done.

"You did this to me," he tells Hauta.

He doesn't know her name, and for a moment expects her to reply, but everything she'd said prior had been lost between his fingers, spoken in distressed foreign tongue. *Injin gibberish*, he'd thought, then. *Savages, they are only savages,* he assures himself now.

The miner tries closing eyes that continue to plea beyond death, but his fingers stripe her face in red war paint, black to the night, the blood perhaps cursed. The young Miwok's eyes refuse to stay closed, reopening with their wet reflections, boring into his soul.

WINTER
1849

THREE IN PENDULUM

PROSPER

Cailloux traded in cycles of wares, buying deer- and bearskin from the indigenous and selling to shivering miners unable to communicate with those not of their own dirt-swathed shade. He had learned enough of the ancient tongue to manage transactions between the ever-dwindling number of Maidu and Miwok, knew various words for food, water, for "white man," for bear, deer, and even spirit, the last of which often blurred between the dead or the drink.

January winter covered the diggings in a layer of what appeared to be ash, for everything the snow touched rested on filth, and could as well be mixed with burnt wood for all the stove fires that alighted after the sun fell below the horizon. It was frosty enough out for the snow to stick, Cailloux figured, yet not enough so to stop the flakes from absorbing clay-dust and rust.

In warmer times, his trading post dealt in loomed rugs and reed baskets, also provided by the natives, as well as in canvas tarps and stakes and provisions often traded to and from other local merchants. But for now, his business was warmth, and business was good.

Before closing, Cailloux made one last transaction with a woman old enough to be a great-grandmother, not that she gave him much of a choice in the matter. Her braided gray-black hair draped over one shoulder, nearly touched her knees. He'd traded with her before, many times, and felt ashamed for not knowing her name. Colorful bands of orange and turquoise spiraled around the single lock, which she'd decorated with beads and feathers.

She insisted he take the bearskin from her back. He couldn't imagine her without it, walking through the snow, back to wherever home may be, possibly miles from Log Cabin Ravine. But even as she removed the beautiful skin, she seemed senseless to the cold, didn't shiver as he found himself doing quite violently.

"You," she said and pointed, "for you."

She pushed the thing into Cailloux's arms before he could resist. The thick fur was not from that of a black bear, but a grizzly, still warm from her own body heat, and the leather on its opposite side well-cured. The woman then pointed to the heavens and smiled, flattened her hand to catch snowflakes and watched as they dissolved.

"I can't take this from you," he said, thinking of all that had been taken from her people over the years. Looked down upon, spat on, mistreated, slaughtered. Her skin the same shade as his when burnt by the sun. In his travels from the bay to the mountains, he'd witnessed an entire village burned to the ground, and now couldn't help but think again of the snowfall as ash.

"No," he said.

Cailloux pushed the fur back to her, but she pushed back with astounding strength. The old woman then said some words in her language he couldn't decipher and turned away.

"Wait," he said, and from his pouch grabbed a handful of coins, an uncounted mix of half-cents and half-dimes, perhaps a few bits each worth twelve-and-a-half cents.

She shook her head no, but he grabbed her wrist and turned over her hand and forced the coins upon her, feeling guilty. Here he was, like everyone else, forcing his ways upon her. He could see that much in her eyes, that she felt sorry for him.

"White man," she said in English.

"I'm sorry," he said, releasing his grip. "Food for you and your family. The money, I mean. I can't just *take* this from you." He then used a word from her language: *trade*.

The old woman smiled again, as flat as any smile can get. Her next words were foreign and songlike. A prayer, perhaps. She turned, dropped the coins on the ground, walked away.

"*J'espère qu'un jour nous trouverons la paix*," he said.

IN the last few months, rainfall had been as sparse as the men working the earth, and so Weber Creek snaked through the land waterless and mostly abandoned, whereas in the months prior men stood nearly shoulder-to-shoulder. There were some, sure, who still put in long hours prospecting and attempting to pull gold from the ground, but most had given up, comfortable wasting away small fortunes on gambling and women while waiting for the next hard rain, which made working the placer deposits much easier. A ghost town of long toms and thirsty canvas water hoses and tired men. Mining equipment lay discarded everywhere, forgotten.

He thought of his wife, buried back home in Bourges, France.

Cailloux had stopped his own efforts at mining. He hadn't "struck it rich," as he had hoped, and as some were wont to say; no, not by any means, but he had done well for himself. Had fifty ounces of gold in the form of dust and flakes as savings. He kept it hidden below his bedroll in the cabin he'd painstakingly built the summer he'd first setup camp in the diggings. But he was a careful man, or so he thought. A businessman. At any given time, he kept on his person only enough gold and coin to get him through the day, for the threat of desperados was always on the back of his mind, a band known as the "Owls."

Hiboux dans le chêne, he thought.

They sometimes went by a longer moniker, "Owls in the Oak Tree," but more commonly were referred to as Owls, for short. They had tendencies to waylay and murder prospectors travelling to and from mining camps along the many forks of the American River, into which the Weber eventually dumped its waters, which fed into the Sacramento, and finally the Pacific Ocean. Whether or not such men would come so far north in the taciturn winter was not worth the risk of ever finding out.

Better alive and poor than wealthy and dead.

The creek would return from the dead soon, he knew, as it had the year prior. January through late February would bring snowfall to higher elevations in the Sierra Nevadas, and heavy rainfall through March, meaning snowmelt and new life to the streams. Once again, the change in weather would bring a boom back to business, a need for provisions other than fur. Men would then need replacement equipment for that which they discarded or had otherwise left out to ruin by way of the changing seasons.

Cailloux, who the bar-keep at the Placer Hotel often called the "Frenchman," as was custom to address a man where he was from, spent his nights at cards and other games to pass the time. During the day he ran his trading post in the center of the mining establishment, so most of the men he saw each night were customers or otherwise familiar faces. He broke even in his gambling, mostly, careful not to lose large amounts to chance, despite a good hand or a string of luck. Drinks were cheap there, the women a buck or two.

He'd seen enough men lose all they owned on a single night of misfortune and drunken stupidity, though, so he paced himself, as he had planned to do this night. Once he'd seen a man squander a few hundred in gold. Not many were smart enough not to go broke. Most drank so hard they'd wake the following morning still in chairs, draped over unfinished card games, a bit lighter in the purse. Indoors was mostly safe, despite one's consciousness, however, for everyone had on him a weapon. Even Cailloux carried a small pepperbox pistol.

"Frenchman!" said the bar-keep.

Cailloux tipped his hat, sat on one of the wooden stools.

Without asking what drink he wanted, a ladle of whiskey was poured into a glass and slid across the counter, and the Frenchman slid back a coin, what the Americans liked to call "a short bit." He thought of the woman as she'd dropped the coins as though worthless. Maybe without using any words she spoke some truth.

In his lap he held the thick grizzly fur, fingers running through it.

A hand then slapped onto his shoulder from behind, and if he weren't lost in thought just then he may have thrown a punch or reached for the pepperbox, but the man was only a drunkard with hot breath. Like the indigenous woman, he recognized the face, but didn't know the name.

The young man sang part of a tune in a lightly Irish accent and couldn't have been more than eighteen or nineteen years old. His hair burned red atop his head and over his lips, his cheeks covered in peppercorn scruff. About as drunk as any man can get before passing out or losing one's meal, he figured. Cailloux had seen the young man running the monte table, remembered him as having an easy-trigger temper. Swore more words than reasonable ones.

"You're the Frenchman," the Irishman said, "that's what he called you."

"Who?"

"The bar-keep."

Oui, je suppose que je le suis.

"Yes, I suppose I am," Cailloux said.

"Come, join us," the man slurred. "We need another in our game."

Cailloux let out a sigh, sipped his drink. The last thing he wanted to do was sit with this man. Perhaps if he stayed silent, the man would leave. But that wasn't in his fortune.

"One game," the Irishman said, "and fill this man's drink!" he called out to the bar-keep, slapping a coin down hard. "S'on me. Ay?"

~

ONE game of Three-card Monte turned into five, and then six, same as the one drink turned into five, and then six. Soon an entire table laughed as money passed back and forth across the table, a mix of men from different countries enjoying each other's company.

Cailloux quickly learned the Irishman's name: Richard Crone. The young man moved cards as though he had done so all his life, and slurred in rhymes thick with accent, mostly as a distraction technique. Next to him sat a fair-skinned man, possibly American, and around the rest of the table a Spaniard who Richard kept calling *Manuel*, whether or not that was his name, as well as two other Frenchmen: Bissi and Garcia, he'd soon learned, who spoke not a word of English. Cailloux translated, if needed, which wasn't often for the simplicity of the game.

The Irishman set out three cards face-up: a three with gold discs, a five of clubs, and a horseman or knight of some kind. He tapped the horse, the "money card," then flipped all three over to their backs. The goal was to keep track of the money card during some quick sleight-of-hand shuffling. The American went first, offering a hefty coper coin, a half-cent.

Richard Crone mocked the small bet and downed half his glass and sang obscenely, tossing one card over the next, over the next, over the next, until they appeared as a blur, lost in the dance of his hands. The alcohol helped with his trick. After the cards purposefully slowed and came to a stop, Cailloux suspected the middle of the three, the one the American eventually pointed to, but when flipped over, the horseman or knight had magically become the five.

"Try again, won't you?"

The American did, won the next two rounds, and then others started pushing coins across the table for their turn.

"One at a time, gents," Richard Crone said, "*ceann ag an am.*"

Cailloux had never heard a Gaelic tongue quite like his.

Each took his turn at the seemingly simple game. The wagers started off small, not a lot of money finding its way on the table, but the bets grew progressively larger. Some were in coin, others in gold, and others in later-fulfilled promises to buy the next round.

Cailloux played three hands in a row, lost one, won two, which started the routine of each player allowed three games before the next. Three-card Monte, in cycles of three.

Winning and losing spread evenly between players over a few drinks' worth of light gambling, but after the tables suddenly turned in favor of the dealer, claimed "Irish luck," the Spaniard mumbled "*Cambiar las cartas*," under his breath and slammed his fist down.

It was understood, by this point, that Richard Crone couldn't speak a lick of Spanish, nor any other language, much like the two Frenchman; despite that, both men laughed.

"What 'e say?" Richard Crone asked. "What am I missin' you find so funny?" He then said words no man right in the head could possibly comprehend.

No one said anything because of the fire behind the young man's eyes, until Cailloux calmly explained similarities between the French and Spanish language: "*En français*, what he said," Cailloux said, "in French, sounds much like '*changer les cartes*,' or 'change cards.' I believe he's suggesting you're cheating and should swap these out."

"*Vous cachez des cartes!*" the smaller Frenchman said.

The other agreed, saying the same.

"In got-damned English," the Irishman said.

The American adjusted himself, spat on the floor.

"Cheating," Cailloux translated. "You hide cards."

"I'm no cheater! Look, you want new cards?" he said, tossing them over his head. The three of hearts fluttered down and landed on his shoulder, which he brushed off. The man had a short fuse, no doubt. He took three new cards from the shoddy deck, from the top: a king holding a sword, a nine with a crease in one corner, and a two of clubs.

"*Pas celui là!*" the other Frenchman said, pointing at the nine.

"Not that one," Cailloux said.

Richard Crone's face turned a shade redder as the nine made its way to the floor. He then shuffled the remaining cards, fanned them out in front of the accusatory fingers. "Choose one," he said, "damned cards don' matter."

"*Vous choisissez la carte,*" Cailloux translated to his fellow Frenchmen.

"*Yo elijo,*" said Manuel.

THE game went on for another few rounds of drinks, and by then the American had bowed out, taking his losses, though he stayed around to watch in a half-stupor. Cailloux had won a decent amount before calling it a night, which frustrated the young Irishman.

"You got a quick eye," Richard Crone said. "You win this next time, Frenchie, and I buy us all a round, what say you?"

"I'll wager that," the American said, sliding in a bet on his behalf.

"I can't argue with that," Cailloux said.

At this point, he could barely see the cards, and in a matter of a single slow blink the three cards began rolling over each other. The king was the money card this time and started in the middle, and he followed it one over the next, up and over, over and up, but his head spun from the drink so hard that he blinked another slow blink and it was gone, lost in the shuffle. The cards slowed, whether in his mind or by the dealer's hand.

Cailloux eyed the one in the middle, hesitated over the one on the right.

"Well?" Richard Crone asked.

"That one," Cailloux said, pointing at the rightmost card.

"You sure 'bout that?"

He wasn't. Could be the middle. Could be the leftmost. His hand moved over each, settled over his original decision, then tapped the middle card instead. And when flipped over, there he was, the king in all his glory. One-in-three odds, a complete guess.

"*Chance des français*," Cailloux said, which got his fellow Frenchmen to smirk.

The young man changed color again, fast as ever.

"Tell me what tha' means or I'll open yer throat," he said.

"French luck," Cailloux said.

"Bar-keep," the American said, overly loud, although those at their table were the majority of customers this late hour. "A round a' whiskeys over here. Put it on Irish Dick's tab. And pour 'em plenty! We're having ourselves a good time, here."

The Spaniard looked uneasy until the drinks arrived, as if waiting for everyone to draw upon each other and fire, ending the night early.

Cailloux cheered his audience and they drank.

"No more monte for me," he said.

"Time to earn mine back, then," Richard Crone said. "*Manuel*, you're in, *sí*? That's how you say it in Mexican, idn't it: *¿uno más?*"

The Spaniard man slid across another coin, a full two bits, downed the rest of his glass, and the cards took off in a frenzy longer than normal. When they slowed and stopped, he pointed with confidence at the middle card.

"Sorry, *señor*, maybe next time," the young man said.

The jack of diamonds flipped over, and with that, the Spaniard was out.

That left the two Frenchmen, Bissi and Garcia, who could pass for brothers, and were determined more than ever to win the damn game. They had mostly broken even in their playing, and whether by Richard Crone's design or by pure coincidence, the next eight games went two wins, two losses, two wins, two losses. Their bets increasing each time. They were due another win, and parleyed *en français*, which Cailloux eavesdropped while in his own half-drunken conversation with the American, who was the whitest man he'd ever seen.

C'est notre victoire, maintenant ou jamais.

Et si on perd?

Nous ne le ferons pas.

And they were right, Cailloux realized. The odds were in their favor. Now was their chance to strike and to strike hard. He'd bet high if he were in their boots. They wouldn't lose, or so the odds predicated.

"What are they sayin'?" asked the American.

The room quieted as the smaller one, Garcia, untied a pouch from his belt, then tossed it on the table. The sound was enough to make anyone curious to look inside. Richard Crone broke that curiosity, then stepped back after cursing to himself, then added some words in Gaelic.

"That's a lot a' dust," he said. "A lot a' dust."

"Yer kiddin' me," said the American, leaning forward.

"Gold?" Cailloux said. He warned them in their shared secret tongue not to bet so high, saying in so many words, "I have more than that stashed in my cabin, and no way in hell would I ever risk it like that, even with your odds."

"Speak so we can all understand or don't speak at all," the dealer said.

Who would bet such an amount?

Cailloux hadn't realized until now that the entire game could in fact be a charade, a hustle, young Richard Crone playing the long con to these men. Was his shock at seeing all that gold dust an act? He thought back of his own winnings, which wasn't much, all considered. Had the Irishman fought to get them all drunk, with this the ultimate end-game?

No, he thought, *no man would do that to another.*

But then he thought again of the old Miwok woman who'd given him the bearskin not more than a few hours ago, before he nearly drank himself to black. He thought of all the bad things man could do to fellow man, woman and child. Ashamed, he considered the coins he'd offered her in exchange, how she had let them fall through her fingers into the snow. What were they worth, really, if he, Prosper Cailloux, were willing to waste them all in a game of chance?

Not chance. A manipulation.

If Richard Crone accepted the bet and won, he'd win the entire amount and the two Frenchmen would leave empty-handed, but if he accepted the bet and lost, he'd have to match whatever that bag contained, and would either have to give up the gold or his life.

Cailloux spoke as quickly as he could to the older of the two, "*Je sais combien de temps il faut pour collecter un tel montant, car je l'ai fait moi-même. Quelque chose ne va pas avec ce jeune homme*," and then realized doing such a thing wasn't so wise, for he was then warned.

"I will not hesitate to cut out yer tongue," Richard Crone said. Out front of him was a long bowie knife, which he'd produced with remarkable speed for one so drunk.

The American put a hand on his sidearm.

Manuel, if that was his name, scooched back his chair.

Richard Crone leaned forward, waved the long blade in front of Cailloux and said rather calmly, "I swear, Frenchman, I will gut you inside and out if you don't tell me now what you just told yer friends here. You know each other, don't ya—"

"No," he said. "I said I wouldn't if I were them."

"All those fancy words just for that?"

"French is an obscenely lengthy language."

"That may be, but it's not yer decision to make, now is

it. Ask them if they're serious about this bet. If I catch any hint a' meanin' otherwise, you will taste this blade."

"*Il aimerait savoir si votre pari est sérieux*," Cailloux added, and for the Irishman's sake, addressing him, "I told them you would like to know if their bet is serious."

Bissi and Garcia both stood, eyed the cards like hawks.

"*Pouvez-vous le faire correspondre*," said the older one.

"Can you match it?" Cailloux translated.

"Ay," said the Irishman. "And if I don't, they can have my life."

The cards danced one last time across the table after a few more words, the horseman starting on the far right this time, as Cailloux and the others at the table concentrated on the money card. Richard Crone didn't even look at the cards at first, simply shuffled them and stared the men down, and when the cards slowed to a stop, Cailloux was certain the horseman had returned to the middle, though the redheaded fellow was rather sly with the hand.

Bissi conferred with his partner, or brother, and they whispered only to each other. The younger of the two nodded, then pointed at the middle card.

Richard Crone flipped over the only black card.

"You just got broke."

AN inch of snow had fallen when Cailloux and the American staggered out of the Placer Hotel together. There was no confrontation over the exchange of funds, as he had expected from the weapons drawn. Even the bar-keep seemed uneasy, perhaps had a longrifle ready. The two Frenchmen simply swore *en français* and spat onto the table before they left, and the Spaniard followed, everyone going their separate ways. Morning might have turned over by the time Cailloux stumbled into his cabin, lit a fire, curled within the bearskin, and fell into dream.

HE was out for only a few hours and half-dazed in an imaginary encounter with a band of Owls when his breathing came to a stop. Someone's hand covered his nose and mouth, forcing his eyes open in a suffocating moment of panic. A black bandanna covered the face in front of him, but he recognized those boring eyes and shade of skin. Richard Crone had called him Manuel.

"Make no outcry on pain of instant death," someone said behind him. "You unnerstand?" said the voice. "Promise not to scream and he won't slit yer throat. Blink if you unnerstand."

He did so as the desperado let go. The only noise Cailloux made was a gasp for air. Once he had a few breaths, a blade pressed hard against his neck, enough to draw blood and sting. The kerchiefed man's face pulled back from his own, revealing the revolver in his opposite hand, the open mouth of the barrel pointed at Cailloux's gut. Both his hands were steady.

"Say not a word and you'll live through this."

He recognized the slightly-sobered voice. He'd known him only as the American, a dirty miner who dressed like most in the diggings, thick beard and handlebar mustache, one who could easily blend within a crowd in his layers of sweat and mud-dust. He had never learned the man's name, never thought to ask. Might as well not even exist if not for his words.

Prosper Cailloux took in his small and now crowded cabin. Two other men stood guard at his door, the Frenchmen who'd lost their gold: Bassi and Garcia.

Richard Crone, is he a part of this?

"Almost thought you was a grizzly when we opened yer door," the American said. "Scarred the tar outta us, nearly got you shot afore any of this." The man could barely stand he was so inebriated, but that didn't stop him from rummaging through his provisions, the entire room tossed. He sweat heavily, despite the cold.

"Where you keep it," the man said, "the gold."

"Gold?" Cailloux said and was slapped hard.

"The dust you blabbered on about."

A soft golden glow filled the room, but not from the woodstove, which still offered warmth as snow and a chilly breeze swept through the open door of the cabin; instead, the room was alight by a flickering candle the American held in front of him, which caused desperado shadows to dance over the walls, for that's what these men were: Owls.

"It'll be light out soon," the American said, "maybe a few hours. If you want to see the sun again, tell us where you keep it. Where is it?"

The Spaniard leaned in close again, said "*Déjame destripar al cobarde, o al menos déjame dispararle*," but the language was lost to him.

Whatever he said wasn't pleasant; that much was certain.

"Not if he complies," said the American. "The man wants to gut you like a deer," he said. "Tell us where you keep it and I won't let that happen, and we'll be on our way. Easy as that."

A hand slapped across his face again, bringing heat.

The candle nearly went out.

"You got three seconds or I let this man do as he pleases."

Prosper Cailloux, still waking, tried to make sense of it all. He considered his options, considered his future or lack thereof. His trading post was a profitable business, but his gold, what was that worth to him? *Pourquoi avais-je ouvert ma putain de bouche?* he self-chastised. Yes, he'd brought this all on himself, had opened his mouth, the whiskey making him stupid. The men at the saloon had gone their separate ways after, but there was always the consideration that they had all conspired against him. Not that it mattered now.

"Three," the American said. "Two—"

"It's under me," Cailloux pleaded. "*Sous moi, sous mois!*"

"Under you?"

This drew their interest. Both Frenchmen looked over their shoulders, then, and the youngest stepped inside the cabin while the eldest kept watch.

Three sets of anxious eyes.

With his palms held to the ceiling. Cailloux shifted his weight and moved to the side. Before he was off completely, the American turned up the corner of his bedroll.

"Clever," he said.

Beneath where he slept each night, Cailloux had loosened four wood planks that helped compose his floor, and within a cavity he'd dug in the earth, hid a small chest that contained his savings. Fifty ounces or so of dust and flakes. He'd panned the considerable amount of gold the year before his claim at the creek had all but depleted of the yellow metal; ten times what the two Frenchmen had wagered on their final bet.

The cabin was well-crowded, so the Spaniard took another corner of the bedroll and pulled it outside, tossed it awkwardly in the snow.

By the time he returned, Cailloux's secret was exposed.

The American whistled, said, "Bissi, come look'it this."

And then there were four sets of eyes staring upon him and his stash of gold, all aglow like the flame of the candle, each with a look of a once-good man gone mad with fever.

"I think you just got yerself broke."

A fist slammed into his jaw, then the bridge of his nose, another in his chest, and suddenly a melee of snowclad boots kicked him bloody and unconscious.

A smokey-orange sun gave birth to the morning as roosters called out worship. The clouds had all but dispersed by the time Cailloux was able to stand, the snow already melting. A cling of picks rang out against rock in the distance. The next storm would be worse, he knew, with miners getting in final labor before the worst of winter was upon them.

They'd taken it all, even the grizzly fur, his provisions, everything worth taking. He woke piecing the night together and pulled out a tooth, shivering. If he had a mirror, a well-beaten and hideous man would stare back. They'd left him alive though, barely, a miracle in itself.

Luckily, he hadn't frozen solid overnight. His fire had gone out, his door left open, and one of the desperados had taken the boots from off his feet. He quickly warmed his blue toes for fear of frostbite and made make-shift shoes from shreds of canvas and rope.

Make no outcry on pain of instant death …

Those words haunted deep, same as the indigenous woman's last expression had burned into his mind. Her grizzly fur, a gift to the "white man" trader: stolen.

Cailloux imagined her walking through the storm in her moccasins, not much on her but decorative clothing, not even shivering, and as he thought of her, he made another small fire in the stove, for at least they'd left him wood. He warmed himself until the shaking stopped.

You have a trading post to run, he told himself, *et chanceux d'être en vie.*

He was indeed lucky to be alive.

CAILLOUX made enough before noon to purchase food and bandages. He wrapped himself in layers of wool and deerskin as he worked his trading post, everyone asking what had happened. Mauled by a bear, perhaps, for that's how he probably appeared on the outside, how he felt on the inside. Anger soon ate away at his stomach. It was his own foolishness, his own idiocy that had let the events of the night and early morning transpire. And so, he starting telling his customers the truth of what had happened in the saloon and what had happened after.

Robbed by four, he recounted: an American, a Spaniard,

two Frenchmen. Held at both knife- and gun-point in his own home by desperados in the diggings. He gave their descriptions, if only so they could be more cautious and not follow in his footsteps. Miners began to believe his unbelievable tale, worried for their own safety, for the wretched Owls had yet to come so far north and were still rumored to roam closer to the soon-to-be roiling American River.

"What he look like, that American?"

"I seen that Mexican feller."

"Those two Frenchmen, Bissi and Garcia? I know of 'em. Name like Garcia, not sure he's even French. They setup camp by what's left of that injin villiage 'bout two miles northwest'a here."

"Talk to the saloon keeper," Cailloux was told. "Tell him what happened."

It took everything he had to walk into the Placer Hotel that afternoon, and it took three other men to offer their company, picks slung over shoulders. For all he knew, those who'd jumped him could have returned to the Placer Hotel, awaiting such an encounter. But the place was empty at such an hour, all but for the owner and a young boy no older than ten mopping what no one wants to mop off a floor. The keeper of the establishment listened, and later recounted the tale to some of his friends who had business on Log Cabin Ravine.

Everyone knew everyone in the diggings.

"These criminals are in no haste to leave," the saloon keeper said to Cailloux. "They came back early this morning, in fact, threated me with certain death if I disclosed anything about the matter. Richard Crone may have been hustling both you and those men the other night, but it seems *they* in fact worked you. Crone's not a part of it, no. He's a hot-head gambler, sure, but he's no *Owl*. Probably not even old enough to know what it is to be a part of such a group. Doubt he'd heard of 'em other than rumor."

Word quickly spread from miner to miner, until the affair was well-noised about, and within hours a mob had gathered. An alarm sounded, of sorts, if only figuratively. Vigilantes popped out of nowhere and everywhere all at once, those with sidearms and pistols and longrifles and scatterguns and blades and other weaponry scouring the creek and camps in search of the men who went by their descriptions. Those who mined in the diggings would have none of it.

"Ex-convicts," one man said of the two Frenchmen.

"Don't know his name, but know his face," one said of the American.

"This place needs law."

"We're as good as any law."

"Those men need to be dealt swift justice."

The bickering went on and on among those involved in tracking them down, and within a few hours two men were brought to the center of the main thoroughfare, dragged by their feet: the Spaniard, still wearing the black bandanna around his neck, and the American, whose belt had come loose during his struggles, pants gathered around his ankles; he wore a familiar pair of boots, and had the bearskin wrapped around him, which he clutched to as if naked beneath. The two were found together, it was said, exactly where it was supposed. A short time later the eldest of the two Frenchmen was dragged among them, the youngest nowhere to be found.

Three of the four.

"These the men who did this to you?" someone asked Cailloux.

In a daze, he nodded. The chaos had erupted so fast.

"There's a fourth," Cailloux said, "another Frenchman. Could be this one's younger brother, maybe a cousin, for they have the same eyes and brow."

"Where's your brother," someone said, threatening with a hammer.

"*Où est ton frère?*" Cailloux translated.

"*Je n'ai pas de frère*," the man said, and spat.

The man who asked the question spat back, in his face.

"He says he doesn't have a brother," Cailloux said.

"What about *him?*" another said, pointing the tip of a pickaxe at the only man who pleaded to be set free, mumbling about rights and fairness and whatnot.

"I'm not a part'a this," the American cried, his voice creaking. "I don't know these men, yer mistaken," he said, and other such lies.

No one believed a word of it.

The Spaniard understood nothing spoken to him. He stood in silence, until the stock-end of a longrifle punched into his stomach and bent him over. He crumpled to his knees, the air taken from him. Cailloux understood the feeling, not so empathetic. Seeing his fate, the first of the two Frenchmen, Bissi, knelt on his own.

Cailloux walked up to the American and punched him in the face, stripped off the boots, which were his, and also the bearskin. The shivering man fell to his knees in what was left of the snow. He was bare-chested, pants still at his feet. Every joint of his shone red amid the white.

"These belong to me," Cailloux said to the crowd, "part of what they stole." He sat in front of the American, unwrapped the canvas and rope from around his own feet, and put on the boots. "And so is this," he said, wrapping himself within the grizzly pelt.

They had beaten him unconscious, had taken everything.

"*Où est l'or!*" he screamed into the man's face

The American only cowered, cold.

"Where's the gold?"

"We found one of these on each of the accused," one of the miners said. He held out three smaller bags of gold dust. "Each weighed the same. Each about twelve-and-a-half ounces. We weighed 'em. And this." He held out a larger empty bag. They musta split equally, four-way."

"Where's the rest?" Cailloux asked. "*Où est le reste?*" He put the three bags into the larger one, then addressed Bissi. "*Où est Garcia? Dites-moi, ou vous et les autres mourrez.*"

"*Que voulez-vous dire?*" the man said and smiled.

"What he say?" someone asked.

"Nonsense."

ALL three men were stripped of their clothes, all but their skivvies. Another man caught for various crimes was added to the line-up and likewise embarrassed. There were perhaps a hundred or more in the crowd. Cailloux would forever remember the date: January 20th. With no judge present over law, a jury was chosen among citizens, and it was sentenced that each of the three robbers would receive thirty-nine lashings apiece, their punishments to be issued the following morning. The other was charged the same, no matter his crimes.

Richard Crone was sought after for questioning, but the interrogators found no fault in his doings. He still had on him his winnings from the night prior and took much shaking to wake from his drunken slumber. Apparently, after he'd gone home for the night, he'd finished half a skin of whiskey or other such spirit. For all Cailloux knew, the Irishman could have been next to have his gold stolen, for he was none too quiet about his winnings.

The man had a mouth.

With three-quarters of his savings returned, and the men apprehended, Cailloux could breathe easier. What he had was still a large sum of gold dust and flakes for a person to own, but he hoped the fourth quarter would turn up, along with the missing Frenchman, who, by now, had most likely run. He was not found by nightfall, presumed gone. And no law presided to dish out a warrant for his arrest.

SUNDAY morning, the 21st, a day of rest and day of worship, the same crowd as before gathered in front of the giant oak which grew out from the hay yard. Why this place was chosen to deal out the punishments was unknown by any in the crowd, or so Prosper Cailloux discovered, though it was assumed the hay would help soak up the blood.

A guard of twelve men stood with loaded rifles pointed at the bare backs of the five prisoners, and they were ready as ever to fire if any decided to flee.

The Spaniard gestured signs known only to the Owls; he was indeed a desperado. The elder Frenchman, Bissi, kept his hands out front, tied like the others, but made no such signs. Cailloux was surprised to see Garcia there as well; he was the fifth. Apparently, he'd been tracked down, though the gold never found; he had either refused to answer questions, or couldn't because of the difference in language. The American cried out in desperation until someone gagged him. As for the other man, he was treated the same for his malfeasance.

Cailloux thought of that word, then, for it was derived from French: *mal* meaning *evil*, and *faisance*, meaning *activity*. An evil activity for all involved. For the briefest of moments, he thought of shouting "Fire!" in English to spark a reaction from those with rifles, thus ending the lot by the power of a single word. They deserved such fates, four of them, at least.

All five men were lined up, side by side.

"Heard this transpired over poker," someone said.

"Monte," said another, "in the El Dorado."

"Happened in one of the saloon tents," said another.

The Chileno was flogged first, his back opening in red smiles. He made not a noise, only closed his eyes and grimaced, took the pain. The lashings were so harsh he fell over on the thirty-fifth, receiving the last four unconscious. Even as they flogged the next prisoner, men treated his gored flesh with strips of cowhide. Wounding him at first, then treating those wounds.

"Placer Hotel," said Cailloux.

"Nah, not there. Robbed a Mexican named Lopez."

The eldest Frenchman, Bissi, was a much larger man by comparison, yet his back opened with ease, striping red. He gritted his teeth, cried *merde!* and other such profanities. He, too, fell flat on his chest when the number of lashes went beyond reasonable, but he was able to rise on his feet and take the rest standing. Garcia was not as strong, and took his punishment next, followed by the others. The American stayed upright, perhaps because of his rotundness, but became silent after fainting, and took a majority of his lashings unaware. His back bled the most.

Thirty-nine lashing was the punishment, for forty would kill a man, or so it was understood.

Scarlet against the snow-covered hay was quite a horror.

"Serves them all right," someone said under his breath, "specially the Mexican. Can't believe he nearly beat to death one of his own."

"They nearly beat me to *my* own death," Cailloux said, but no one seemed to pay much attention to the beaten man whose injuries had caused all this. "Robbed me in my sleep."

"Heard he killed a young injin girl afore this and got away with it."

The elderly woman's voice burned into his mind.

You, she had said.

Cailloux took great interest in all that transpired. He imagined himself raking those flogged backs with a massive set of paws, thought of the indigenous woman, her long lock of braided hair off to one side, wisdom etched onto a face wrinkled with age, and wondered if that's why she gave him the fur, to give him strength as these men were drained of their own.

The hay yard was a good choice, for the men bled heavily under the ominous oak.

"The diggings don't need men like these," said another.

"Wake him up so he feels it."

Floggings continued until each took thirty-nine lashes. But before it was over, Richard Crone came up to Cailloux, tapped him on the shoulder. Startled, he turned, found the Irishman equally entranced, and holding out something for him to take: the horseman, the first of the money cards. Cailloux took it, and the young man disappeared into the crowd.

Those holding rifles lowered their aim, for no man could run from this, not any longer. When asked to stand, none could, the youngest still flat on his face and the Chileno out cold. It was understood that once they regained strength, they would all leave town, never to return.

Cailloux couldn't help but wonder if they would comply.

Visible heat rose from their wounds like morning snowmelt.

The American and the other were hauled off to be treated, for they'd been beaten severe. Too weak to stand, the three with names attached to them were carried off as well and stretched out upon the floor of a neighboring structure, backs to the ceiling so their wounds could breathe.

DESPITE all that had happened, backs torn to shreds, the two Frenchmen were spotted a few days later in one of the tent saloons, or so Cailloux had been told at his trading post. With his own wounds far from healed, most of his chest and face bruises, and despite his gold kept elsewhere, he never could shake the threat that they might want to kill him. He still lived where he lived, after all, and all four men knew the location. He hadn't slept much, knowing they were alive.

What would stop such men from coming after me? he wondered. *They were asked to leave the diggings, but what would stop them from killing me outright?*

"'They would not live to flog another man,' Bissi had said," he was told. "I'm guessing he meant those who did the whippin' but those words could be aimed at you and those who served their punishments. If I were you, I'd be careful. I'd watch my back."

"You're sure it was him, and Garcia, too."

"Heard and seen 'em myself."

"The Frenchmen."

The man nodded and said, "Still bled through their shirts from the lashings. They were drinking whiskey, just the two of 'em, boasting. I was at the floggings, same as everyone else."

"What about the other two?"

"You mean other *three*."

"No, I don't care about the Chileno, only those who did this to me," Cailloux said, motioning to his face, "and robbed me at knife- and gun-point, nearly killed me."

"Didn't see any of 'em at the tent. Cold out, and late, so not many men was there round the fires, but *they* was. Saw that Manuel fellow too, maybe the day before. Couldn't tell if he was comin' or goin' but it was him, lone. Haven't seen the fourth, but I'm sure he's here somewhere. Where else is he to go?"

Asking around, others reported all four in the diggings.

Since the initial incident, Cailloux never went anywhere without his pepperbox pistol loaded at his side, as well as the bowie knife he'd acquired in trade. He'd practiced drawing, some, and pulling out the blade and stabbing the air. He was anything but a gunslinger, nor skilled with a knife. He wasn't much of a threat at all, but having weapons eased his mind.

"What happened to that fifth man?"

Cailloux wasn't worried about that one, for no one had seen him after the floggings, either dead or well on his way out of the diggings as instructed, maybe headed farther west.

ANXIETY stayed close until a few weeks later when a second date burned permanent in Cailloux's mind: February 12th in the winter of '49. An officer of a neighboring community and a few of his appointed deputies rode in on horseback, and Cailloux approached at once, telling his story in short form, about the gambling, the armed robbery, the lashings, and described all four men.

"They were told to leave," he said, "but what's to stop them?"

"All four are desperados," the officer said matter-of-factly. "*Owls.*"

The two Frenchman, the American, and the Spaniard, who in fact went by the name Manuel, were suspected of robbery and attempted murder elsewhere, and stealing horses, which by itself was punishable by rope. "All this occurred last fall on the Stanislaus River," he was told. "Pursued ever since by me and these others."

It didn't take long for the officer and his deputies to rally vigilantes.

By late afternoon, Cailloux was asked to come to the hay yard.

THE officer knew one desperado by face, two by name, and pointed them out one by one. "That one's Manuel, no doubt, and the big guy is Bissi, known in their organization as a 'lieutenant' of sorts, like in the army, and I recognize that ugly feller," he said of the American, "couldn't tell you what he goes by, though. The Owls have all sorts of passwords and sigils and such, even communicate in secret hand-grips, which does them no good when tied up."

He approached the bloody line-up of prisoners, for they'd been beaten in their capture, old wounds reopened. Their hands were bound in knots of rope, and they were put on their knees as before.

"What's your name?" he asked the nameless.

The American spat blood.

"Guess that's we'll call you then," the officer said and spat on him. He then turned to Cailloux, who wore his bearskin. He hesitated at seeing the fur, said, "These the men?"

"Three of the four, yes."

"We couldn't find a fourth," the officer said, "so Garcia's most likely skedaddled. Someone will catch him, eventually. Always do. Not much of a threat out on his own."

The charges placed against all three were substantiated by not only Cailloux but other witnesses, and by the officer himself, but amounted to nothing more than *attempted* robbery and *attempted* murder, and horse-thievery, with no overt act other than those alleged.

As rumors spread of this second arrest, a crowd once again formed, and doubled in size to more than two hundred angry men in a matter of minutes. Before dusk, the gathering had organized a jury, had appointed a *pro tempore* judge: a man from Sacramento by the name of Grimshaw. "You sure you want to do this?" he was asked once or twice, but he was certain.

The three accused of the older crimes, and not leaving as instructed for their latest, were too weak to attend their own sentencing, and so they were tried once again in the open air to best appease the aggravated crowd. The trial lasted thirty minutes at most, before the judge put to vote a single question addressed to the mob as a whole:

"Are these men guilty of these crimes?"

An eruption followed, calls of yays and ays and likewise.

Cailloux threw his hands into the air, invigorated by the mass-assembly. To others, he must have resembled a rather brutal-looking fellow with his collection of cuts and bruises, his neck nearly sliced open and scabbed over, a tall man made larger by the pelt, a man whose face was composed of hatred and rage and various bruising colors. And so, when the *pro tempore* judge asked his final question, "What punishment shall be inflicted?" which hung in the air for quite some time, Cailloux was the first to call out, both in his mind and with his voice.

"Hang them!"

The proposition was seconded and met with nearly universal approbation.

All but for one man who made his way up to the front during the commotion that ensued. Edward Gould Buffum, a soldier and a miner known by many, and a journalist of sorts. He stood on the stump of pine to put himself above everyone else and argued against the majority.

The officer shook his head, as if signifying there was always one.

"In the name of God and law," Buffum protested, "we cannot have such a course of proceedings. Not here, not ever—" Hundreds or more voices and disgruntled murmurs drowned him out, and once again it grew quiet.

"We should hang *you*," a voice called, "if you don't step down from that perch and desist from further pathetic remarks." This garnered laughs, then riots.

The man stepped down, his words not so powerful.

Six inches of snow covered the ground as winter started its second attempt to fill the Sierra Nevadas with enough ice to fuel the spring. The sun was out and shining, but colder than a hell frozen over. Every breath spoken came out in puffs of white smoke.

"Hang them!" the crowd chanted, as if the entire diggings burned.

THREE thick and oiled ropes were procured and thrown over the largest limb of the oak outside the hay yard, one for each of the desperados. Those captured, anyway. The ropes dangled in the breeze, swaying gently in the cold. In a line, the prisoners were marched out of a neighboring structure used as a make-shift jail, for the diggings never before had a need for one.

All were on their way to enter scenes of a new eternity.

The ends of the ropes were looped, tied off with some sort of slipknot that would tighten when pulled, each lariat tossed over a neck.

Cailloux held his tongue, despite wanting to curse them on their way out of this world. *Brûle en enfer*, he wanted to say to the Frenchman, so that only he would understand. *Que ta mort soit longue.* "Burn in hell," and "may your death be long." But the hell they were about to endure would be flameless, and their necks would likely snap, offering quick deaths.

No explanations were given to the men. It was just understood by the majority what was about to happen. They were to be strung up and hanged by the neck until dead.

And they'd go out blind to the world.

The Spaniard's own bandana was used to cover his eyes, and similar black bandanas were brought out for the others. The three men stared into their new darkness, looking around the void for light. Vainly, some tried to speak, all barely able to stand.

"*No quiero morir! No quiero morir!*" said Manuel, a kid by the sound of his voice.

"*Ce qui se passe?*" said Bissi.

The American, like Cailloux, held his tongue, perhaps accepted death for all he had done. He'd drained his tears earlier, had finished pleading for his life. At some point he'd wet himself.

Not until the wagon rolled out did anyone speak.

"Hang 'em till dead," one man said.

"Hoist them up by the ropes," said another.

"Let the bastards suffer."

"*Interprète*," said the Frenchman. "*Qu'est-ce qui se passe? Interprète!*"

Cailloux was not the only one capable of interpreting for the Frenchman, for there were many from his country in the diggings within this crowd. Likewise, there were many who understood Spanish, but chose not to speak or even listen to the Spaniard. Attempts made to be heard over the infuriated mob by the soon-to-be dead were drowned out anyway.

The officer and his deputies pinioned each man's hands behind his back, and in turn led them to the back of the wagon and helped them onto it, an act which should have been performed well before the bindings and blindfolds. The American kicked out, connected with the shoulder of one of the deputies, who reacted by punching the man in the nose. Both the Frenchman and the Spaniard struggled as well, lost in the dark, lost in translation.

Soon enough the desperados were lined up shoulder to shoulder on the wagon, a good three or so feet off the ground, and positioned so they stood at the end of it, facing the crowd, the toes of their boots over the side. The men wobbled, but were held upright by deputies behind them, per chance one might slip off the edge and end his life prematurely.

No one said a word for the next several heartbeats.

The deputies jumped down from the wagon.

Cailloux savored the moment, had changed as a person because of it. Never before had he witnessed a man die, though he'd come close himself. *You*, the old woman's voice haunted. He could still smell the woman on the grizzly pelt, and wrapped it tightly around him, heart racing.

"Damn you all," the American finally said," every last one of you."

"*Ce qui se passe?*" the Frenchman said.

What's happening, indeed, thought Cailloux, *qu'est-ce que c'est.*

"Our lives are coming to an end," the American said, "that's what's happening."

The entire gathering held an extended, collective breath. The hangings would be the first in the dry diggings, and no one knew what to make of it, afraid of what this once rowdy but otherwise peaceful establishment would become. Three were about to be hanged, and men had volunteered to hold the ropes as anchor; an entire community about to end lives.

The Miwok and Maidu, what would they make of this? Some were in the crowd, Cailloux realized, watching out of curiosity but not showing interest.

Hesitating, he thought. *An entire community hesitating.*

Without priest or prayer-book, the oxen pulling the wagon were gently whipped into movement, their own necks hanged by yoke, and they ambled off, ever so slowly.

Spooked horses would have been a better choice.

The three guilty men teetered the opposite direction, tips of boots holding on for as long as possible, and then all three men angle-fell simultaneously into the night.

Not a single neck snapped, due to the speed at which the wagon moved away from them, and so all three instead swung as their human anchors held on tight, dragged through the snow, slipping, regaining purchase. The Frenchman's anchors lost control of the rope entirely, and he crumpled to the ground, got to his feet long enough to take half a step before he was pulled back up into the air. Three sets of legs kicked at the air.

Still, no one said anything.

The Spaniard kid died first, and his bowels let out, then the American, who stained both sides of his canvas pants the moment the legs within them stopped moving. The Frenchman held out longest, mostly because he'd required two hangings, but also because of his build, but after a minute or two, his legs stilled and the three hung in failing pendulum.

The officer held up his hand, an instruction to hold the ropes until his signal. He stared up at the dead, as did all, and held the silence a few minutes longer until their fates were certain.

Cailloux finally let out the air trapped in his lungs.

THREE graves were dug on the north side of the creek, ready to receive three bodies, far enough away from the bank for those in the diggings not to worry about heavy water flow flooding them or contamination. But the graves stayed empty for three straight days, for the bodies were strung in the oak as a reminder of what could be done to those with black hearts, and they were not moved until the bodies started to rot. The only men to give any notice to the dead were those who brought picks and spades to first dig the holes, then fill them with dirt. And as the heavy snowmelt filled the streams between spring and summer, a new wave of gold fever spread through the valley.

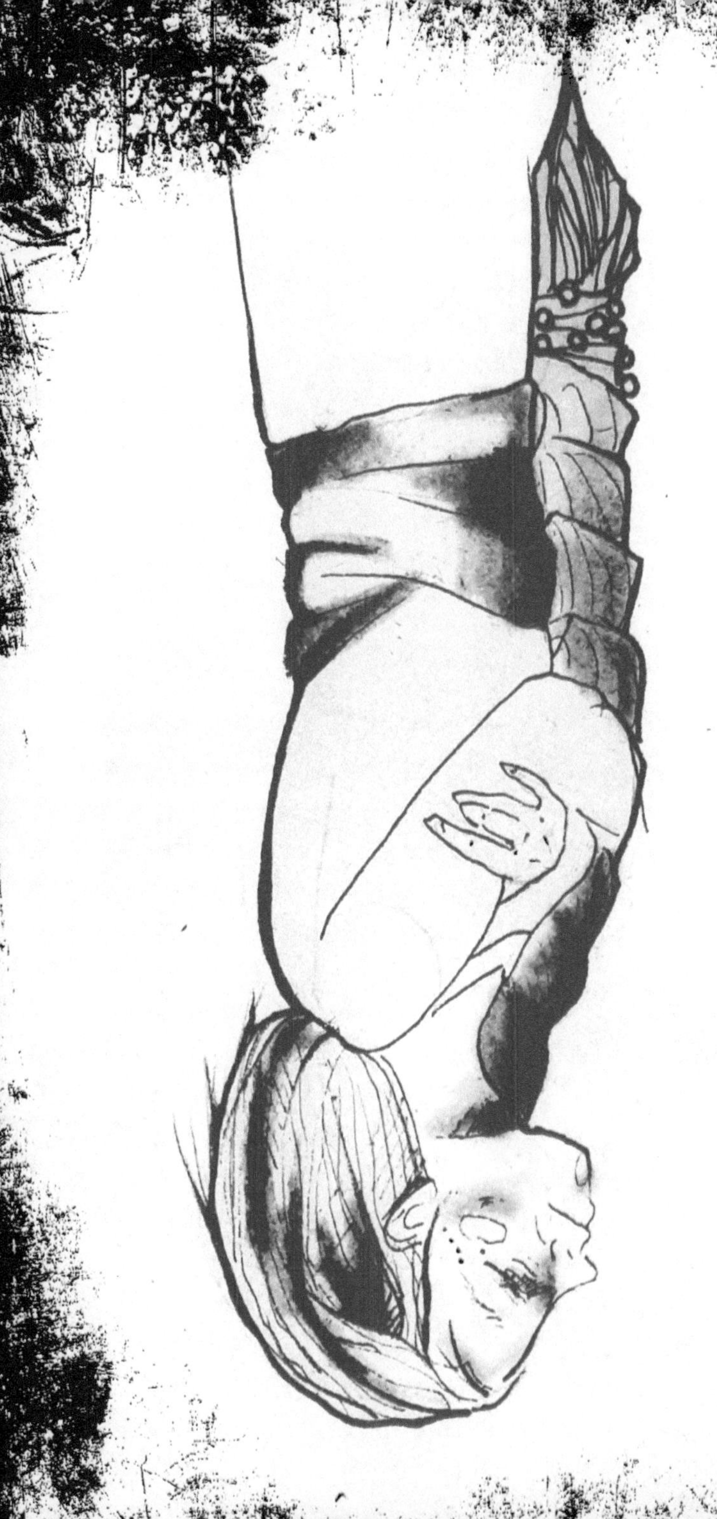

SPRING
1850

A GILTED ONE

RODE to the center of the diggins harder than I ever rode afore. Pre-dusk meant the judge was on his way out for a good long while, and not even my father, a hard man, could convince him to stay long enough to find reason to hang Cole Mullins and the man called Slade.

Cole Mullins and his demon stole two half-filled buckskin bags of gold from our claim, all we had, and Judge Lynch implied nothin could be done about it. So what good was he? Why even have a judge? And my father, where was *he?* Same place I'd always find him.

"We brand our bags, on the bottom," I told the judge. "Same as the cattle we once had." I tied my mustang to the hitch out front of Hunter's Express cause there was room, caught him on his way out, though I couldn't imagine why he'd need such provisions.

"What's your sigil?" he asked.

He meant the letters, and perhaps couldn't read so I pointed at my horse. She wore her saddle, the fender branded with the initials BAR: Benjamin Alexander Read, same my father.

"Why isn't your daddy telling me this? You are not yet even a man."

"Fifteen and some," I said. "More man than Mullins."

This was partly true. Cole Mullins had lost an arm, cut off below the bicep from a round that tore through, lodged in bone, and turned infected. He was sick most the time and skinny, like me, and a full half-foot shorter. A small man. Maybe five-four in boots. A hundred pounds rain-soaked. I outweighed him by at least the heft of what he and his partner stole.

"Listen, son—"

"Read," I said. "My name is Read, same as my father."

"Well, Read, I am going to tell you what I told Ben when he recounted this sad tale earlier, same as I tell every prospector spouting similar stories. This territory only got statehood a month ago. We ain't got a well-established jury system here, not yet." His hands did their best to encompass the entire town. "And any trials held are barbaric. We don't have ourselves a courthouse, not even a jail. All we got is that tree."

He pointed at the massive oak across the way by Elstner's hay and wood yard. Rope dangled from the largest branch, a noose on the end, a warning perhaps. I'd never seen men hanged but heard stories. The gangly arms of the tree nearly touched the ground in places.

What the judge didn't understand was how badly these two needed to be hanged, and I had it in my mind to make it so. It wasn't just our gold was the problem. Cole Mullins was a dangerous man, even with only the one good arm, and his partner seemed rooted in pure evil, having carved more than a baker's dozen notches on his wrist, like chisel into stone to tally each man he'd killed. They scalped Indians for sport, or so I figured, men and women and perchance kids, for I'd seen scalps sometimes tied to their horses.

Some said Mullins was friends with the young Mississippi riverboat gambler, Richard Crone, who steadily ran one of the tables at the El Dorado Hotel, which was run by Elstner—who ran most business on the thoroughfare. People had many nicknames for the Irishman, such as New Orleans Dick, or Irish Dick, or the horrid Bloody Dick, a terrible name. He went by many a *nom de plume*, as the French would say. To be seen in conversation with him meant one was up to no good, and Cole Mullins was seen with him often.

"What do you know of Richard Crone?" I asked the judge.

"Read, that was long ago," he said.

"Did that incident have anything to do with Cole Mullins, or Slade?"

"You weren't there," the judge said, "and neither was I."

Rumor had it the first to hang in the diggins—three men at once—resulted from a man who'd lost his poke of gold by way of blade at Richard Crone's table. This was back in one of the round tents, before the Irishman had started to hustle cards in the El Dorado. Throats threatened to be cut, or whatnot. Guns pressed against temples. I don't know for certain. All stories passed from one mouth to the next, so who knew what was right and what wasn't?

Way I understood it, without any man with a badge, an impromptu citizen's jury made themselves known and vocally fated the three accused, and so they hanged them, simple as that.

Some say more had hanged since then, but that's how stories can bend with time, how a place called Dry Diggins changes to Hangtown and suddenly there's fear of the rope.

But this particular hangin tree needed new lives to turn dead.

"You related to Charles or William Lynch?" I asked the judge.

He smiled and said, "I get asked that often."

So, I said, "So is you?"

He said, "So is I what?"

"Related."

I knew he wasn't, but also knew it would rattle him some. What I disliked about him most was that he was a well-dressed man in a not-so-well-dressed land. Look around, and all you see any given day is dirty men with brown and tired faces slopped in mud. Not the judge.

"Only as far as surnames go. Look, son. You're old enough to understand what's needed to prove ownership of what you gather, and likewise to prove *de*-ownership."

"Theft."

"Yes, thievery," he said, and spat against the wind how no man should. He wiped tobacco juice from this mouth with the back of his sleeve and swore at the splotch he made and said, "I'm heading back to the Gate—"

"The gate?" I said.

"Golden Gate," he said, as if I should know what he meant. "San Francisco harbor was just incorporated. Lots of nimwits are coming from elsewhere and leaving their ships in the bay. Headed here, or to Coloma, though this place is dryer than most when it comes to diggings. Well, I'm going to the coast, and on my way, I'm stopping at the diamond springs to meet the rest of my party because the way to and from is not safe traveling alone. Keep that in mind."

I visibly repulsed as he patted my shoulder.

"Words of wisdom," he said. "Desperados, Miwok or Maidu, any number of horrid things'll put you to an end. And between here and there I am to sentence four Indians for the murder of Martin Hopkins. Guess you don't know who that is. What I'm saying is that I don't have time for petty theft claims. There's a man in the bay who killed a dozen men and—"

"But Slade—"

"Ah, yes, the mysterious man everyone calls Slade, *just* Slade, though no one's ever seen him wandering town. A mystery man. A ghost. I've heard it all before, stories of this or that and what have you and I don't believe a single word of it."

I stepped in front of him, and he shoved me aside.

"What if I can prove it, that they stole from us?"

The man guffawed, spat again, this time downwind like every man should. He untied the horse next to mine and put his foot in the stirrup, swung atop the ugly thing. His mustache and beard was striped brown from what he failed to clear.

To claim the bags was easy enough, but neither my father nor I could find Cole Mullins and his ghost partner.

The Mullins claim had been left abandoned, already taken over by another. Seen it myself. If we could only find them, link Slade—

"I'm not coming back for at least two months," the judge said, "maybe longer, but you find out they took you and your father's gold, well, put a hole in each filthy man and take back what's rightfully yours and be done with it. The only two laws when I'm gone is *alive* and *dead* and all that matters is whose gun breathes smoke and doesn't fall next to him."

"I'm not a killin man," I said.

"Neither am I," he said, the way any good politician lies.

The white sun haloed his head, but it was the heat of hell that burnt at his back, the devil and his dark silhouette. The man got me red furious.

The judge may not have ever put a round into a man, nor fired a pistol—not even sure he carried one for one wasn't on his belt—but he'd had plenty of men killed with his rattlesnake tongue over the years. From what I heard from others round the diggings was he'd sometimes whip the horses or oxen that carried the cart that dropped those he sentenced to hang till dead, that he'd stay until legs stopped sputterin if the falls failed to snap necks.

I looked at the tree, then, same as he did, then at him as he looked at me, then at my horse and he at his horse cause their eyes perhaps had more trust than our own at that moment. The black depth of Nugget's left eye reflected a young man, a boy lost for purpose.

"Want some advice?" the judge said, and I didn't, and told him so.

I wanted to tell him he could go hang himself.

"Cole Mullins, if what you say is true, he's long gone by now. Lost his arm a while back. And I have reason to believe he and the man you call Slade are two separate worries, one not associated with the other."

"And he'll lose his other when we catch him," I said of Mullins.

The judge laughed, spat again.

Lookin at the sky, perhaps to help him imagine what he was about to say, he said, "An armless man … makes you wonder how he'd manage holding his pants up for a piss."

This got me to smile, which I guess meant the man wasn't all bad.

"Haswell's the acting sheriff, but he's away on business and no one's seen him in days. There are officers here, if you can find them," he said, "but formal law is powerless when those in charge of protecting are like the ones here. Supposed to keep in check the scoundrels and desperados infesting places like these, but they don't, because they are corrupt, so justice is often administered by miners and simple folk. I can only help with high crime, and be prompted to do so, but what you're selling's not severe enough to warrant a hanging."

There's a reason, I guess, certain men are capable of pullin triggers and others find the guns too heavy. His clothes said this about him. Not a scuff on his boots. Not a swatch of dirt anywhere on his wears. His saddle, silver-studded, like his spurs. I guess you could say he was a well-mani-cured man, a little queerly dressed compared to those he so often sentenced, and he wouldn't offer to sentence another anytime soon.

I noticed his longrifle on his saddle as he mounted, the way I adorned mine.

"Cole Mullins and Slade or not," he said, "best to keep digging."

By this I'm not sure if he meant for gold or for trails, but the glimmer in his eye was another type of message, like the noose, but one full of sadness, aimed to keep me safe in respect of my age, perhaps on account of what we'd gone through just to get here.

"And stay away from Richard Crone," he said, then added, "and the El Dorado, if you're a smart boy, or any of the tents, for that matter."

And with a smile of his own, he gave the reins in his hands a tug and circled his horse, rode toward the sun, in a race with it too, for it took more than a few hours to get to the springs on four legs. Another mounted man appeared out from between two poorly-made shacks and sidled up next to him, and the two kicked into their rides. They left a wake of dust.

I wanted to ask if he'd seen my father inside the market, or the Boomerang saloon, but knew I'd have to see to that myself, which is why I came into the center of town. Saloons, especially the tents, were not the places for boys, but often one my age or younger stumbled out through the swing-doors, drunk, or with that wild-lost dreamy-eyed expression from lustin over women twice their age—women old as mothers. I'd often gone in to find the man who made me. Sometimes I found him, sometimes not, but never with whores.

There weren't a lot of women in the diggins, maybe half a dozen. And there weren't many not-yet-men like me. I knew all three by name, and all were as weathered as their fathers. They'd come from the east, having lost their mothers in childbirth or in their travels west.

All names know each other in the diggins, and as if to prove that very fact a man rolled backward out the open maw of the Boomerang, vomited, and landed hard, slid back, looked at me, tipped the brim of his hat, said, "Read," and I said, "Wright."

"Isn't that something," he said.

"What," I said, "you tossed out afore dusk?"

"Read and Wright," he said. "I can do neither."

"I can do both, but it's another kind of write, spelled—"

"They's the same to me," he said, and regained his

feet. "What good are words anyway unless spoken?" Cards slipped out his shirtsleeves as he stood, and he snatched them up with a smile, tucked them inside a pocket. "I'd rather stick to odds and ends, if you catch my meaning."

"You're lucky you wasn't shot dead," I told him, and then, "It seems you have card-skills ahead of you. Real card-players don't need to cheat. You seen Benjamin Alexander Read in there?" I eyed the doors.

A brown-leather knapsack flew out after him, landed at his feet. He picked up the bag, looked inside and sighed in a way that meant all was there, probably not much. He nodded kinda sideways.

"Yes, or no?"

"You know he's in there," he said, and dusted off.

So, I went inside, got hit by the sour stench of spilt spirits, of well-worked men, their shirts soaked clean through by sweat and drink, the spunk of tobacco spat and smoked, kerosene lanterns with black wicks in desperate need of oil the way each spent man needed a refill of liquor. Some begged at the bar, and that's where I found my father.

"Papa," I said and shook his shoulder.

A tumbler of placid brown waited afront him. He stirred, but only enough to flip the side of his face that touched the bar. Though somewhat asleep, he held his drink. He'd bring the back of his hand across a face if anyone tried to take it.

Two bar-keeps worked behind the counter. One stacked new bottles on the shelf behind them while the other walked toward me, asked "What's your poison?"

"How old you gotta be to drink?"

I'd never tried spirts, except for the whiskey my father sometimes rubbed on my teeth when sick from the wicked. I'd always liked the way it tingled and made me salivate.

"Only 'quirement's money," he said, but he could see it in my eyes I wasn't about to buy spirits, only wanted to talk to the man laid out across the bar.

"Papa," I said again, and this time he heard. He always heard.

"What, Read?" he said.

For as long as I can remember, he never once called me by my first name, which was his own. Always Read, like everyone else, or *boy*.

"Judge says—"

"I already talked to the judge," he said.

"And?"

"There's no *and*, Read. Never is." He straightened on his barstool, formed into the shape of a question mark, then less bent and added, "You know why I'm here."

"I do, and it's why I came."

"John," he said, loud enough so the bar-keep with that name turned back to him from what he was up to under the counter. There was a shotgun there, I knew, a sawed-off, for my papa had told me as much, but the clank of glasses meant he was otherwise busy. "John," he said again, less of a slur, the 'J' more pronounced. "Another round."

"You still have half a round in front of you," the bar-keep said and laughed, "but long as you're willing to pay I'm willing to pour."

"Not for me," my father said, "for my boy."

"One for the boy," he said.

"Know what? Make it two. I'm still parched."

He clunked a tumbler next to my father's as my father slapped a few coins on the counter and slid them across. Two coins, two glasses. Behind the well-dressed man, arranged on the shelves, were bottles other than whiskey: absinthe, cura-cao, bitters, as well as gin and brandy and ones labeled 'sugar' and 'peppermint' and on trays some lemon-peel and leaves.

The bar was the draw of the room, a tide of alcohol ebb and flow, but with people. Some sat on stools, like my old man when I found him, slumped or snorin.

My father downed the drink he had left and slammed

the glass on the bar, motioned with his finger to fill both tumblers, and the bar-keep upended a bottle into one and then the other. Two fingers' worth. It was more than drinks, I knew. My father had prepared for two things: what *he* needed to do, and what he needed *me* to do.

"It's about time you became a man," my father said. "No more *boy*."

I took one of the tumblers and he took his and we lifted and clinked them together. I was about to sip when he put his other hand across my forearm.

"You look a man in the eyes when you offer cheers," he said, and then, "Let's try that again," he said, and this time I made sure we connected.

His eyes were much like my horse's—full a trust. They bore into me like I'd never seen them do afore, and in those depths I saw an older version of myself.

I was about to sip, but he again put a hand across my forearm.

"We are not going to *sip*," he said.

"No?"

"No. We are going to take it all," he said, which I knew meant more than the fire that would soon burn into us. "You and me," he said, "we are going to get back what's ours. We are going to hunt down Cole Mullins like the wild animal he is, and whoever he's running with, and we will take it all. What's rightfully ours, at least." Even as he spoke, he sobered, though how many drinks he had in him was another mystery.

The secret about my father is that he's better a shot when inebriated, even better when plastered. The more booze, the better his aim. He was hard on the drink, I knew, to prepare for what was to come, what we was about to do together as father and son, and he wanted me to not only share this liquid courage, but to become the man he'd always wanted to raise.

A hard man.

He nodded, his eyes on mine, and I nodded, my eyes never off his, and we raised our glasses at this uncheerful of cheers and each took a drink and as I started to sip he tilted back my glass until we each finished the horrid conflagration in our throats and slammed them down on the counter and when we was finished he smiled as I grimaced.

The bar-keep knew we was done but lifted the bottle a good foot, a way to ask without words if we wanted another round, but my father held up his hand, and so he took both glasses from us and wiped the counter under them with a rag and returned to his under-the-counter work.

"Read," my father said and grabbed my shoulder, firm, quite opposite from the encounter outside with the judge.

As he held on, mostly for balance, the drink burned deep. So hot my eyes watered, and I had to wipe them with a sleeve so as not to show tears.

"You did fine," he said and let go. He slid off his stool and made as if to crumble at the knees but righted himself, adjusted his belt and holster.

He wore a gun tucked in the crack of his pants behind him, which he sometimes slid to one side or the other to place in better reach. He could shoot with either hand, though he was better with his left. And he could fire two at once, I knew, in tandem, but preferred the simplicity of a single firearm at his side. He'd taught me to shoot against the hillside at the backend of our claim, but I was no good with guns other than a rifle, only hit rocks and dirt, no jars.

Afore we left, he slid two bits across the counter, one for John and one for the other behind the counter. Worth twelve-and-a-half cents each, it was a decent tip, but we was low on funds and unless we got at least some of our gold back we was in a world of hurt.

The diggins was dry indeed, like its name implied.

After news spread of the yellow metal in '48, there came

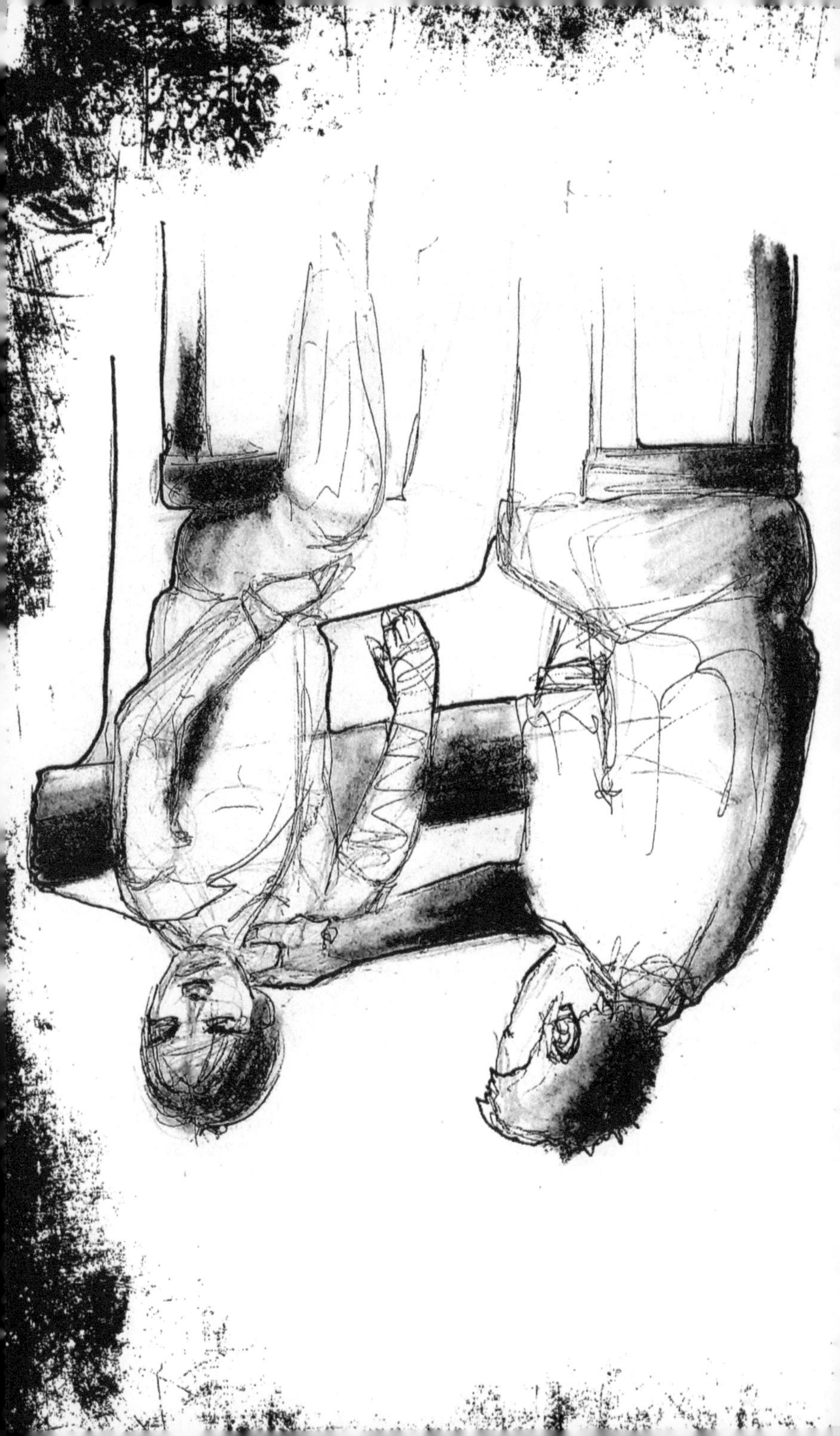

a stampede to the foothills. Gold-fields, some called it. The name of the county itself, El Dorado, meant "the gilded one," but where was all the gilt? Where had it all gone? Deep in the rocks, we knew.

We'd been promised fortune by word of press. Nuggets the size of horse hooves, hence the name of my pony. Gold one could simply pluck from streams by hand, or by nickin one free with a bowie knife from the rocks. But by the time we arrived from Springfield, Missouri, like so many others, the ones afore us had already snatched the easies, and so the work left was harder than implied. Some died to come here, and those who didn't now worked whole days for close to nothin, and sometimes whole days for *absolute* nothin.

No, what we found in these diggins was terrible work that could break backs, with pick-axes and pans and whatnot to find what those before had left behind: dust and pebble.

We'd staked our claim legally, our wooden sign four feet high and plainly visible, as per custom, and once we found gold, we established both a placer and lode claim with the proper papers to back it. All that was really needed was to bury the end of a spade in the earth, but such terms could be argued over. The last four months, we'd depleted our supplies, and what little money we'd brought with us. We'd built a cabin, paid for the supplies needed to extract from the ground and from the water we passed through our site, but for what, two half-filled bags?

That amount could get us by for another four months if we parsed it out like food rations for the starved, but now even that—what we wanted to save—was gone. Took by Mullins and the man called Slade, or other men he ran with. It was up to us to take it back.

"I don't want to kill him," I finally said.

"Neither do I," he said, and I could tell he meant it well enough. "The last thing anyone should ever have to do is take another life, but we'll do whatever's needed, and if that means firing a pistol at another man, it'll be by my hand, not yours."

I thought of my rifle, which I'd left next to my bedroll. I couldn't imagine takin aim at a person. I'd dropped a deer, and plenty of squirrel, and once a fowl, but the thought of otherwise wasn't in my blood. No one could mine murder outta me. Handguns were meant to kill men, no other purpose, and I'd only ever fired my father's just to know how, and cause he'd wanted to teach me properly should I have to defend myself.

My father wasn't like other drunks. At nearby tables, people spat on the floor, not in the spittoons, and they grabbed at ladyfolk as they passed. He never sacrificed gold or coins or cash money over games of monte, nor faro, like those nicer dressed. Mexicans seemed to prefer monte over other games in the saloon, but my father and I only ever played for fun after supper. The deck had forty-eight cards, while some at the saloons only had forty.

"Money's worth dying for," my father once told me, "but only if it's a necessity to live. Nothing's worth gambling away to something as stupid as chance."

He'd also once told me, for he frequented the saloon often, that sometimes in the forenoon when the gamblin was slack, gamblers—the *professionals*, not those who simply *gambled*—would stand from their tables and go for a drink at the bar, leave large sums of money at their backs without care. Piles of gold and silver and stacks of coin. They played games such as Faro, Monte, *Rouge et noire*, and *lasquinet*. A man could lose his cattle, his ranchos, hard-earned gold, and other possessions, all in a matter of moments.

"Shows you what money's worth to some," he said as we walked by such a table. "Those who don't need it seem to have it most and don't mind not holding it, while those who need it most have trouble holding onto it in the first place."

To see money exposed in such a way was madness. The law of *meum et tumm*, 'mine and thine,' was strange to witness firsthand. Private property flaunted yet known by all that to touch what wasn't yours could get you shot dead. The last man killed in this town, in fact, was over a game. The dealer had cheated, sure, but what dealer didn't?

I guess that's the same gamble as life.

"Care for a drink?" a man asked as we passed.

My father turned to him and gave him a womanly curtsy and said, "Already had a drink and don't have any coin but thank you kindly sir for the consideration."

"Generosity and nothing more," the man said.

"Not today, maybe the next," my father said.

"Who was that?" I asked with a tug on his sleeve.

Never afore had I seen my old man pass on a free drink. Never afore had I heard my father utter such elegance in speech. A man usually short for words, long for silence.

"Strauss," he said under his breath. "A well-off man." As we distanced ourselves he added, "He's come from the bay. His business was first canvas, for tents and whatnot, but he's since struck in another way, making pants of the same cloth. Made these," he said, and pat his thighs, and I learned then he hadn't curtsied but shown the man his pants.

I'd always been afraid of places like the Boomerang, or the El Dorado Saloon, which was once the Placer Hotel, and thought of such places as where ruffians and desperate men gathered, but everyone inside was desperate in another kinda way. It wasn't such a scary place, but where one could go to escape the fears outside the diggins, where men sweat and bled and struggled to make ends meet. Which I guess is what my father did each time he came for a drink.

"Where's my damn horse?" my father said as we walked outside. He swung the French doors wide, and they came back to hit him in the rear but it only pushed him forward a step.

"Your horse?"

"My horse."

He put his hand on Nugget, stroked her mane, rubbed the ears. He looked around, perplexed, maybe wondering if he'd rode Sasha into town or if he'd walked.

"Last I saw she was at the claim, grazin."

"Yours can carry us both, I guess," he said.

The mustang wasn't strong, not yet, but strong enough in a pinch. My father ran his hand over his own initials and then readjusted the stirrups, one side then the other, then put his foot in one, lifted one leg over and nearly fell over the other, righted himself. He patted Nugget as if to let her know it wasn't her fault. He took his foot out the stirrup long enough for me to get myself up there with him and I rode behind and held his waist.

We passed through town unprovoked, a town mostly constructed of cabin-sized places, most made from ponderosa and sugar pine taken from the mountains. Some were just shacks full of wares with canvases draped over shells, merchants with product.

We looked ridiculous, I knew, my father's legs over each side, nearly to ground, but no one in town took much notice. "Home" wasn't far, but the ride felt long from the awkwardness of it. Nugget walked as drunkenly as my father steered her. His own horse still stood where he'd left her in the field next to the enclosure once used for cattle. We'd fenced some, but it wasn't yet a corral. Enough bailing wire around posts to enclose them, though.

"Couple hours till full dark," he said, and hopped down. "Hurry on. Best we ride out fore it's nigh too late to see out here. Grab some waterskins 'case we end up stuck."

I slid down after him and went inside to fetch the rifle and dry-bread and other things like we discussed. He said I most likely wouldn't need the rifle, but take it to best be safe.

"And have a sup of water," he called out, and I did.

He prepared the horses while I gathered, and swigged from the bottle at his side. What was in it, I don't know, but it was hot like what we'd drunk.

"Never met a man called Slade," he said when I returned and hopped aback Nugget, "but Mullin's a damn coward. Cowards cower with cowards, and I'm guessing neither are armed if they're desperate enough to take from a man and his boy."

He said this to keep my mind at ease, I figured, but to go out armed, even to a man with only one arm, was enough to make me jittery.

"You got spares?" he said. "Ammunition?"

"Here," I told him, about ten or so in my pouch.

He said, "You ready."

And I said, "Ready for what," not as a question.

This was a thing we had between us. Every time he asked if I was ready, me sayin 'for what' was always said in a way that intoned it wasn't a question but that I was ready for 'what,' for anything that *could* be 'what.' When he asked me four months ago if I was ready to pack our lives in Missouri and head west, after Mom died, I'd hesitated, afraid to leave behind the only life I knew, but told him, "Ready for what," and he smiled just the same.

He took up on his horse and I followed.

2

"**SOMETIMES** the best information is from those behind a bar," my father said. "Everyone comes for drinks, and everyone talks. Part of the bar-keeps job's to listen, and John said, fore you came, that he'd heard two men who sounded like their descriptions talking Weber Creek, a little west of here, near the Jones claim. Could be planning to take from the Jones too, but I'm guessing not. I'm guessing they plan to set-up camp close then head off in the morning."

My job was to listen as we rode, so I listened.

"I figure it'll take us three-quarters of an hour there, three-quarters back, and by the dip of the sun I say we have two hours before it's too dark to ride. Full dark when we return's not what we want, no doubt, but we can camp with what Sasha's carrying if need be. She's got two bedrolls on her and our saddle blankets're big enough unfolded to huddle under."

Like the judge, we raced the sun. We trotted some, and ran on straighter paths, but as we neared the trail that led to the part of Weber where he thought they might be hid, we slowed at the crack-sound of lightnin and a cry. The cloudless sky got each of us to glance at the stars that poked through the early night, but then the lightnin cracked again, followed by another cry.

"Someone's being whipped," my father said matter-of-factly.

He dismounted and with his hands informed me to do the same. He put a finger to his lips and after which the two of us tied our horses by rein to the low branch of a smaller version of the great white oak. A small god-hand that reached through the earth.

The crack came again, and again, until the man on the other end stopped his noises all-together. I reached over my back, then, and swung the rifle to my front. I held it, soldier-like, perhaps in reaction to my father, who unholstered his pistol. He pushed at air for me to stay back.

I followed him anyway, but not so close.

The nearer we got to the water, the darker it became though it was still light out, until it got almost too dark to see ground beneath our feet as the ravine swallowed us.

"That thing costed me a hunnerd dollars," a man said.

The pit in my stomach told me 'the thing' in ruins was the man they'd beat.

"How they learn," said another.

They was still a ways in the distance, their voices carried to us over geography by the wind. We stepped softly so as not to send our position back to them, as quiet as mountain lions. Soon the smell of smoke wafted toward us and the orange-red of a small campfire strobed.

Two men in nothin but skivvies stood next to the flames to keep warm. They had started to dry wet clothes on a propped-up tree branch, perhaps worried how cold it might drop and how much longer it might take to cook their wearables. One held a whip, which he began to coil. He was done with it and cursed under his breath.

"They's warm enough," the other said.

"They's still wet is what they is, and I'm not wearin no darkie's clothes."

Neither man was Cole Mullins, and neither was Slade.

I shifted in order to see better when a branch broke underfoot. Both men startled and stared my way, and then my father's way not far ahead. I had three men who looked right at me but only my father could tell I was a person and not some critter of the night.

Close to naked, neither wore nothin close to weaponry.

By the water, near the creek and covered by a canopy of forestry, there was no light save the fire-flicker. They couldn't see out to us, but we could see in to them, so we stayed silent.

Both men glowed.

"Who's out there?" the ugliest called.

He walked past the clothes and grabbed an oilcloth slicker that hung on another branch and put it on. His hair a mop of tar. The other man grabbed for the still-wet clothes by the fire and hurried on a ratty pair'a pants. A holster lay in wait on a large rock, but no man reached for it just yet. For all they knew, we was just a skunk or coon.

Unfortunately, I sneezed.

The one who struggled to dress said, spooked, "Who the hellfire's out there?" and the other closest to the gun yelled, "Show yerself!" and made his way to grab the gun but my father stepped into the clear to reveal himself and cocked the hammer back on his pistol.

"Woah-woah-woah," said the ugly one.

"This your camp?" my father said.

"This yours?" said the other.

"I guess it's neither of ours, then."

Since my father held the gun, we had the advantage, so I put a round in my rifle, though I could hardly see a thing, but managed under the duress. I then took the position he once took moments ago and aimed not at either man but above them case I needed to make a point that my father wasn't lone, ready to light up the night with what the scrawnier man had called hellfire.

"How many of you's out there?" said the ugly one. This close, I could see his teeth had been kicked in perhaps years prior. A few jutted out at angles.

"Seven," my father said.

I am six men, I thought proudly.

"I call bull," said the other.

"Beside this pistol here," my father said, "there are six others, long rifles too, pointed right at you, each ready to rain upon you should you go for that gun there."

The man closest contemplated with his eyes.

"I still call bull," said the scrawny one, and he moved for it.

I fired right above his head. The shot was closer than I meant, the rifle not sighted properly, and so a round popped the bark of some tree which pelted him. Either the echo of the shot or shrapnel caused him to flinch. I noticed then they had no horses.

"How long you gonna keep whippin that man?" my father said.

To his left: the back of a dark-skinned man, darker than I'd ever seen afore, sprawled over a downed tree. His back a criss-cross mess of open wounds. He was dead but for subtle movement. As if to prove he was still capable of breath, he wheezed in the cold night air and let out a strange choke sound. For a moment there was only tree limbs high above that scraped against one another, and wind through their branches.

"Asked you a question," my father said.

"Till he learns properly his place in this world."

"And what place is that?"

Neither answered.

In the darkness, in the quiet, the six other men, who was me, reloaded his rifle and pointed the smokin end toward the more evil of the two as my father kept his own barrel pointed at both men at once, it seemed. He inspected the poor fella they'd tortured. The man with the whip let it drop, as if to say it wasn't he who'd lashed the man bloodily.

"You know Cole Mullins?" my father said.

Only the uglier of the men responded.

"Yeah, I knows him."

"Where's he?"

"In the woods, pointing a rifle at you. Now ain't *that* a tricky situation."

I ate my heart, but knew deep down the man was a liar.

"Tell me where you last seen him," my father said, not buyin it either.

"I last seen him this morning."

I watched as my father leaned down to the dark-skinned man. He whispered a word or two in his ear, but none of us in earshot of normal voice heard what was conversed.

"What're you saying to that black n———!" he said, though he said the word.

The ever-dark night detonated with a sound much like an explosion of dynamite as a round buried into the man in the longcoat. He was forced back by the shot, but remained on his feet, then grabbed at the red that wanted so bad outta him. He turned, almost theatrically, to check for an exit, but the round had buried into him and so he fell to his knees.

"You done killed me!" he said. "You done got-damned killed me."

"You done killed your got-damned self," my father said.

Never fore had I heard him talk in such a way. Never had I seen him shoot a man.

The scrawny one held a pair of shaky hands up high and said, "I seen him oh please oh god don't shoot me like you done him. I seen him later than morning he was gathering up his stuff from the camp next over and—"

"Where is he?" my father asked, almost politely.

"I swears I don't know his whereabouts, but what I say is true, he done grabbed all his stuff and last I saw he was the next camp over talkin with the Irishman, the dealer."

"Where?"

"About a mile south or east, I don't know which direction is which, but he's that way," the man said and pointed downstream. "The old Weber camp from which the creek's named."

The shot man cried out in agony, a long unhuman wail.

The other pissed himself.

"Help this man to his feet," my father said.

"What?"

"This man your friend whipped. You're going to help him to his feet."

"That's no man, and the one you shot's not my friend."

Reluctantly, the one in only half his pair'a pants made his way toward the poor fella. His scrawny hand reached down as if afraid to touch the dark skin, but after the barrel aimed his way next, he did as told. He staggered, wiped his hands on his knees and spat only cause he had tobacco in his gums and needed to spit.

The dark-skinned man did his best to stand on his own, his back flayed open in five or six places, but he stood with pride. The same vibrant red as any of us inside.

"What's your name?" my father asked him.

The man only shook his head, looked at the one not yet shot.

I knew my father wanted me to stay hid, so I stayed hid.

"These road-apples aren't going to hurt you any longer," he said, and meant what the horses sometimes left behind in piles. "They try to take anything but another breath and I'll fill 'em with holes. You gotta name?"

The man as dark as pitch squatted down, wrote with his finger in the dirt.

"Lemi," my father read.

The man nodded with a painful expression. He was hurt bad, I could tell, even from afar as I was, breathed what seemed not-enough-often. Firelight bounced brown and gold off his chest as he turned. He opened his mouth, and all was red inside, for they'd cut out his tongue.

My father said with a grimace, "Which one of them did the cutting?"

Lemi pointed a shaky finger toward the man whose piss stunk the night.

We all watched the scrawny man's mind explode out the back of him. Black fanned out in the dark against the rock. He fell straight as a board on his side, hands still held above him. A third new eye above and between his others. Sober than most, my drunk father had killed him.

Then quiet, not even the hoot of an owl or flight of nightbird.

Two steps forward and my father was at the other man he'd shot in the belly. He took his time to reload and did it right in front of him so he could watch. But when he raised the pistol, the dark-skinned man let out a sound and approached him, gently put a hand over my father's forearm the way my father had done to me at the bar afore we drank.

Lemi shook his head no.

My father understood the unspoken word and grabbed the holstered revolver the other had tried for and unholstered it, held the weapon out to Lemi to take.

"Stand up," my father told the man who sobbed on the ground.

"You done shot me! I'm dyin."

"Stand up."

I watched from in between the trees as the dark-skinned man took the revolver from my father. The man on the ground slowly regained his feet, clutched his stomach as if life would spill outta him. He lifted his fingers to reveal a dark and deep wound.

"I wasn't going to kill you," my father said to him, "nor your friend, but what you two done is a justifiable offence. The round I put in you was aimed true. Would have lived after digging it out of you, but now you're gonna stand and die like the man you aren't."

"What is you, law?"

"Open your eyes," my father said. "See the man who kills you."

I thought of the judge and what he'd said.

Life and death is law.

Out here we was on our own.

The man named Lemi circled round, as if about to give a verdict to the guilty. Each of them bled: one from the back, one from the front. The man about to die indeed opened his eyes, enough to haunt me forever. He welcomed death and smiled right at it, wide.

"Go'on," he spat. "Kill me, n——!"

Lemi hefted the revolver, showed everyone he knew how to use it properly. He finally stopped alongside the rock where the other would soon feed worms, perhaps so as not to cause a ricochet. He raised the fat barrel and held it steady, the end creasin the man's forehead, the same spot as his partner, then he did what was unexpected. He fired to the side, blew off one ear, then followed him to the ground and shot off the other ear. Not to kill him, but to leave him deaf.

A sense for a sense, perhaps.

The man fell onto his knees. He tried to scream, but couldn't find air, his hands over each side of his head. He bled through the gaps between fingers, stomach folded onto itself as he hunched, like his partner. Even if he could scream, he wouldn't hear now or nevermore.

Shirt in bloody tatters, Lemi holstered the revolver and looped the belt around his own waist. The gun his now. He squatted again and wrote on the ground with his finger.

"Read," my father said, to bring me into the open. "My son's here with us," he said, so as not to startle him at my presence. "He was watching our backs this whole time."

I joined them by the fire, and I seen what he wrote.

Then I saw the man's cavernous wound.

"No," my father said to the question written there and sighed. "He'll live."

Gunshots was common, so we wasn't too worried, yet the three of us knew we shouldn't stay long lest someone get curious of the noise. They didn't have much in terms of possession, and so we left it all there for others to scavenge should any others come like hungry vultures. The fire still smoldered, though we pushed down the logs with our boots. And we left the shot man there next to the ghost of his dead partner.

The dark-skinned man looked around as if to wonder where he might go, but my father said, "You're coming with us, long as you need."

We walked the path we'd come in as our light faded. The canopy of trees was as bleak as candles in a darkened room, but we only had maybe a half-hour afore the ground would prove too dark to ride. I held my fist high to measure what was left of the sun.

"We need to dress those wounds," my father said to no one in particular.

When we got to the horses they was still there, not spooked by the gunshots.

"You ride?" my father asked him.

Lemi nodded. There was a thing about him. I could tell he was a well-learned man. He could write, which meant he could read, though he could never again talk on account'a his tongue. The post office in the diggins had opened not long ago, and they had paper and pen and ink. Maybe he'd share his story with us if we could afford some.

"I can ride with you, Papa," I said, and untied Nugget and handed over the reins to Lemi.

"You're a good man, Read," he said.

There was more my father wanted to say, perhaps to apologize for all I'd seen, but goin in we knew we had stepped away from innocence. My father opened his mouth, closed it. His eyes said what his mouth couldn't, and I nodded. I knew what he'd say.

3

WE got back to the claim soon as the sun finished its death behind us. Could barely see, but Nugget and Sasha was anxious to get back. I watered the horses the second I hopped down cause they hadn't had any to drink since the creek. We had on hand two covered buckets filled from the spring north and they drained the first and wanted the second, but I wouldn't let them have it all. The man named Lemi was thirsty too and he drank, and we drank, the three of us with cupped hands and just as greedy as we pulled water to our mouths.

My father paid no mind to those dark hands in the water, and so nor did I. We left enough to heat for coffee, then hobbled the horses for the night, none of us saying nothin but knowin what needed to be done. I thought then that it must be painful not to talk. Lemi seemed nice, even helped store the saddles with the other tack.

"What kind of man takes another's tongue?" I asked my father.

We hadn't talked about it on the ride. The three of us simply rode, emptied our canteens, used some to wash hands cause four of our six hands was bloody.

He pulled me aside, away from Lemi, and said, "A vile man."

And I said, "Think he done something bad?"

He said, "No. I bet he knows what they didn't want spread, is all. I reckon he's done nothing bad. I see it in his eyes. They hold a truth that wants out."

Lemi waited as we talked, looked off to the horses, his back hunched from pain. Who knows what he had on his mind. He could hear us, no doubt. The night seemed lost for all other sound. His back bled, and needed tended to, so my father led us inside.

"Come on in," my father said, motioned with his hands. "Let's get you clean."

The oil lamp lit the cabin in pale orange. With its light it felt a bit warmer inside. I unrolled one of the travel bedrolls the horses had carried and made a place for Lemi in the only place I could, under the canvas-covered window. Not too comfortable, but a bed. Three made a small room smaller. It beat the hard ground, though, and I'm glad we didn't have to. I'm glad he wouldn't have to sleep in that bastard camp no longer. Perhaps he was thought of as *theirs*, though my father was firm that no man could own another, other than by debt.

Slavery was banned in California by its first governor,

in a much heated debate, but no skin other than white was truly free in the west, red or black or brown or what-have-you. The last thing a person wanted in the west was to be of a color, lest be killed by a cold man drained of color. My guess is the men my father shot had tried takin ownership.

The quiet caused me to turn to the doorway. Lemi hadn't yet joined us. My father took no notice, or perhaps took notice unnoticed. He squatted next to the woodstove to make a fire to cook with, but not for food, not at first. The dark man could stab him in the back, smash a rock over his head and end him, but my father expressed no worry, and I guess that was the point, not to show hostility to our guest. He placed a cast iron on the stove for water, took to his duties.

Lemi stood outside the doorway as if afraid, as if the cabin were a trap he'd spring. The man took a few steps back to let darkness swallow him and stood with his back to us. He could walk away, and we'd never see him again. It was his choice. Freedom meant he could choose one direction or the other, and unless we gave him that freedom what good was we to not let him have it? He caught me through the window and smiled at my curiosity, then tilted his head to the stars. He seemed to pray, though his mouth didn't move, and I caught myself wonderin if words was needed to talk to a god.

I tried to ask for help in the past, about my mother, but no gods ever listened.

My father tore into the silence with a meat knife against a section of linen, made strips he tossed in the water as it steamed. He clanked his pocketknife in as well, the sharp one. Soon he had a fire arage in the metal beast in front of him and the water boiled what was put in it. He stood and stared into the pot, all hypnotic. I watched the flames lick out the vents. All three of us stared at something, least for a while.

My father held one of the big wooden spoons in the water a moment, then used it with another utensil to scoop the knife and set it on a clean cloth he'd earlier put on the table. He fished the strips of linen next and hung them to drip on the floor not touchin nothin. Last he took his hipflask and took a swig. He held it out, but I put up a hand.

We waited, but our guest stood within the open door.

After the water, my father heated bean soup and crumbled in bacon from the morn, and the smell was what finally brought Lemi inside, though this was after a good long while. I was into the cards on the table, not a game, just to shuffle and arrange by number and color.

"We'll eat," my father said, "but not till we set you right."

My father eyed the bandages, then Lemi eyed the bandages.

Lemi showed the whites of his teeth in a grimace, but only cause it hurt takin off his ruined shirt. Most of it stuck to him. When freed, he crumpled it to a ball, dropped it on the floor cause there was nowhere else to put it. He made as if to say some words, then seemed to remember he couldn't, and I couldn't help but wonder how long he'd been without a tongue.

He sucked in breath, let it out, a mad wind.

"Let's see what they done to you," my father said, and twirled his finger for him to turn around so as he could assess the damage.

The man gave us his back, which he contemplated over, and which was in shreds. Six slashes bisected the skin that shoulda otherwise connected him. I never seen wounds so deep. Bits'a gravel clung and there was bruises like he'd been beat or thrown to the ground.

"Take this," my father said to him and then held out the wooden spoon.

Confusion hit me only long enough to realize it wasn't for the pot.

The man took it, knew what it was for.

"And you might want some of this," my father said.

He meant the flask, which the man also took. He knew what it was for too, unscrewed the cap, took a long swig, then another. He didn't grimace, which meant his tongue had mostly healed, cut off years ago, perhaps. He handed back the flask but kept the spoon.

"Read, fetch more whiskey."

I knew where it was and got it for him. I never seen my father drink in the cabin, only used it for medical purposes. The moment I handed him the bottle he uncapped it, motioned to the spoon. Lemi bit onto it, not hard, not yet, but when the spirit ran down his back and fell a shade'a pink onto the floor, he coulda broke it. He made no noise other than relief.

I took a dirty rag to the floor as my father used his pocketknife to pluck out the gravel, dropped pieces like gold into his open palm. He spread the wounds, peered inside.

"This will hurt some," my father said.

He wadded one of the cloth strips he'd boiled, tipped the bottle over it to soak in some of the liquor, waited for the spoon to return to the man's mouth, then used it to dig into each ravine.

Lemi's back arched the other way, but he knew what needed to be done.

My father had boiled maybe twenty or more strips of linen, some long, some short, and they steamed on the table and as he placed them over the open wounds. Only bandages we had. And when it was finally over, the longest cloth was wrapped round and round him, completely opposite in color to his skin, same as the whites of his eyes, his teeth, and he turned to my father, held out his hand, fingers skyward. Not for a handshake, but for the flask.

My father smiled and they each took a pull.

I took a small pull as well cause it was insisted upon.

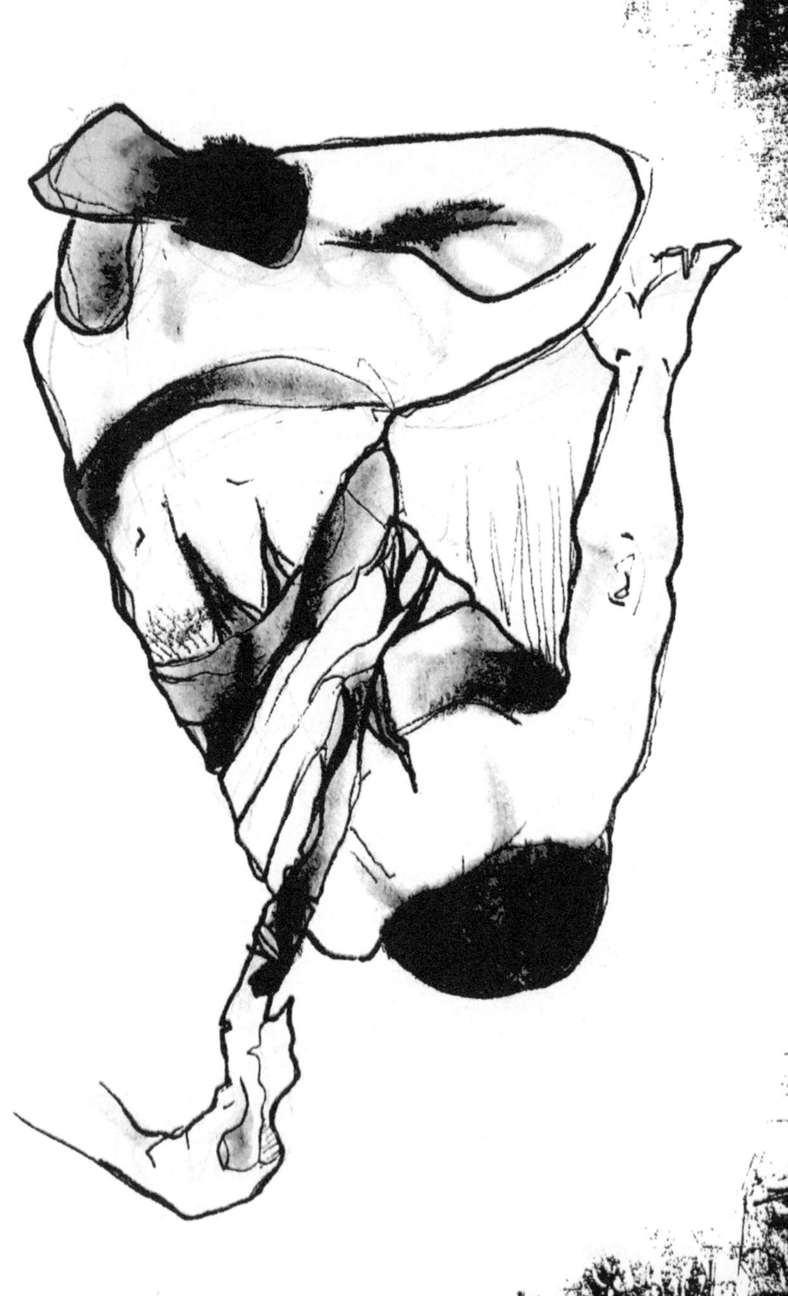

Then my father did a peculiar thing. He walked outside just then, bent down and scooped a double-handful of earth, brought it inside, dumped it on the floor and moved the lantern to the mess he'd made. He knelt on his haunches, wrote "FOR TALKIN" with a finger. My father could write some, though usually had me read on account of my namesake. "You's gonna read," he told me long ago, and we both learned. We both grew into our names, me perhaps more so.

Lemi had nothin to write right then, but we knew it was for whenever.

He took to sleep on the bedroll, his back to the roof. He may have passed out but started in his dreams come supper. Bad dreams, from the look of it. Only out an hour at most. His back spasmed like stones skipped over a stream, and we ate without him. He bled through the make-shift bandages the moment they was put on, though my father wanted them on awhile longer, and after we ate I cleaned the cast iron so he could boil more linen.

When Lemi woke, we sterilized again. More bandages, more whiskey, but no more need to pebble-mine with the blade. My father washed his hands with a cloth and took up thread and needle, sewed the widest of chasms in rugged X's that disappeared into the man's skin as he bit on the spoon. The next bandages soaked a bit less and stayed more pink than white.

"In the morning we'll see about proper medicine."

"How we gonna afford any?" I asked him, but he didn't seem concerned.

It was full dark when Lemi was ready to eat, and to talk. He simply got up and sat afront the dirt on the floor, soup cup in hand. We followed him, the three of us circled like we was gathered round a fire ring. The slow wheel of time turned. We talked only with our eyes for some time, but then my father broke the silence.

"How long they think they owned you?"

In the dirt, Lemi wrote in cursive, "long enough," then brushed his hand over it so he could write again, "cut out my tongue," and erased it again.

"When'd they do it?" I asked.

He shrugged as if so long ago he couldn't remember.

"Well," my father said, "they can't own you now, and never did to begin with. One is dead, the other just as good as with that round buried in him. Can I ask you a favor, though? Can you write not in cursive? I'm not the best at reading cursive."

Lemi wrote: "left for dead," brushed it away, wrote: "but not."

He meant the man my father shot in the belly.

"Sometimes men like him need learning. All night he's gonna think about the things he's done in his life, all the bad things, wishing he hadn't. He'll be thinking those things till he dies. I knew when I shot him it wasn't fatal, or I would have aimed higher. The plan, before seeing what they done to you, was to dig out the round and make him talk. Could have shot out his heart, but that's not how the stars fell."

There was a long pause, then my father continued.

"You could have ended him just the same," he said, tapped the middle of his own forehead, said, "so why didn't you? You were in the right to take his life."

Lemi looked at his bedroll, at the gun he'd placed there, same one he'd used to take the man's ability to hear. He nodded, slowly, as if he'd wanted to kill him but couldn't.

He wrote: "eye for an eye," and brushed away the words.

"Hearin for talkin," I said, and each of us smiled.

Lemi wrote: "why?" and pointed at my father's chest, then at mine.

"Why were we there?"

He nodded.

"Cole Mullins and the man he runs with," my father said, "they took everything we had, in terms of gold, everything we gathered over last four months at this claim.”

“Two bags’a—” I started to say, but he put up a parental hand.

“Our savings,” my father said. “Were they liars?”

Lemi wrote: “about?”

“Their whereabouts, and their business.”

Lemi shrugged, then wrote: “still time.”

“Time?”

Lemi wrote: “to prod.”

“You think we should go back, in the morning.”

Lemi shrugged, cleared the floor, then wrote: “sleep.”

The man was tired and rightfully so. What he’d gone through, both now and then, I can only imagine, though I tried hard not to. And it was true, if the man my father shot, the one still alive, still let out wheezes of breath come sunrise, he could be prod more. My father could bury a finger in the shot wound to get more words outta him. He’d talk loud, unable to hear his noise.

My father contemplated. I could see it on his face.

“One more question,” he said, “then we can all bed down for the night, though I’ll be up keeping watch the next few hours. In the morning, soon as the pharmacy opens, we’ll get you what you need and you can either be on your way or stay with us. We have enough besides that gold stolen to fix you up right. Doctor’ll know what to do.”

The man openly cried in front of us.

“Like I said before, you can stay as long as you need. You decide to stay and mine the diggings, what we find will be split three ways: you, me, and the boy. Two-thirds is our share, of course, as this is our claim and having a third set of hands will only add a third to what we find. I guess my question is, are you a man of trust? I see the good in you, same as I see it in Read. I’m not saying you’re ours. *Amigos. Compadres.* Men working together, is all. Any man say otherwise, and he’ll quickly learn he’s wrong.”

Lemi pointed at his chest, as if to say 'Me?' and my father nodded.

My father said, "But I lied just then. I have two questions and that was just the first. The second is, will you help us find Cole Mullins and the other?"

Lemi thought a moment, made a gesture of a gun with his hand, pointed it toward the open door and pulled an imaginary trigger, as if he'd shoot for us.

I pantomimed a noose around my neck and pulled a rope that wasn't there.

"No," my father said and laughed, "we don't want either man dead unless they have to be. When we find those cowards, we'll take back what's rightfully ours and be done with it. They want to resist, well …" and with his tongue outstretched he tilted his head and pretended to both hang and put a round put in his head. And that was the end of our parley.

Lemi took to his bedroll and me to mine, and until my eyes grew too heavy to hold them up any longer, I watched as my father stood guard by the open door. He wore his gun belt with thumbs hooked on either side. For a moment I thought he might rest, but his only movement was to get his leather hat from off the table. He saw me watchin him and winked.

4

I AM not even sure if my father slept that night, cause he was in that same spot when the sound of a coyote let us know it was sunup. He seemed rested, like he'd cat-napped on his feet.

"Mornin," he said, same as I responded.

Lemi slept soundly on his stomach, hands propped under his head. He hadn't moved from what I could tell, and until his chest rose he appeared dead to the world. The bandages had held through the night, and not much more blood had seeped.

We fried us some eggs from the half-dozen we had and let the man dream. Two eggs for each of us and two for our guest, but we left our guest's meal plated on the table for when he woke, which my father said might not be for hours. And so, my father, Read Sr., wrote in the dirt on the floor: "GONE" and "TIL NOON" with an arrow that pointed toward the meal.

"Where we goin?" I asked as we saddled.

"To prod," my father said, and I knew what he meant. He meant back to Weber where we'd left a dead man and a not-so-dead man. We had hours anyway till the general store opened, for the sun was yellow on the horizon and wouldn't represent itself as hot-white noon for some time. "That's if he lasted the night," he added.

I said, "What do you suppose he's ponderin?"

He said, "Ponderin?" same way as I said it.

"The man at the creek, the one still alive. You think he's thinkin of all the bad stuff he's done and trying to set them right?"

"Mayhap," he said, "if he wants to die a better man."

"Won't ever make it right, though, will it?"

He left my words in the air. He always instilled in me there was both good and bad in the world, and that good outweighed bad by far, but I always seen the scales of right and wrong tilt the other way. I'd witnessed bad men and their capabilities. Might be more good than bad in the world in terms of numbers, but what the bad weighed seemed a lot heavier. A dozen good things could happen, but one awful thing could tilt the scale hard.

What the men at the creek had done to Lemi would take a thousand great deeds by a thousand great men to even out the good vs. bad.

"How will you prod?" I asked.

"He'll be shivering with fever. That round in his gut will need to come out if he ever wants to cool, if he wants to live. Might not remember who we are, on account of the dark and his shock. Maybe see us as a boy and his father come to fetch water."

"Is that why you wore the hat?"

We rode side-by-side, so I only caught one side of his smile.

"I figure he's been suffering long enough not to spook upon seeing us, and that he'll not go for another weapon should another be in their camp. I imagine he's where we left him, doing his best not to bleed out. Once he waves us in, we'll make ourselves known and he'll be sweating more ways than one. He'll tell us anything we want in order to survive."

"And what if he don't."

"Then we'll prod harder till he does."

"And what if he don't after that?"

"Well, I guess he'll suffer the same fate as his friend. Not that I'll shoot him, I mean. *Eventually.* Killing him was up to Lemi, and he chose not to and we should respect that."

"There's one problem," I said.

"What's that?" he said.

"Won't he not hear us," I said. "His ears was both blowed off, the barrel right next to him. Hearin for talkin, remember?"

"I guess we'll need to adapt, find a way to be heard."

I knew what he meant by those words, but none of it mattered cause when we got to the clear of the creek we could see straight through the trees and scrubs. Only the scrawny one remained, dead, and on his side.

My father checked their camp first, then waved me in to join him. The colorless scene from the night afore had regained its color, black for red: a spray of blood and brain matter against the rock, stripes on the ground from Lemi's back, a puddle where the man in the longcoat sat and held in his stomach where we'd left him.

The camp lay abandoned and tossed awry: cups and utensils and food scattered about as if molested by coons, two daypacks with not much left but dry goods and half-empty canteens, a few picks and gold pans with flakes of yellow still reflected by sunbeams that passed through the canopy of trees. Wet clothes had turned dry on the line yet were covered in dew.

"How you reckon it's safe?" I said.

"He left a trail anyone could track," he said, and pointed at a break in the foliage. Some of the leaves splotched red. "And we have the advantage. Won't hear us following him."

Poison oak was common, and the oily leaves often changed dark as scarlet in the heat as they clung on their overtake of the trees, but what covered the brush parted by hand was shinier than any natural poison. The man's path was dotted on the ground, too, as if he'd plotted his past travels on the map called earth, not to mention boot tracks in the mud.

Only thing my father took from the camp was a bag of ammunition that matched the gun now in Lemi's possession, which he pocketed. There was a rustle in the trees above as he took it, and we both startled but we found nothin but a trio of turkey vultures on branches high above, wings outstretched to dry them of the wet morn. They awaited their next meal.

We filled our canteens in the water and drank and filled them again.

I followed my father as he parted the brush and fought through it. The blood had fallen heavy at first, but as we made our way what seemed north-eastward it thinned and so we slowed our pace to match in case we was upon him. Manzanita scraped our ankles. We made such a canal in our travels that we'd easily find our way back to the hobbled horses.

Then about a quarter-mile in I stopped as my father held up a hand, and then I heard who we pursued. A moan, some swears, a stumble and crash. Maybe twenty or so yards afront of us.

The way my father called out "Coward!" meant he no longer cared if the man knew who we was at first. The way my father said it was a reminder, a threat of his capabilities, but we both knew the man we chased was deaf.

Another moan, another crash, another swear.

We pressed on, my father with the pistol at his side, me with the rifle slung over a shoulder so as not to snag it in the brush, until we came to a pressed-down grassy area.

The shot man no longer wore his slicker. He wore not much at all as he lay on his back with his face to us. One hand held his stomach, the other he held out as we approached.

"Please help me," he cried.

"Where's Cole Mullins?" my father said. "How are you two in business and how are you affiliated the man he runs with?" He pointed the barrel, but it didn't do much good.

"Please," the man cried. He spoke as if the gun was imaginary, and loud as if to talk over its fire, and in an octave higher than he had the night prior. He kept watch over his shoulder, frantic. His eyes sank in pits of deep black, drained of life, of will.

I pointed my rifle at him cause it seemed the right thing to do. Might have a gun with him, hidden in the grass, or a bowie knife. Could be an act, an attempt to draw us closer.

"Where's Cole Mullins?" my father said again.

"You's the man who shot me!" the man cried.

A bush far behind him moved unnaturally and I nearly fired, leaned forward even, but my father put a hand on the barrel and slowly brought it down. He cocked his pistol, raised it to whoever intended to make his presence known.

"Is that you, Cole?" my father said. "Show yourself. We outnumber you ten to one and we're primed and ready to fire upon the lot of you."

Right then a brown cub meandered out from the bush, no bigger than a sack of grain, followed by another. Two bear cubs. I'd never seen bear cubs afore.

"Oh, gawd," the man cried, and backpedaled.

It was then I realized, and my father too, that the path we'd followed had been too wide to be made by man alone, the brush too trampled, and it was then we noticed the tracks that lead into the clear, as well as the mark clawed into the deaf man's leg just below the knee, hidden before from the way he sat. Gashes as wide as fingers.

He'd been dragged.

My father lowered his pistol and put a finger to his lips to intone we was to stay as quiet as the dead. He then turned and pointed the direction from which we came, patted at the ground to tell me without words to do so slowly and without sound. Spoke without words.

I listened to his hand-language and nodded.

"Please help me!" the man cried. "I dint mean to do what you think I did to that n—— to that man. Thomas, he done it, he done cut out that man's tongue cause that darkie was smarter than him two-fold, not me. I just whipped him good for not doin as told, is all. Slaves is used to whippin and that's all I done to him. Please don't leave me out here."

His noise brought out mamma bear, biggest creature I ever saw. The grizzly smashed through the trees on our left, mere feet away. She let out a roar to scare the stripe off a skunk and rose on her hind legs. Seven or eight feet tall if it was an inch. Our pal with the stomach wound pissed hisself right there, knickers spreading with the yellow fear that made him.

I aimed and my father aimed.

My father lowered the pistol and I lowered the rifle.

There was nothin we could do for the coward. He was good as dead, and though the beast afore us was made of nightmares she was still a mamma bear, a wild creature with instincts and a want to protect her young. The ground thudded as she landed on all-fours. We left him there to feed her cubs, all he was good for. He was fodder and deserved such fate.

The scale of good and evil tipped one way or the other, and whichever way didn't matter, not to us. If we fired we was as good as dead too, but we still had work ahead of us and this man didn't. The grizzly'd take a round or two and turn upon us before we could fire seconds.

"Don't leave me here," the man cried.

The mammoth bear let out another roar as the two cubs disappeared into the trees. She advanced on him, and we withdrew, slow as we could not to cause more than a twig to snap beneath us, and so we watched as her giant mitts lashed out, removed the round from his gut and more so, and then lashed out again, takin some of his throat and his voice.

"That bear was twice the one we saw in the tent," I said when we was safe.

My father didn't say nothin but nodded.

Not long after we first came to the diggins, a man by the name of Ben Nickerson tried to bring a grizzly to what's now the Blue Bell Café. Strange man strutted in with the damn thing leashed round the neck, he with the lead rope, along with a donkey in tow to carry all his wares. He'd come to the diggins to gain his gold by other means, to stage fights. Maybe he raised it from a cub. No matter, public opinion wanted no bear, so he was outed and soon returned to start a canvas tent saloon, which stood bigger than most other places. No one knows what happened to the grizzly. For all anyone knows, he let it go. Could be the same bear as this one, grown.

On our way back, we found the man's pants, shredded, as if torn free from his body. In the small pouched tied to it were a handful of schillings, and a note with only two words scribbled, childlike: HANGTOWN CRƎƎK with the E's backward, and Cole's initials after a dash-mark, as if he'd wrote it.

The creek is what ran through most of the diggins, why people came to it in the first place. Weber Creek, actually. It's why we came. Promises of gold found easy as river rock.

"What's it mean?" I asked.

My father shrugged and said, "Could be where they're going. Could be where they've already gone." Another mystery.

"This is Weber Creek," I said.

In the bushes next to the bloody clothes was a thin layer of well-worn rawhide with a black line drawn drunkenlike down the middle. Half a map, I knew, cause of the shoddily-drawn nautical star in the corner. He'd either dropped the map or had it on him before it was torn from his possession. Had a different penmanship than the note. The N, E, and W were curlier, as if supposed to be cursive. There was no S, and the fork of the E pointed to the east, as it should.

"Where's the other half?" I said.

And if this was indeed a map of the creek, why not label it as such on the front, not have it written on a separate note?

We looked around for the other half, but it wasn't meant to be found, and so we drank our canteens dry and didn't make mention of what we'd seen moments earlier. Instead, we headed back to the camp and scoured what they'd left behind. The vultures were already at work on the man's gut. They flew away awkwardly at our approach, wings as long as my arms.

The few bags the dead men had left behind didn't amount to much. They had no gold, no coins, nothin of any value, not that we would have taken it. We was there only for what was ours, the gold, and they didn't have it. They knew of the coward Cole Mullins though, and whether or not Slade was the other he ran with, I wondered if they knew of him.

The dead man stared back as if he had more to tell us.

"The next camp over," he had said before dyin, and I relayed the memory to my father, who nodded. He bent over the man and tried to push down his eyelids, but they wanted to remain forever-open to ponder life, and so my father pulled out two of the coins he'd found and placed one over each socket. I'm not sure which version of him left me more unsettled, and if I could guess, this was my father's original intention upon taking the coins.

"For the ferryman," my father said.

I didn't know what to make of that and didn't ask.

We was about to head back when my father tilted his head, then reached around the dead man with the silvery-round stare. Saw something he earlier hadn't, what the man had tucked into the back of his pants like a handkerchief.

Another map, it seemed, but blank. My father held it up to the sun, scratched at a smudge, then handed it to me.

"Let me see the other, too," I said, and put the torn map atop the blank one. "Same leather, thin as parchment." I turned it, admired the sun as it still rose, and pointed the tops of them the direction I figured to be north.

"Crude drawing," my father said, "but it's definitely Hangtown Creek. Weber. This jut, here," he said, with a finger on it," is where the creek enters town before heading west.

The smudge he'd tried to scratch with a fingernail was not a smudge, I determined, but a dollop of black ink, as if a fountain pen had been pressed against the blank canvas too long. This second piece of leather was completely blank but for that imperfection.

"I don't get it," I said.

"Maybe there's nothing to get."

"I mean, why have a map at all if nothin's on it but the creek? No reference points. What purpose does that serve other than to know what way the water flows?"

We pondered this for a while, then I folded both small enough to carry in my saddlebag, and we made our way westward along Weber, not a creek-walk, but alongside the water, quietly, lest we come upon the two we really sought. We'd already found two of Cole's associates armed, one of them, anyway, and might find others.

After some time, we came upon the adjacent camp, at least what was left of it. The fire they'd left gave off warmth, but my father said they'd most likely left at sunup. No hoof-prints in or out, only foot-prints that suggested they were headed the opposite direction we assumed they was headed after takin our gold. Not *away* from the diggins, but *toward* it.

And so, we returned with our horses in silence, the horror long behind us.

5

FORENOON we rode into the middle of Hangtown. Lemi could still be asleep in the cabin, for all we knew, or gone, but we passed by and stopped in town for supplies, none-theless.

"What if he takes—"

"He ain't gonna take nothin," my father said, "and ain't much for him to take if he wants to take. But he ain't gonna take nothin. Everything we own in terms of gold is here." He patted the pouch tied to his belt where a second pistol could go. Maybe where a second *should* go.

"You think Lemi knows more 'bout Cole Mullins?"

"I think he might."

We tied our horses outside Empire Theatre, an adobe-faced construct that stood like a sentinel in the middle of the diggins. Sometimes we'd go there for stage plays. This time'a day, it was all but abandoned. All other places to tie a horse was taken, so we walked from there.

"How much we got left?" I asked.

"Enough," my father said, and that was the end of our conversation. The way he said 'enough' meant it *wasn't*, that we'd be hard up soon.

"We got enough to buy supplies for Lemi to write with?"

"We do," he said.

And so that's the first thing we looked for: an ink vial, some sorta quill-pen to dip, and a blank book with wood-pulp pages. I almost asked if we should hold off till we knew he was still there, at the claim, but thought better of it.

The most expensive of what we bought was a tincture in a tiny glass bottle with a stopper at the neck. My father slid bandages across the counter, and a quart of whiskey to either drink or use otherwise, and it was all paid for with an assortment of coin. He looked at me the way a father remembers to look at a boy, then asked how much for the hub wafers in the jar behind the counter. We rarely splurged on things such as candy, but he slid a coin the same size as the wafers across the counter in trade for half a scoopful. When he handed them to me, the man behind the counter put together my true age by the smile on my face and slid the coin back.

"Made from a lozenge cutter," the man said. "They come from Boston, Massachusetts of all places. My favorites are the brown ones. Chocolate."

"Much appreciated," my father said and tipped his hat.

We tried licorice and clove and chocolate, but couldn't figure out the other flavors, one some kind of mint. After having a dozen between us, the chalky things all tasted simi-lar. I put what remained in my own pouch, and we each wandered town with differing coin purses at his side. We bought eggs and apples from Asa Cleavenger's grocery, then returned to the horses.

We'd gone into town for two reasons: to shop, and to spot the men we was out for in case they was dumb enough to return. What we purchased went into the saddlebags, with my father's free hand at the ready should he need to fire his pistol, and me with my free hand on the strapped rifle, but mostly to keep it from jostlin around. Sometimes my father would hop off Sasha, hand me his reins and say to wait while he looked inside. He returned each time downtrodden.

The way we rode, we passed the oak out front Elstner's hay yard.

"Used to call that *The Dreaming Tree*," my father said after I couldn't seem to keep my gaze off its branches. "Long before it was used for hanging."

The rope swayed in the breeze.

"Why?"

He considered the question thoughtfully, then said, "I don't know. I guess old names eventually die once new ones take over, or are forgotten, and since now everyone calls this *The Hanging Tree*, well, the only dreams this tree creates now are nightmares, so there's no use for it having its old name."

"Is it true," I asked, "five men were hanged?"

"Three," he said. "I was there."

"You was? Where was I?"

"Sleeping," he said. "You weren't much older than twelve or thirteen, and it happened long after dark. Some things not every man should see. Hell, I'm nearly three times your age and don't think I should have witnessed such a travesty."

"I want to see Cole Mullins hanged," I said. "And—"

He pulled back on his reins and stopped so that I'd have to back my horse. He stared up at the tree, in wait for me to join his side. The problem with Nugget is that I haven't yet trained her to walk backward, so I lead her in a not-so-wide loop to get her alongside him.

Another lesson from my father was in store, it seemed.

"I do," I said. "I want to see a rope round his neck."

"I don't," my father said.

"And why not?"

"No man should ever be hanged."

"Cole Mullins deserves to be hanged. And—"

My father laughed at this, and said, "What, cause he took something wasn't his? Cause he took two half-filled bags of gold dust from you and me?"

So, I said, "The other night, you shot that man dead and he didn't do nothin to us. You *ended* him. And together we left the other dead to a bear, his ears all shot off by a man we don't know who's now in our cabin. What's the difference in shootin a man and stringin one up?"

So, he said, "You seen what they did to Lemi," not as a question.

I nodded.

"You think they deserved what they got?"

"But Cole Mullins and the other man *stole* from us."

"You think they deserved what they got?" he asked again.

He meant the dead men. I considered then nodded, then added, "Bible says thou shall not kill, nor steal, nor covet thy neighbor's goods," and I was about to go on, but he stopped me.

"Bible says a lot of things," he said. "Those commandments, they have an order, but you think some are more sinful than others?"

This was what my father liked to call rhetorical.

"What are they?" he said.

"In order?"

"In order."

We had a family bible brought with us from Missouri, an old leather-bound thing mostly come apart. He knew I knew the sins. We only had that book and two others, and I read it first page to last I don't know how many times. The commandments were underlined long ago by ma, he told me, for she'd underlined all the important scriptures.

"I am the Lord thy God, thou shalt not have any strange gods—" and before I could go on and recount the others, he stopped me again.

"Idolatry," he said, then, "golden calves. Every man at the diggings worships gold in one form or another. Now go on, what are the rest."

I counted them on my finger as I went along, first my thumb, then index as I said, "Thou shalt not take the name of the Lord thy God in vain."

"How many times you hear a man say *got-damn* round here?"

"Countless. Then there's the one about the Sabbath."

"You know what day today is?" he said.

I didn't and shook my head.

"Not many do, and those who keep track are miners. Preachers, too. Reverend Hosford, a Methodist, preached weekly here, right at this very spot until a proper church was built, but his main interest is gold. And Reverend Joseph Meek in Coloma. Their places of worship are built now, sure, but empty come Sunday, and they spout often to their own deaf ears."

As my fourth finger rose, I said, "Honor thy father and—" but couldn't say 'mother.' Then there's the one about the killin, and then the one about adultery."

"Judge Lynch is a religious man," he said. "How many men you think he's killed, not by his hand, but by his *word?* How many men you see coming out the Boomerang or one of the tents each day having had a woman other than his wife? Not a lot of women here, I know, but think about all the wives left back home waiting for their husbands to return with fortune, and then think again of those men you seen. And how many times have you seen the judge with his arm around another woman wasn't his?"

I seen it plenty.

"Thou shalt not steal," I said, in need of the other hand, and then rattled off the others in quick succession, lastly, "Thou shalt not covet thy neighbor's goods," which I gave emphasis.

"They have an order," he said, "but some have more weight than others, and like everything else in that book, the words require interpretation."

"What's interpretation?"

"Finding meaning. You're dead set on putting an end to Cole Mullins and the man Slade, or whoever he runs with, but for what?" He held up just the pinky finger on his opposite hand, which I knew was same as the tenth sin, the one about takin goods from others. He held up his other pinky then, to denote the sin I'd first brought up, and said, "A better translation of 'kill,' at least in Hebrew terms, is 'murder.' Subtle in distinction, but important. To kill an innocent man is murder, but to kill an *unjust* man in order to preserve life, well, it's still the same as killing, but not the same as murder. It's not even immoral, in my mind's eye."

"This whole place is sin," I said, which made him laugh. "Whole place is immoral."

"Then you understand."

"But isn't it *unjust* to take from another?"

"That could be one interpretation, but wouldn't it be just as *just* to be able to retake what's ours, our gold, without having to put an end to two more lives? Wouldn't it be worth the risk not having to worry about eternal damnation?"

More rhetoricals.

"When a man hangs," he said, "it's not always as simple as broken necks. Three men hanged from that tree, until dead, and none had their lives spared quickly. We all stood watching until no one moved. We all stood watching as bowels let loose. And, as a reminder, for the next three days, we all watched as they turned to rot, still hanging from those branches."

I'd seen rot on a fallen log, on a dead squirrel someone shot.

We both stared up at the hangin tree, and I imagined not three but two sets of feet danglin from two sets of rope. I imagined cloths over their heads, though I knew who each of them was, but then felt guilty to have such a horrid daydream, though I guess that was my father's point.

The Dreamin Tree, I thought, *with nightmares caught in its branches.*

"So, let's take it back," I said, "what's ours."

6

AS I feared, Lemi woke and had gone by the time we made it back. I surveyed inside. The sun was past straight above us, which meant early afternoon. Hotter than most days. Wasn't till we went outside I noticed what he took.

"He got the damn 'barrow," I said.

After we staked our claim, it was one of the first items we bought to move rock. Could easily hold the weight of a man before a tip. There was cheaper wheelbarrows to buy, but we knew we'd put one to hard use, so we handed over ten dollars to a man in town named John Mohler Studebaker. He came to the diggins from Ohio at nineteen. Wasn't much good at the mines, from what was told to us, so he rented the back half of Baker & Keyser, the smiths, to make and repair 'barrows for better miners.

"And the spade!" I added.

We'd saved this man, only to be robbed.

My father didn't say nothin as a rumble came from the back of our property closest to the stream. Lemi pushed in front of him the 'barrow with a mound a sand and pebble gathered from the creek shore, so high it cascaded over the top on either side. Shirtless, he sweat like I never seen, muscles like boulders. He pushed maybe three times what me and my father could push, the spade poked out the peak. Some of the linen bandages had worked their way down.

He'd been at work on the placer deposit on our section of the creek while we was gone, and from the look of it had been at it for hours and knew the process well. The two dead men must have labored him hard since they first thought they owned him.

Lemi smiled when he saw us, lowered the barrow with a thud and headed to where we spent our time with pans. He held out a pan to us like a meal, showed us what he found.

Seven good-sized yellow pebbles, and enough bits and flakes to fill a thimble, an amount the two of us alone hadn't panned in as much as a full day's work. What he presented coulda paid for everything we just bought.

My father clapped him on the shoulder and said, "Will you look at that," but again not as a question. There was no way not lookin at it, for gold was mezmerizin magic.

Lemi held up a finger, then three.

"One third," I said.

"One third," my father agreed, but then he inspected the bandages applied only the night afore and cringed, held up his saddlebag and added, "let's get you some proper aide. You've sweat through them and are bleeding still."

I handed him a rag to wipe himself dry soon as we went inside, and he soaked it through. I then reached into my own saddlebag. I uncapped the ink and dipped the new quill-pen inside and on the first page in the book of blanks wrote 'Lemi' and underlined it and left a spot for a last name. I pointed to the area, and he only shrugged. He pointed to the word 'Lemi' and then to his chest, as if that were solely it.

"Just Lemi, and nothin after it?"

He nodded.

My father poured into a bowl a small amount of water from buckets he musta filled while we was gone, and dripped in ten or so drops of the tincture, which smelt the way medicine does. He washed his hands best he could and used a clean rag on the stove to stir and soak in the mix.

"What is it?" I asked.

"I don't know," my father said, "but the man at the pharmacy said it would help disinfect and prevent infection. Some Indian thing. Help him out of those old wraps."

I didn't want to, but didn't have a choice in the matter, I knew, so I looked at the man and said, "This is gonna hurt some," because it would.

"Dab the ol' linens first, on his back" my father said, and handed over a plain-water-soaked rag. "And don't go easy. Soak them well and they'll come off easier." He put one of the buckets on the table and tossed another rag inside, then set the new bandages on the table.

The old strips of cloth was already drenched in sweat, and blood, but I knew what my father meant and soaked them as willingly as I could muster. I squeezed water from the rag to cover him good. Made a mess on the floor, but any mess could be later dealt with.

Lemi felt hot to the touch, like his skin was afire, as if the water would steam right off him, but he didn't seem to mind the touch, and only flinched on the deepest wounds. I wanted to ask my father why it had to be me to tend to him, but it wasn't right to ask, not then. I assumed it was to help me become a man, another lesson.

"You want the spoon?" my father asked him, but Lemi shook his head no. "You want the whiskey" he said next, but he didn't want that either.

When the old bandages started to fall on their own, where they wasn't touchin wounds, I slowly peeled them away. The three of us scrunched faces, but only one of us from pain. I coiled the expired ones like snakeskins on the floor where they soaked what dripped off him. Gashes as wide as fingers raked his skin. Those my father had sewn shut held strong and seeped only little.

"Read," my father said, cause I'd been entranced. "Wash your hands."

I did so, but he then thrusted another wet rag into them to tell me I wasn't yet done, the rag he'd soaked in the bowl, the one with the medicine. He pointed with his eyes to Lemi's back, and I knew again what it was he wanted me to do. The tincture or elixir or whatever it was must have burned fierce cause Lemi hissed the moment it touched him, as if the dead snakes at his feet would come alive and strike our ankles.

"I'm sorry," I said, but was then told I needn't be.

The rag turned from canvas-color to red, and so I put it in the bucket and wrung it clear, then stuck it back in the bowl to soak more of the drug. I did all this three times, delicately, until my father said enough and that I done good. And when I thought the horror was truly over, he had me apply the bandages. He wanted me to know how, now and for the future. He showed me the first, and I did the rest till the awful deed was over.

We washed our hands together, and he nudged his shoulder against mine.

I nudged him back.

Then my father tossed the man one of his clean shirts. I hadn't realized till that moment Lemi only had the one in tatters, which was still on the floor. He must have bathed in the creek while we was gone, too, for his pants were cleaner than the previous night. And his gun, still holstered, slept alongside his bedroll.

"You should rest," my father told him. "You're in no condition to do what you did this morning, but don't think your hard work went unnoticed. You're a good man, Lemi, and like I said the night before, this is your place as long as you need it, so make yourself comfortable. If you don't feel like sleeping, you can write. We should know your story."

Lemi spoke without words, thankful for what we'd done, what we'd promised to do for him. He then went to the bedroll and sat, set the ink vial on the floor at his feet, and began to write in what looked like loopy cursive.

"I want to see that map again," my father said, "the one of the creek."

I pulled it from my pouch and cleared a spot on the table, pushed away an empty plate. The eggs we'd left for Lemi had disappeared, and I couldn't help but wonder how a man eats without his tongue, but that was as far as I let the thought wander.

Maybe I'd offer him a wafer later.

We unfolded each of the leathery things onto the table-top, one with a splotch of black, the other with a jagged line to denote water. Crudely drawn, perhaps with a piece of coal. I pulled out the scratch of paper as well, the one with the name of the creek and Cole Mullins' initials.

"It's definitely the creek," my father said. He got up and went to the wood stove and took out a half-burned splinter of wood, used it to mark a place on the map, what appeared to be southeast. "This is us," he said, making a small dot.

"Yeah," I said, "so?"

"So, nothing," he said. "This is us, way down here. This is about where Cleavenger's is, and here's where Studebaker sells, and this is the Empire." He moved his finger along the front to point them out. It was only half a map, so he continued a charcoal line onto the table behind it. "Here's where we first tried staking claim but couldn't cause it was already taken, remember?"

"But why did he have this on him?" I asked. "And this other."

We stared, perplexed, until Lemi cleared his throat. Unaware, we hadn't noticed he'd gotten up from where he wrote to stand behind us. He held out his hand expectantly for the blackened wood and my father handed it to him. His hand swallowed it, but he wrote the word 'legend' on the larger blank flat of leather.

"Legend?" I said.

Lemi nodded, as if that single word fixed all.

"What legend?" my father said.

I thought of pirates and buried treasure and was about to say it could be a treasure map of sorts, when Lemi let out a frustrated grunt and took the piece he'd written on and set it atop the other. He lined up the corners to match and pointed to the word again.

"He means in terms of symbols," my father said. "Not a story, but a symbol."

"A symbol of what?"

My father leaned in close and pulled back. He pointed at the areas where a compass should go if the blank one was also a map. Just below the black splotch he pointed again and said, "There used to be an N here, and an arrow, noting this as North, but it's been weathered or worn away. You can barely see what's left. North is up, as it should be."

I leaned in too and saw it.

"So, they *both* used to be maps," I said.

"No," my father said. "One is a legend for the other."

"I don't know what that means."

"Legends are used on maps to explain symbols," he said. "Triangles for mountain ranges, dotted lines for trails or paths traveled. Lemi's saying this is the legend for the map underneath, one to be overlaid onto the other. This splotch notes something specific. My guess is a rich vein."

"You mean gold."

"Perhaps," he said, then pulled up the corner of the now mostly blank legend, revealing Hangtown Creek underneath.

"Could be a drop of sap, or it could be what they were looking for, those men we stumbled on. If this is north, though, and *this* is north," he said, and flipped to the other, "then none of it makes a lick of sense. They'd have been in the wrong area."

I leaned over him, flipped between the two.

"You're right," I said. "Doesn't make sense. If that black dot's significant, it's nothin special. That's the hill, there, which is nowhere near the creek."

"Could be sap," he said again.

"What you drew on the table," I said, "is it to scale?"

"Mostly, I guess."

Cole Mullins' initials, I thought, and put the scrap of paper on the table, said, "Hangtown Creek. How it's written, the E's are backward. What if this is some kinda key? The fork of the E's pointed west, so what if west is east and east is west?"

He flipped the piece with the splotch on top of the other, so their faces touched. He peeled it back to see where the smudge and the map kissed, which was about three-quarters of the way up-creek. He placed a finger on the table in that spot.

"Here," he said.

His finger touched what he'd drawn on the wood, not directly on the black water, but off to the side a ways where a feeder stream should be.

"What's there?" I asked.

"Cole Mullins," my father said, and I knew he was right.

7

IT wasn't a long ways away, maybe an hour ride, but we packed heavy, with provisions for camp if needed, and food: hard bread, dried beef, a hunk of cheese. Enough for several days per chance things turned sour, pots and pans and such. We took with us full canteens and wineskins of spring water. Nights were warm still, so in terms of cloth we packed light, no blankets.

We wanted Lemi with us, but he was still in need of bedrest and self-repair. And we wanted his story. The only way for him to give it to us without his finger in the dirt for days was to stay at the claim and write. He didn't argue, and I left a few hub wafers in case he had a sweet tooth. We told him where to find the food if he grew hungry, and he already knew where to find water. His bandages would last till we returned, we figured.

"No need for panning today," my father told him. "You done plenty already, and you getting well is needed over the opposite. That's what'll happen if you push. If you're a praying man, it's the Sabbath. There's a bible on the shelf should you want to read the good book."

We took the horses and rode off northbound, passed through town one last time should we find the men we was out for in need of their own provisions. My father asked those he knew by name if they saw Cole Mullins or any man he ran with, and then asked strangers. No one knew where to find him, or least they told us as much.

A wild chase, we knew, but one we couldn't pass.

Four months of hard work was at stake, and that's if they hadn't spent all our gold on booze and whores. We'd take back what was ours, all polite-like if possible, though neither of us thought that would be the case. Take gold from a man, from a family, and there's not much to talk through. There's *take*, then there's *take back*, and we were set to take back.

My father drank his normal amount. A third of the quart gone by the time we made it to the crook in Hang-town Creek that matched the jut on the crudely-drawn map.

"Upstream a ways," my father said. "Three, four miles."

We'd of course drawn a new map so there wasn't a need for two. Like the final three fingers of whiskey still in the bottle, the place we was headed was about as far away.

Three or four miles turned to six or seven, then eight. The map wasn't to scale of any kind. Not lost, thanks to the creek, but out a ways. Dry as dirt so far deep into summer, but a path to follow. We passed old camps and claims, fires long cold. All left abandoned. Tools gone to rust, and some so old the rust had gone back to earth. Bones of eaten or long-forgotten animals, white and splintered like overly-seasoned firewood, littered each camp.

They called it Dry Diggins for two reasons, the other was cause all the streams dried out this time'a year till uninhabitable. Men died if they pressed their luck too long.

"We're close," he said. "I can feel it."

I could too, a gut-shot deep inside.

The horses sweated as we came upon the place marked in secret. A massacre, bodies strewn all about. Some decapitated, most scalped. Men, women, children younger than me. I never seen injins but that's what they used to be, most naked but some in buckskin dresses and other hides. The most well-dressed of the lot was headless, no head to be found. Blood ran brown on the ground and flies hovered over it all, which meant what happened happened long in the past, a few days maybe, the bodies not right, skin like leather.

My father drew his pistol and I the rifle.

We walked our horses in silence and stopped to cover our faces in kerchiefs to keep down what we ate on account of the smell. Ten dead in total, half kids, and a mother clutched a silent babe. Scavenger birds hadn't discovered them yet, but we had. Even the stream was dead, and around it teepee like structures made from tree branches, some topped in mud. A man lay over the long-out fire pit, perhaps pushed onto it while still aflame based on the black spread. None of the bodies held weapons of any kind. All shot dead, then scalped or ravaged or worse.

"What do you make of it?" I said.

"Lots of rounds," he said. "I'm guessing thirty or forty. Could be the work of a few men if they reloaded between what they done."

"You think it's our men?"

"I think it could be. Stay on your horse."

He hopped down, holstered his pistol, wary. He told me to keep an eye out, for we was in a flat area and stood out. He could draw fast, I knew, but I watched the trees as he walked about the slaughter. I let go of the reins and raised the rifle, ready to shoot the first thing that moved, and it was hard not to look at the gore around us, at things no man, no boy, should see.

My father dug into one of the bodies with a blade.

"What are you—?"

"Best not to watch," he said.

I couldn't help but stare in disbelief as he dissected and plucked out what killed the man he crouched over. He spit in his palm, cleaned the round, then held it to the sun.

"Large caliber," he said, "maybe from a five-shooter, I don't know. Based on the amount of hellfire rained down upon these poor folk, I'd say handguns and quick-firing. See how everyone's scattered about, as if caught off-guard? At least two men did this, maybe more. Two men could have taken them down in a single wave with a few guns apiece, then reloaded for a second to finish what they started. Definitely not a lone man."

"What was they?"

He knew what I meant and said, "Miwok."

So, I said, "How do you know this?"

And he said, "Miwok, maybe Maidu. Both are known for coming to the foothills in the summer to hunt, and I never seen Maidu here. Hunting deer or bear, mayhap."

I'd read about Miwok, but never heard of the other till the judge mentioned them when I went on about Cole Mullins and the man called Slade. I knew when Mexico broke from Spain in '21 that their federal constitution granted citizenship to its injins, even those in this area, but mission skirmishes all about took out many soon after, and then what was to become California was conquested by Union forces, and so a majority died from starvation and disease, or were run out. And my father told me a tale over supper one night of a certain 'campaign of extermination.'

He often called what was done *genocide*.

"Was they slaves?" I asked, and he knew what I meant.

"They don't look overworked," he said. "Far as I can tell, they were as free as you and me, peaceful, at least until they were butchered." He stood and washed his hands, wiped them dry on his pants. He handed me his hat and said, "Water the horses."

I reaffixed the rifle and took his hat, and still aback Nugget I emptied some of the waterskin into it, leaned far over her long neck and told her to drink from it and she drank. I sidled up to Sasha and gave her a hatful as well. They both drank earnest. They wanted more, but that was all I gave as I took up the rifle again, thought about genocide.

Long afore California joined the Union, local legislature passed a bill. I read the thing in its entirety. It was well-known, though it didn't make any sense to either me or my father. Ironically called the *Act for the Government and Protection of Indians*, it codified Spain's practice to enslave the natives, but with restrictions. Clauses forbade cultural grassland burns, which we knew was important to their people, and made it illegal to be themselves in public if not 'employed' by a white man. Another clause made their testimonies irrelevant in a case that involved a convicted white man. Extermination, no doubt.

I tried to imagine how many red-skinned lived in this

land prior, perhaps tens of thousands, hundreds of thousands, even, I don't know, and how many 'white-skins' was here now, if we could be labeled as such, maybe a few thousand or more. Then I thought about how those two numbers got themselves closer and closer together.

"Read," my father said.

"Yeah, Papa?"

"What do *you* make of it?"

I made a lot of things of it, though I didn't know what of it was right, and I told him as much, and he said to take it all in, to *see*, with my mind.

"Why scalps?" I said, "and why that one's head?"

"Some men pay a bounty," he said. "Proof of death. Some think the natives don't have a place in this land, though it was theirs before it was ever ours. Some pay five dollars per."

"Who?"

I could tell he didn't want to say but said anyway.

"State government types, people who think they're savages. Do they look like savages to you, these people?"

"No more than you and me," I said.

"So, what do you make of it?" he said again.

Whatever happened was awful. I imagined women and children pulled from beds, from chores, strange men takin hold of their long hair, with no way to defend themselves other than to put up their hands or use bows and arrows or whatnot, only able to communicate fear as they was gunned down in front of each other, thrown over coals.

I threw up, then wiped my mouth.

"I figure I was right."

"Right how?" he said.

"That Cole Mullins and his partner should be hanged. If not for our gold, for this, if they done this. This can't be legal," I said, hands spread about, "all this unnecessary death."

"It matters who you talk to about law," he said.

"What do we do?"

My father pocketed the round. He stood, took in the scene as if to figure out how to best handle it. There wasn't much whiskey left from the quart when he tipped it back. He swayed, both from the drink and from that which surrounded him. Enough spilt blood in the dirt to coat a barn, as if seeped up from the ground. Seemed like enough blood to fill fifty men. He let out a long sigh and put his head to the sky.

"We talk to the law," he said.

A scrawny man walked out from the brush then and before I could think I raised the rifle and aimed at the bulk of the body as I was taught and fired a single shot, which exploded the pine behind him in a spray of bark. My father turned on his boot heels faster'n light and drew his pistol and cocked the hammer back with his free hand in a fluid motion and aimed where I aimed but didn't let loose and for a second I thought he misfired.

The man I almost shot, and my father almost shot, stumbled out with hands raised. He wore a patch of hide over his loins and nothin else, had either scars or paint on each of his thighs, and dark sun-tanned skin. He looked how these unfortunates must have looked a few days prior. About as old as my father. He approached, either in shock or both deaf and blind for neither my shot nor the sight of the pistol deterred him.

"Easy," my father said, either to me or to the Miwok.

He lowered his pistol and holstered it.

I reloaded, juggled the reins of two horses in need of water. I'd never fired at another man, not to kill, and so I too was in a state of shock, my heartbeats like hammer blows. It pumped all the way into my throat, and I found the pulse hard to swallow.

What if I'd shot him? What if I'd killed him?

The thoughts fluttered through me, but still I reloaded.

The injin said something beautiful.

My father held out his hands, peaceful. He was much taller, by a foot or more, so he knelt. A sign of respect, I can only assume.

"We are not going to hurt you," he said.

The Miwok kept talkin in his language, not necessarily on a path to my father but toward the dead woman in front of him, then to a boy about my size. His hands composed gestures in accordance with his words. His tone was soft, rhythmic. Perhaps he recounted the story of what happened to his people.

Genocide, I thought. *Eradication.*

Suddenly 'injin' felt as wrong as 'red-skin,' for they was both what my father called *derogatory* terms. From then on, I told myself, I'd refer to them as Miwok and nothin more, knowin deep down we was the savages. Not my father and I, but our people: the white man.

I finally lowered the rifle, my hands and whole body in shakes.

"Who did this?" my father said.

The Miwok man looked at those slain before him. He had been shot, too, a graze on his left shoulder, not too deep. He was here for it. Seen it all. Hard to tell if he could comprehend what my father had asked.

"You understand what I'm saying?"

The man blinked slow, eyes not wide but in fright. He made his way to a girl, maybe ten, put a hand on her and said some words in his language. A name and words to put her to rest, it seemed. He put his fingers in the mud-blood around him and made a mark on her cheek, some kind of symbol.

"The men who did this," my father said. "What did they look like?"

He looked at my father, stern, and pointed a finger.

"Like us," my father said. "White men."

After he said some words neither of us knew, the sad

man stood, his voice as gentle as song, and he held out his hand with two fingers raised.

"Two men did this," my father said.

They each spoke different tongues but talked.

And as he used his foreign words, he made his hands into pistols and pretend-shot all around him. He pointed his twin barrels at those on the ground, swiped one across his shoulder and smeared the blood there. He'd been shot at least a day or two ago, but the wound was open enough to streak red, or perhaps his long nails sliced it back open. He ran his hands through his hair and my father said the words for him in our own tongue.

"One of the men had long hair."

"The second man," I said. "What he look like?"

The Miwok man looked at me and then around. Then he put one of his hands behind his back and then with the hand-gun mock-shot the man in the cooled fire pit, then the other without the head, a few others.

"Cole Mullins," I said. "It was him."

But with only a single hand this meant the other did the scalps and took the head. I couldn't imagine a person takin hold of someone's hair in order to cut it clean off.

A sound whistled past me and the horses. Before I knew what it was, another Miwok the same build made his presence known. He was notchin another arrow in the bow he pointed my way when my father told me to lower my rifle, which was half-raised but a threat.

The one who recounted his story with his hand-signs and incomprehensible words turned to the other and put up a flat hand, which was enough to put him at ease. The other lowered his bow. The two talked for some time.

"You seen where they went from here?" my father asked. "On this map," he said with it held out front. "This is us." He pointed to the spot, slid his finger southeastward toward where we came from, "And this is the diggings."

They pondered, then pointed upstream.

"Cave," the grazed man said.

The other shook his head and said, "Mine."

They pointed again and tended to their dead, and my father and I stood in disbelief at their use of our language. We knew enough not to get in the way of their terrible task, nor to offer our help, which they made clear as day the moment we tried. We offered food and water instead, but they didn't want any from us. They said some words in their language that seemed to imply we should feed and water our horses so that's what we did.

"We goin after em?" I asked.

I already knew we wasn't.

"No," he said. "I know that mine. Been to it before. A few miles north of here. Stripped clean, so they're most likely using it as a camp. No one's ridden into town carrying scalps and such, or it would be known. Only place they can claim bounty is in town, so they'll be coming in soon enough. No need setting ourselves up for ambush riding into them, and they're obviously well-armed. They wouldn't think twice killing either of us."

"What can we do?" I asked.

He stood there a long while as we grained the horses.

Both of us thought hard what to do.

"We get the law involved," he said.

"A corrupt law," I reminded him.

8

EARLY dusk fell upon us. We rode a steady pace back into the diggins. By then, most places had closed but the Boomerang and so that's where we went.

My father had sobered to a point and ordered a drink.

I chose to abstain, said, "The law here?"

And it was meant to be in fun, but the fun fell when he said, "Law's always here. At the table, there, playing cards."

Two men sat across from a dealer, one with a badge, in some kind of old military jacket from the American side of the war. The other man was Mexican. Whatever game they played, the stakes was low. They quietly pushed in coins and tried to read each other's faces more so than their own hands. Maybe poker or some other game. Both spat as often as they could. Each with an empty drink.

The bar-keep knew my father well, so when his glass emptied he made to fill it, but my father bade him not to.

"What do you know about the officer, there," he asked.

The bar-keep eyed him and shrugged.

"He a good man?" my father said and slid one of the smaller of the nuggets Lemi had panned. Wasn't much, but enough for answers.

"There are no good officers in this town," he said, and took it. "But the one you imply is the least of the worst. I'm here more than he's out there as law. For a price, he's good."

I knew what that meant but it didn't mean I had to like it. The judge had said as much about the law when he left for the springs the other day.

"What's he drink?" my father asked.

"Same as you."

A twirl of his finger told the bar-keep to pour a few fingers into a tumbler. He stared at it hard but didn't partake. Instead, he told me to stay where I was and made his way to the game of cards. He offered the drink to the officer, and it was accepted with not much more than a nod.

A woman sat on the stool next to me in my father's absence. One of those situations where you don't want to look but are forced. Half her skin wanted outta her dress, not that she wore much of one. She smelled of perfumes.

"What are you, twelve?" she said.

"Fifteen and some," I said.

"You want to be a man?"

I shrugged. She meant what I thought she meant and leaned forward to show me more of her. I looked past her to the table. Couldn't see much other than mouths under hat brims in conversation. The game two of them played went uninterrupted.

"What is you, queer?"

Even if I was or if I wasn't wouldn't have mattered. I didn't want to be in this place but it's where we had to be. I told her I was just a boy, not interested.

"I could make a man of you," she said, "for a price."

The goin rate in Hangtown, it seemed.

"I don't have no money," I said.

That was enough to make her leave.

"What can I get you?" the bar-keep added. "And don't mind her."

"Like I told the woman, I don't have no money."

I meant no disrespect, just knew that he'd overheard. Those behind counters tended to overhear things.

"Your father paid 'nough for more than information," he said.

I looked at the bar behind him, at the arrangement of bottles and barrels. Only certain drinks I knew by color, but with so many lined up they all seemed similar.

"What's doesn't make you like *that?*" I asked.

"You really want to become a man?" he said and smiled.

"I guess. Some day."

"Your father's a drinking man and has good taste. Fire, I believe you called it."

Burned like a hot-white coal.

"Maybe this is what you need," he said, and reached for one of the more clear liquids. It had a yellowish hue. "Smell this," he said, the lip of the bottle held under my nose.

"Licorice," I said, "like the candies, like fennel."

"Lot stronger than candy."

He poured me a swill. Couldn't have filled more than a few thimbles. It smelt the way the licorice-flavored wafers tasted, only ten-fold.

"For sipping," he said.

It hit my lips strong and stayed long, tingled.

"Doesn't taste so strong," I said.

"Stronger than anything your father's ever had."

He left me the bottle in case I wanted more but what I had was plenty. What I had made me dizzy enough to wonder if he'd drugged me, but it was just a drink.

Another card game commenced across the way and again my father didn't play. He spoke freely, as though the Mexican next to him wasn't able to translate, as if the dealer didn't matter.

Must be growing late, I thought.

Outside it was the golden hour, a color we all sought at the diggins. I wondered what would happen if someone walked in and shot up the place, like we'd seen at the dry creek, but it was custom to wear one's weaponry. Two armed men walked in and sat at one of the tables.

There was lots of Mexicans, I realized, and a few some called yellow-skinned—the Chinamen—but the same shade as most of us who weren't as tan as those from the far south, those we'd broken from in the war. Here, the war no longer mattered, all that stuff fought over not as worrisome as the pursuit of gold. Those here all sweat the same, all but the already-wealthy, who never sweat much other than from hot weather or excessive weight.

When my father stood, I stood. In their discussion he shared the note with Cole Mullins' initials, and the new map we'd made. Wasn't much for evidence but told a story.

My father came to me and said, "What are you drinking?" mostly curious.

I looked at the empty tumbler and said I didn't know.

"That man'll help us?" I asked.

"I don't know," he said, same as me. "I told him about the scalps that might be coming this way and he said he knew about a bounty but that no one's brought any for reward."

"It's sick," I said, "to buy another man's head or hair."

He grunted in agreement, cleared his throat.

"But he also said he'd question them about our gold should they come in to claim that bounty. I told him our story, and about our branding on the buckskin bags, and he seemed to regard me as honest. Maybe he appreciated the drink, I don't know."

"If Judge Lynch was here," I said, "as much as I want to hate him, he knows proper law and wouldn't stand for the things we seen. Nasty form'a currency, scalps."

"Unfortunately, he's not here, so that man I spoke to is all we have other than ourselves. He did say if they come onto our claim again and try to take what isn't theirs that it's our right to take it back by force."

"Same as the judge told me," I said.

"And we will, should they be unjust like that," he said. "I need you to be one hundred percent honest with me, Read. You swear you saw them take our gold?"

He'd believed my word alone up till that point. Only I had seen them come in then ride off with it. If a father can't trust a son by word, what good was their relationship?

"I swear to my grave I seen it."

"Cole Mullins and Slade."

"The man I first saw had his arm cut off above the elbow," I said. "Watched him struggle to mount his horse, which was black as his heart. And there's only one man in all the diggins with one arm and no other. I saw the second from the back as they rode off, hair as black as Mullin's horse. Somethin heavy and dark dangled from his saddle, like an onion sack. I seen the man called Slade at the Swinford Store once when you sent me by myself, and the two looked alike from the back, hair as long as Nugget's mane and oil-slicked and dirtier than mud, like he pig-wallowed straight outta the depths of hell."

He laughed, believed my story, same as he had afore.

"I just wanted to hear it again," he said.

"We should head back." I meant the claim.

We'd been gone long, which left Lemi on his own. He had a gun, sure, but there's no self-protection while asleep, and Lemi, like my father, needed more of it.

9

I WAS right about the need to return to our claim. Bad things coulda happened if we'd stayed in town longer, for we rode upon three figures on horseback. They admired our cabin from afar, arms outstretched, either to point at things with hands or with guns. Small as bugs from so distant. Then they saw us. Two yah'd their horses and left a third in dust. Even this late, it was hot enough for mirage. The dry air made them float.

Too distant to make out faces, though the one who stayed longest wore a wide-brimmed hat. Either that or an arrow through his head. A spider-leg bent to it, a second man's arm in long shadow of the sun, as if from afar he acknowledged our presence. The third turned, then sped off.

"What do you make of it?" I asked.

He made big of it, cause he kicked Sasha hard and tore off. With one hand he steered her straight then grabbed both reins and either the horn or swell of the saddle, I couldn't tell which, and with his free hand drew his pistol. He kicked her again to ride harder and she made powerful sounds only horses make when they run.

I was no good with gun on horseback, but I got Nugget

to move almost as fast, stayed far enough back not to eat the dirt tossed up from the hooves. We wasn't far from our claim, so the run was short and soon we both found ourselves in a trot then slowed to a halt.

The cabin was all shot up.

"Lemi," I said under my breath, and made to get off my horse, but my father said not to, said to stay back and to draw my rifle and be on the lookout in case there was more.

My hands shook, but I did as told.

He hopped down and left his reins in a dangle over Sasha's saddlehorn in a way that would be easy to grab if he had to quickly remount. I'd seen him fast-mount many times, a fluid motion to jump and swing himself up and over. He tried to teach me, but I either ended up with a foot in Nugget's side and crumpled on the ground or slid on my belly clean over.

At first, I thought we might be on a chase after them, but my father's hurry was to our home. The three men disappeared, no smaller than stars winked out by daylight.

There was perhaps a dozen or more rounds put into the side of our cabin. Some took out chunks of wood, some simply holes. A gun pointed out the window and shot aimlessly.

"Lemi," my father called. "It's only us. The others are gone."

The man popped his head up.

"You okay?" my father asked, as if he forgot Lemi couldn't answer with words, then, "Wave your hand to let us know if you're okay."

His hand waved, but he remained low.

We waited, though we knew not for what. I guess what we waited for was nothin cause nothin meant our lives. We watched the path they'd gone. We listened to the wind. Soon as we felt it was safe, I tied off the horses and we went in, my father first.

Things inside was busted up, not too bad. I expected Lemi to be shot, yet he was not a holey man from some miracle. One of the buckets on the counter dripped the last of its contents to the floor, pierced through and through, a small nick in the stove behind it.

"How long were they here?" my father asked.

The question wasn't for anyone. He just said his thoughts.

"Why would they come back here?" I asked, "and who's their third?"

"They know we don't have nothin left, so I'm guessing they come for you?" he said, pointing at Lemi. "You see their faces?"

Lemi nodded.

"You recognize their faces?"

He nodded again, then held up two fingers.

"Two of the three, then."

Lemi smoothed out the dirt on the floor, wrote with his finger: "those you seek" and then smoothed it a second time, wrote: "stole from you." He held up three fingers.

"Who was the third?"

Lemi pointed at the open book on the table. He'd written while we was gone, a few pages' worth, and in loopy cursive, almost calligraphy. From the look of things, he'd been in the middle of words prior to the chaos. His story, least up to this point in time. The start of him.

"Read," my father said. He meant both me, and for me to do such.

He moved to the door, gun still drawn. The only way in or out. They'd have to come through him to get to us was his point. He checked the chambers to make sure he was full up, and messed with his belt pouch to ready for reload should the need arise. He held his pistol in a way I knew meant he didn't expect their return. And, of course, he drank.

I flipped to the first of the pages and read what was wrote:

A man by the name of James Thorp bought me in Atlanta, Georgia for ten dollars. He paid for three in total but sold the others for the same to close friends, one apiece. This was in '24 when I was about your boy's age. One of the others was my brother, the other our same age but not right in the head from blunt injury.

The purchase was not aimed to make me his servant, nor was that the aim for the others, but to provide us work and shelter, which is not custom in Georgia, nor surrounding states. The man who bought me understood this, as did I, though I know not what happened to the other two for they moved far away.

How the words came outta me wasn't so elegant, but I relayed their elegance to my father The best damn script I ever saw. Some of the words I struggled over, but I got the gist of most by those around em. A well-learned man, indeed. I was about to ask how a man such as Lemi could be so well-learned when my eyes caught the word 'educated.'

Mr. Thorp had his share of slaves, but they were never treated as such, nor spoken to in a manner of disrespect, which I had been accustomed to as a child. If anything, we were well-fed, well-dressed, and well-edu-cated.

I was taught, like the others of my color (though none were children), to read and to write, and was offered the same schooling as the Thorp siblings. We were seen as equals by all but the oldest, who was twenty-three years of age. I can share with you the rest of my upbringing but you would benefit now from knowing how I ended up in this godforsaken land out west.

Twice as many years as I was old passed and it was winter of '37—

"He was only thirteen years old when he was bought," I said. The math was simple enough for me to do in my head. I couldn't imagine money ever exchanged for life.

—when Mr. and Mrs. Thorp both took ill with Cholera, one of their youngest, too, and by '38 all three of them were buried in their family plot, leaving the oldest boy in charge: Henry.

He was an intimidating young man, and not as forthcoming to those of my color, often mistreating us. He worked us hard all hours of day, fed us scraps, though the treatment was better than what we were accustomed to in the lands from which we came.

We continued our education in secret, practiced our hand at writing and often borrowed books from the library to finish by candlelight in the late hours of night, sometimes till morning. But when a silver candelabra went missing, we were blamed.

"What's a candle abra," I said, as if it was two words.

"Like a holder for a candlestick," my father said, like it was one word, "but fancier. Holds more than one at a time. I imagine a candelabra looked much like an octopus, though I'd never seen either in my life. "It's spelt another way," I said, but kept on.

Move the hand of time around a few more years to the spring of '48 and by then the other Thorp children had died from various disease, one of pneumonia, leaving only Henry Thorp to run an unfruitful plantation. He wanted nothing to do with the place, though, and migrated west after selling to a buyer.

He'd heard of the rush that brought most men to California and brought me and his other workers-turned-slaves with him for hard labor, though I am the sole survivor of my color from our travels. We met up with three other families headed west, as well as their working men, and by the time summer burned hottest the man who owned me caught something respiratory; that and typhoid took out most of those traveling alongside us.

We lost nearly all our oxen, left two of three wagons to the dust of the desert, and put down our horses as a food. Henry Thorp lived through his illness and saw us through to the diggings.

"The third man is Henry Thorp," my father said matter-of-factly. "He's come now to take back what he thinks is his: you. We tried taking back what was ours, found you, and now he's come back to take what he thinks is his."

He repeated himself, as he sometimes did to figure things out.

Lemi looked sad as my father said a few more words, as if to preach.

"No man owns another man," he said, "and if he thinks he does he's not right in the head, not breathing right and perhaps in need of a few holes in his chest to let out such bad air."

He stood silent awhile as I skimmed some of the harder words, like 'respiratory,' 'typhoid,' 'pneumonia,' and practiced them in my head, along with the words I thought I knew but had all wrong upstairs. I wanted to be as learned as Lemi. I wanted to write as elegantly and in such wondrous display. Then I saw a name written on the next page when flipped and my heart fluttered. Suddenly I was lost for words, even to read.

"Is that all?" my father said.

There was another page, and so I read on.

He is in business with the men you seek: Cole Mullins, and another man I've never heard mentioned by name, which I believe is the man you call Slade. The two men you killed were deep in the pockets of Henry Thorp since we first arrived. They were in charge of watching me the night you put them to rest.

Where the others were headed that night, I don't know, but those you saved me from I knew as Francis, and Dirty Jack. The former is the one you shot; he cut out my tongue a year ago. The latter is the one who slashed open my back by whip. He was a bad man, like the rest. I cannot thank you enough for coming to my rescue, and I cannot thank you enough for providing me aide. I am forever in your debt and you have my sincerest grati＊

The words ended, cut off mid-word with a splotch of ink on the page as if he'd held the pen there too long, and I said so. I both wondered and wanted to ask what happened.

"You owe us nothing," my father said, and it made me proud.

"The other man," I said, and scanned the page for his name, "Dirty Jack. He's no longer 'live neither." When Lemi looked at me the way he did, as if to ask how I knew, I said, "When you was asleep yestermorn, we went back to ask more questions, and a grizzly done dragged him through the woods and carved out his throat, stopped him from talkin afore he died."

Lemi didn't smile at this as I thought he would.

"They'll be back," my father said. "We should be ready."

What my father needed was sleep. I told him I'd take first watch.

"I don't think they'll be back tonight," he said.

"Why you suppose not?"

"The way they rode off at first seeing us."

"So we go to the law," I said, "Again. We tell the man you spoke to earlier what we saw, bring him here at sunup and show him how they shot up the place. We have first-hand witness from Lemi, and you and I both saw. We give their names. The law takes over."

My father considered, took a swig.

"I'll take first watch though," he said, "in case they decide to come back this moment, and you can have second with Lemi. The two of you wake me the moment you even suspect their return, the moment you hear hooves. And you wake me a few hours before sunrise no matter how deep into sleep I fall. Throw water on me if you have to."

"You think they're headed back to where we saw the grizzly?" I asked. "The camp, I mean. You think they know what we did to their men? My guess is they already know."

They'd know about Francis, if he was still there and not dragged away like the other. A bear couldn't cause a bullet wound, though could have done all the other damage.

He said, "They came here, so they know."

"And they musta found Dirty Jack, what's left of him."

"I figure so," he said.

The visuals looped in my head, the horrible things we'd seen the last few days: the hurt they put on Lemi, what the grizzly had done in an angry god's wrath, but also what we'd seen of the evil these men were truly capable of—the savagery of what they done to the Miwok.

They'd kill us the same unless we, or the law, put a stop to them first.

"That man you talked to at the Boomerang," I said. "You think he's a good man."

"He's all we got besides us," he said. "At least until the judge comes back."

"The judge is gone for least two months," I reminded

him, but an idea struck me, and I blurted out, "We could ride to him. He may be at the diamond springs, may not have left yet. He said he's to sentence four injins for the murder of Martin Hopkins on his way to the gate of the bay or whatever he called it. We could ride out first thing in the—"

"We'd need another horse," my father said to cut off my ramble.

"Another horse?"

"To ride as hard as we'd have to, we'd require three horses, one for each of us. There's no way we'd leave Lemi. Also, they'll know if we left, the two of us, and they'd come after him. They are smart men and will be scouting us out, watching for us like we're watching for them."

"Maybe the law can ride out then, or we can send a courier for the judge."

"That's a fine option, the courier."

"So, the officer stays local," I said.

"The three of us will stay together for now," he said. "Sunup the three of us will ride into town and hire us someone who can ride fast. He'll go to the judge in the springs or follow his trail wherever he's headed and deliver our message. If we can find him, we'll bring the officer I spoke to back here. Lemi, you're good with words and most legible. Can you take a note?"

Lemi joined me at the table, carefully tore out a page. He fed the thirsty pen a drink of ink at waited as my father thought of what he should write on his behalf.

"Judge Lynch," my father said. "This is Benjamin Alexander Read. You are well aware of our situation at Dry Diggings, but this is no longer about our gold." He either waited for Lemi to catch up or hadn't yet thought of the words. "Cole Mullins and his men—at least five, though two are now dead—have committed heinous acts requiring your immediate attention."

He said all this from the door as Lemi scratched paper.

I studied his ability, wondering if he'd teach me.

"Not only have they slaughtered Miwok for the sake of scalps—and might I add there is an officer in Hangtown accepting bounty for such—but have beheaded a man."

My father waited a long while, though it didn't take long for Lemi to find himself in wait. We hadn't told him any of this till now, so his eyes grew wide. He put a line under 'hang' as if to imply what he wanted done to the men, what we *all* wanted done.

"And they took a man into slavery, which is not allowed in this new state of California. We now have this man under our care. His name is Lemi, and he received deep lashings for no reason other than for the bastards' own enjoyment. They removed his tongue some time ago to keep him from talking of what he knows about them, but what they don't know is that he is a well-learned man. He writes this message, as I have asked, if only to prove a point."

A long silence from my father meant the room filled with the angry noise of the pen. I watched as Lemi took the words and made some better, able to edit on the fly.

"We have proof, the three of us, of their crimes. This very night, the men aforementioned shot up the cabin on our claim with intent to kill, but the cowards have since rode off. We suspect they will return, and we will put an end to their lives to save ourselves."

He then added, after some time, "We are short on money—because they still have our gold, of which you are fully aware—but we have paid a courier to find you in your travels and deliver this message. You are promptly needed in the diggings, in *Hangtown*," he said with emphasis, and after another break for Lemi to catch up, said, "We have contacted an officer of the law. We hope he can put a temporary stop to these men. You must return at once. Our dreaming tree is ready to wake once again."

10

WE spent the night in turn at the door. As I took second watch, my father took to Lemi's bandages. Old for new, the same sterile care. We ate beans again between all this, and I had to be reminded once or twice to keep my eye out the door, for my curiosity was the wounds, which seemed to have healed some, even in short time. The new bandages stayed more white than red, rather.

There was a woman selling mincemeat pies in town, and I thought of this as I ate the beans. Perhaps after we got back our gold, or after we prospected more, we could try one of those pies. Something to look forward to other than dyin, cause that was also on my mind.

Fully-clothed, my father laid back on his bedroll, covered his face with his hat. Wouldn't sleep much, I knew, but least he could rest, 'long as I stood guard. Lemi stayed up with me the first few hours, though he was tired from his body, which had overworked itself to mend.

"You teach me to write like that?" I asked him in a whisper. "When all this settles down, I mean, when we no longer have to be scared of what's out there."

Lemi put his fingers together in a way that suggested someone with a pen in hand and he scribbled the air, then pointed at me.

"I read and write," I said. "My father, too. Nothin like that, though."

He pointed at his chest and nodded, which meant he'd teach me, or maybe teach both my father and me, which also meant he was with us for the long haul. It took time to educate.

To know that our two had turned to three was a comfort in numbers: three pairs of hands instead of two, three sets of eyes. Each of our lives had changed the second we crossed paths.

I'd always wanted a brother, or sister, even back in Missouri before my mother died. She and my father had tried, twice, but the world didn't want more Reads. It wasn't possible now, not ever, for my father loved my mother in a way so as he'd never love another. Since we'd come to the diggins, he hadn't even made a pass at a woman, not that there was much to choose from. Men outnumbered women nearly a hundred to one in California.

"Someday you'll understand," he'd told me, though I couldn't imagine how.

Lemi was old enough to be a father figure, I knew, but something told me I'd never see him as such, that he'd be more of a much-older sibling goin forward.

He pointed at me and put his hands together against the side of his head to ask if I was ready for sleep. Eyes heavy, I yawned. He yawned.

"You sleep," I said. "If you want, I'll wake you when I wake my father."

He nodded affirmation, then took to his bedroll. I watched as he loaded his handgun before he rested, which reminded me to check my rifle. I'd fired but hadn't reloaded.

Whether or not my father slept was beyond me. He most likely heard it all, both our conversation and our reloads. He was a light sleeper, which is why I'd laughed inside at his mention of water tossed on him perchance I *couldn't* wake him.

"I can hear you wake," he'd once told me.

And I always believed it. The man could hear the soundless.

I stayed up for hours, just stared out the door at the black night. An oil lantern flickered yellow behind me, but I could see as far as the trees in either direction. My father thought it best to let the oil burn. Cowards would think twice if there was light.

Movement startled me only once outside, some cat or

raccoon in search of food. I aimed my rifle when it first made a sound, but it scurried. I tasted fear in my throat, which soon turned to anger. A part of me wanted Cole Mullins and the others to show their faces. I'd remove em from this world for all the bad they done. *Me*, I thought. Everyone would say, "Those evil men was put to a stop by none other than little Read, a boy of what, fifteen?" I'd go down in history.

When an animal's hurt and unfixable, you put it down to end its sufferin. I figured if you flipped the situation, the logic still rang true: if an animal *caused* endless sufferin, it was best to end them, to put them down, fast as possible, to stop their spread of hurt.

I didn't know till that moment, while I pondered those sick men, but I had my father's gift. I heard the very moment he woke. I heard what wasn't there, his somnolent breath.

"Read," he said, gentle like.

"Nothing but the night," I told him.

"How long's it been?"

I looked out at the stars, considered their rotation, said, "It'll be dark a while longer. Figure you have a few more hours you can rest. I promise I'll wake you as you said, a few hours afore sunup. You need the sleep, Papa."

"Lamp needs more oil," he said.

He sat upright and stretched, and I told him I could do it, but he stood and made his way to the table anyway, lit a candle, blew out the lamp. I watched as he filled then relit the lamp with the dandle, blew out the candle. Same routine I seen him do countless times. We was like the flame, in a way, one of us needed to light the other. But my father must have figured it was a different kind of dark out, which warranted not two flames to shed their light, but the both of us to stand guard, for he joined me at the doorway and peered outside, holstered his pistol in a way that allowed for a quick-draw.

A father and his son, on lookout. Both of us in wait for the sun to rise.

We didn't talk, just enjoyed the warmth of each other's company, our breath like smoke in the cold. Moonglow shadowed bats and even the silent flight of an owl.

"What do you make of his story," he said, with a glance over his shoulder.

Lemi snored a bit, the way my father sometimes did.

I believed his story and said so. I wanted to read more.

"He seems like a just man," my father said.

The men never came, not the ones we waited for. The next few hours seemed impossibly long and stretched to what felt like four but then the birds sang.

⸕

THE three of us rode into town. We took our valuables, case they decided to finally show and loot while we was gone. They could put more holes in the place, but what good would that do? Then I thought of them burnin our home and relayed my concerns.

"All we need is here," my father said, which meant us.

"I guess," I said, and thought of all we'd left behind.

Smoke, in my imagination, was fierce, all our possessions burnt and adrift in the wind. A rage a' fire. I could almost see in in the distance behind us, like a premonition, but there was only clouds over the direction we'd come, none dark. The smell of smoke was only that of the smith, the crackle of flames drowned by his hammer as he pounded metal.

Not a white man we passed didn't glare at Lemi as he rode Nugget lone. Some spat at the sight of him, the ugly come right outta them. Tobacco trailed and stained many an unkempt beard, clothes splotched and splattered.

No one seemed to care about their appearances, not a thought put to it, yet most made it clear they wanted *others* to know what *they* thought. My father and I got looks too, just for having Lemi with us. Not towed by rope, but alongside us on horseback. They was afraid of him in terms of equality. Saw him not as a person but a freed possession. Lemi rode with his gun in plain sight, so maybe that stirred them also. Maybe it was the fact that he wore one of my father's shirts—a little small—cause his was so torn.

The officer was nowhere to be seen, but under the oak we found a young man, no more than twenty years of age, who agreed for a decent sum to ride hard to the diamond springs. He asked to read the letter first to know why we was so urgent. Soon after he got to the end, he looked at the dark-skinned man with us and then at me and part of his soul fell outta him. He wasn't like the others. I couldn't help but wonder about his own story, what made him.

He took the coins offered—not much of our funds remained from the sound of the bag at my father's side— and smacked his horse on the rear and yawed her into full gallop. The young man would either find the judge for us or we'd never see him again. The sadness he expressed gave me hope he'd at least try to track the judge down and send him our way. I couldn't imagine the judge and his posse ridin as hard back into town, despite the news. He shrank into the curve of the trail he rode and then was gone.

The note hadn't mentioned Lemi's skin, only that he'd been taken into slavery. The omission was on purpose, but what white man had ever been cast a slave?

"How long till he returns, you think," I asked.

"Hours," my father said, "*if* he finds the judge where he said he'd be. Could take days or more if he's already left for Coloma. Judge Lynch has his hands full, no doubt, but our note should steer him in the direction where his services are most needed."

"Here," I said, to state the obvious.

I looked up at the tree, as if it called me to do so. The rope was gone, and so part of me wondered if it was even there the day I spoke to the judge. I figured it hadn't been. Why would anyone leave a rope danglin? The tree hadn't been used in years to hang a man, yet in my memory the rope had waited ready and desirous. Perhaps I'd conjured the noose, then, its swing in the breeze as imaginarily alive as the toys I used to play with.

When does imagination leave a person? I wondered.

The outstretched limb had once killed three men side-by-side-by-side, but in my mind's eye I'd only seen the one rope, not three.

Would three be used again? I wondered.

Lemi had been called to the tree as well. He stared at the gnarly branch with a snarl, as if in remembrance of the knots once strung there; he cleared his throat, as if strangled. He'd seen men hanged, I knew, same as my father had. The way he looked at the tree, he knew firsthand why the diggins was renamed not so long ago to Hangtown.

The dreaming tree, a nightmare oak.

All three of us took in its claw-like grasp of the sky: a giant's hand pushed free of the earth to reach for the clouds, to clench the heavens in the slowest motions of its growth. It held both the sky and us for who knows how long, maybe a solid minute or two.

"Read," a man called, and both my father and I turned.

The stalk of a longrifle swung at him, knocked him clean in the head and missed mine by a matter of inches in a way that I felt its wind. I held tight to his belt and nearly fell with him to the ground as Sasha rose on her hind legs. I leaned forward and grabbed the horn, then the reins, as she came back down, almost atop him.

I eased her then drew my rifle at the man who'd struck him.

Lemi unholstered and pointed at another.

Weapons was drawn at us as well, three or four or more from the men who'd come up behind us, a not-so-instantaneous snapping of metal much like pine needles popping in a campfire, everyone set to pull triggers. Men across from us, as well from afar. The awful sound of eminent death ceased in under a second, and then the black eyes of barrels moved from face to face to face, theirs to ours, ours to theirs. We was well outnumbered and outexperienced. I knew this, and Lemi knew this, so we both lowered our weapons, and they soon followed.

The sound of guns again, but to disarm.

No one wanted a shootout in the middle town. No one wanted to shoot a young boy in front of his father.

The man who'd hit him was the officer from the bar.

"What's this about?" I said.

I turned Sasha—much too big for me—in a slow circle to take in the scene. There was five men total circled round us, but only the officer I recognized. One wore a badge, a gangly man with an unfortunate face, the others just men rallied together.

My father had fallen hard, unconscious. Blood soaked the dirt under him. Not dead, just out cold. Even so, in that fraction of a breath before he hit, he'd drawn his pistol, fell with it in hand and his finger next to the trigger. He'd drawn at the sound of our name, knew by its inflection as trouble. At first, I thought he'd pissed himself, but his whiskey had spilt, the glass cracked under him. Drunk, he wouldn't have turned as fast. Drunk, he might still be conscious.

"What's this about?" I said again.

"Your father's under arrest," the officer said.

"My father's done nothin. Under arrest for what?"

The officer put the tip of his boot on him, lifted my father's head perhaps to make sure it was indeed the man he'd meant to strike, or maybe takin pleasure in what he done. He smiled an ugly smile and knelt, pried away the pistol and threw it aside. Once hot with autumn morning sun, my father's face now collected brown, same as the ground. The officer looked from my father to me, then at Lemi and pointed his finger like a gun, pulled a fake trigger.

Someone spat. Someone always spat.

"He took what wasn't his," the officer said.

"The judge said law's corrupt," I said, "and he was right."

"Judge ain't here," he said.

"He will be soon enough, and he'll set this right," I said.

"There's nothing to set right," he said. "Gord, tie this man up and make sure he can't get loose," he said. He meant my father, and the gangly man did as told.

The appointed officer or deputy or whatnot named Gord took a thin rope he had on him, and he pulled my father's hands back, tied them together in a mess of loops and knots. He didn't know much about rope, it seemed. He then took the leather coin pouch from my father's belt and poked inside and that's when I raised my rifle a second time.

The moment I aimed I had the spread of guns pointed my way, same as earlier, same rattle of metal. Lemi either cleared his throat or coughed in the swirl of dust but didn't draw.

"Get your hands off him," I said.

I peered down the sight so that the side of his head was targeted, no more than six feet away, no way to miss. The round would take most his head clean off. I knew the others wouldn't fire 'less I fired, and they knew I knew, which meant my threat was as empty as I wanted this ugly dried turd's head to be. Only *I* knew I couldn't go through with it, though a temptation.

The officer in charge held up a hand, patted the air, and his minions lowered their weapons in turn. The last was the man directly across from me, seen only in periphery.

"No one is going to fire," the gangly one said, "not even you, son."

"Take a coin and find out," I said.

"Easy," the officer in charge said, "everyone settle down, easy. Gord, get your hand out of that man's pocket lest this kid blow your face off by slip of finger."

"Won't be no slip," I said.

The man about to be shot said, "Someone's gotta pay these men for their trouble. We hired them, and someone's gotta pay."

"Get your hand outta his got-damn pocket. Do as the boy says."

He was definitely the one in charge. Even though I held the only weapon pointed at another man, his tone kept the others calm, all but the one.

"What's your name, kid?" the officer said.

"Read," I said.

"Read?" he said.

I nodded and said, "That's right. My name is Read, same as my father, there. He taught me properly how to shoot, same as he taught me when it's right to aim at another man and when it's not, and this is one of those moments where's it is."

"Gord," the man said, just his name, and that pulled his hand away.

I lowered my rifle, slowly, but before I had time to even think to bring it up again the gangly man pointed his revolver in my general direction and cocked the hammer and whether or not he planned to fire didn't matter none cause the officer in charge drew his own as fast as my father would've and shot him clean through the heart. The red welled faster than I ever seen.

The other men expected more, but there wasn't any; their arms angled in mockery of chickens, hands frozen either at their holstered weapons or upon their lowered rifles, but the event was over as quickly as it began. A flash of heat made me think I was dead.

"Dammit, Gord," the officer said, and then, "I thought you'd be smarter than that, you stupid sonofabitch, but you wasn't." He shook his head, and the next moment plucked the badge from the dead man's chest, flipped it like a coin to the one closest, said, "Learn from this idiot."

The other tried to catch it, dropped it in the dirt, swore, and put it on.

"What's your side of the story?" the officer asked, "you and the n———."

I told him I didn't care for the word and he promised not to use it again. Then I told our story in brief. How he'd already been told about the theft of our gold, about the slaughter of the Miwoks north, and the scalps. How we'd hired him, his very self, to act in the judge's absence to find the men who done such. I said all this mostly for the sake of all the others in earshot. I said that what he done to my father was not fair nor just. Cold-cocked, they call it. I then shared my suspicions of who filled his purse, the only explanation. We'd paid a sum, so the others we sought must have paid him more.

He laughed, as if knowing I'd say this, but I went on.

I told him, and thus the others, how a courier was already on his way to fetch Judge Lynch, and this seemed to concern him. I didn't say how long ago, made it sound as though it coulda been *days*, for I knew he could simply send a man or two after him.

"He'll be back very soon," I said. "Any time now."

My father also taught me the art of white lies and when to use them.

"Well, looks like we have one man's word over another, doesn't it?"

"One good man—my father, there—and one bad," I said. "The man who paid you for *justice*, he Cole Mullins?"

"Whoever he may be," he said, "he rightfully owns this man you call Lemi. Has the paperwork. Seen it myself."

"No man can own another man," I said.

"Depends on where you're from, and he happens to be from the east where such ownership of slaves is legal."

"California condones slavery," I said.

"Does it now. You realize *condone* means to *excuse*, to *overlook*, to *ignore*? Did your daddy teach you as much? To condone is to tolerate, son. You're only pleading against—"

"Only my father calls me son."

"Read, fine."

"It's not what I meant, then," I said. "California does not *allow* one man to own another. The state may be new, but the act is banned according to the governor."

"I never heard of such law," he said and scratched his chin, as if to ponder. "Doesn't mean *you*, all of what, thirteen, fourteen—?"

"Fifteen," I said.

"—yes, fifteen then, that you are not *right*. This— this man, here, what's believed is that he in fact belongs—with all the proper paperwork—to a man from the east who claims your father killed two men looking after his property while he was away on business."

"Business," I said, "what business? And stop sayin property."

"I'll say what I please, and his business doesn't matter."

"Is his business to steal gold."

"Did your daddy kill those two men?"

I hesitated, but answered nonetheless because my father wasn't in the wrong to do so. "Only one, and it was justified. Saw it myself, and him too," I said, and pointed a thumb over my shoulder at Lemi. "It was fast and clean and just. Bear got the other."

He laughed, and so did a few of the others.

"A bear, huh."

The way he said those three words made it seem as though it could be possible. He hadn't seen firsthand what had been done to him, otherwise he woulda known.

"A grizzly," I said. "Saw that too. She had with her two cubs. The man was dragged from their camp to the woods. Wasn't clean, nor fast, but it was as *just* as the other man's death. He was alive when we left him, though his partner was not, and on the 'morrow we paid this second man a visit to ask him more questions about the gold taken from us, but he was gone." I thought of my father, how he shot him in the gut, dead if not treated, but decided to leave out that part of the story. "We followed his blood, saw the bear."

"And did your friend, here, *bear* witness?" Some of the men laughed at this, though what he said was dumb, and when they stopped, he gave Lemi his full attention, not talkin *to* him but *at* him, through me. "What does the— What does *he* have to say?"

"He can't talk," I said.

"And why not?"

"The man my father killed cut out his tongue to keep him silent, from sayin what he knows about the men you really should be out for. They whipped this poor man to tatters. Took us since all that happened to set him right enough to ride. Both men deserved to die."

"This true?" the officer said, this time to him.

Lemi nodded.

"Open your mouth."

He did as was told, and after a moment no one wanted to see his maw. Whether or not the officer could decipher the wound was new or old didn't seem to matter. What mattered was my story, and I was just a boy and the only voice, which meant nothing to any of these men.

"Tell you what, son," he said. "Until the judge returns, *if* he returns, I'm going to take both these men. This town don't yet have a jail, so I'll think of something suiting."

"You can't just—"

"I can and I will," he said, and slowly raised his pistol horse-level, not to lay down fire, but to show that he could. "Doesn't matter if you like it or not, but I'm the appointed law while the judge is away, and my deputy, here … what's your name?" he said to him.

"Tommy."

"Deputy Tommy is going to rope Lemi, same as he did your father, and we are going to take them both into our custody and without altercation while you run off home, where you will stay until all this irons out, you hear? Those men won't be coming after you. They only want what's theirs and to be done with it."

"What about what they took from us?"

"You don't have proof they took your gold, now do you?"

"The judge—"

"The judge ain't here, now go on."

I watched helplessly as Lemi handed over his gun, which no one seemed to put together once belonged to the men my father shot and was in trouble for, the very gun used to deafen the one he hadn't killed.

Lemi slid down from Nugget, let them tie him.

A freed man no longer free, a captive.

I slid off Sasha but only to take Nugget's reins and hop on her instead, to lead the other back to the claim. Two of the sweaty men not badged sat my father upright, reaffixed his hat. There was a nasty gash above his ear, blood dried tacky all over him. He was about to awaken and find himself in a world of hurt, and sonless.

"Where you takin him?" I asked, unanswered.

Others dragged the dead deputy outta sight.

The blood on the ground left in their absence reminded me of the Miwoks, who'd soaked what made them into the earth. What once pumped through them had dried a deep brown, yet the blood I stared at now reflected sunlight and shone as red as the anger that filled me.

They told me to 'get' like one would a dog, to 'go on home kid.'

But home wasn't home without my father there. I felt like the boy they made me out to be, all lonesome. Lemi, too. They took both from me, even our money.

"Where you takin him?" I said again.

There was nothin to do but juggle both horses, let them do what they planned to do, as I tried to figure a way to best handle the situation.

The officer didn't say a word but pointed with two fingers from the brim of his hat. End of the path, he meant. Past the Boomerang, far past the Empire structure, past a half-dozen log-cabins and horribly-built things. Most days the path down the middle of town was a slog of mud and holes from miners digging right there in the thoroughfare, but the last few months the weather had been hot and dry, most digs abandoned. Where they set to take him was the last wooden structure, long too abandoned, soon to serve as a jailhouse.

"We don't have no food," I said, and this was mostly true.

I could fend for a couple days if needed.

But to be alone?

The officer circled his horse to mine. He dug in my father's pouch for a coin, a single coin, and flung it my way. I caught it, half a bit, not enough to even buy hard bread.

SUMMER 1850

12

WAS custom in the diggins, and known well, that if you raised a weapon at another, be it a rifle or handgun or blade, it meant you intended to kill. Slight rise of a barrel could cause another to draw sooner and take a shot, the matter settled upon the other's death. Pull a blade and you better cut or be cut. I guess I was lucky I wasn't shot dead for takin aim at the officer, despite how I felt about him and his men. And it would have been right for him to kill me, or at least seen as his right. Even the judge would have been in the officer's favor had he done it.

Many a men died over gold, and money, but despite all that, Hangtown was rather laid back for a place of such potential. Firearms checked at the door, for the most part, knives kept sheathed. No one wanted to die earlier than they should cause life was hard enough. Men worked sunup to sundown on week-days, clothes full of sweat and head full of grit, and by week-end most sought worship or spent what they'd made in less favorable places. To gamble was to waste it all away, my father said long ago, and that's what I seen most do; though to drink was another way to lay wealth to waste, and he taught me that too with his unquenchable thirst.

I stayed long enough to see where they took him, followed on horseback, my father's horse in tow. It musta been Monday or Tuesday cause the town was in full effect.

"Are you sellin'er?" a man asked from deep within a hole, and I told him no as he carried on with his dig. He looked as though he were diggin his own grave, for the hole was big enough for a coffin. He stood knee-deep in diarrhea-colored water, and lifted out a bucket, which he passed to another who washed its contents onto a rocker, the empty bucket passed back so the first could change to baler to rid what welled around him.

This land once proved as easy-rich, but those days had passed in a matter of a years so the real hard work could commence. We'd come in the hard years. Anywhere you looked, men in groups of two or three or up to seven worked together on the creek that split the town. Beds of ravines now wrinkled the faces of the hills, the creek bed, and all the flats. Even the hills had been spared their pines, all cut to stumps to make lumber needed for cabins and equipment. The creek itself had been altered and no longer ran its original course. Just about obliterated. It's once flowing waters, per those here long afore us, had since been diverted and distributed. Countless ditches on either side, water now goin to what my father called 'long toms,' with canvas hoses like snakes to feed them.

Picks and pick-axes and shovels hacked at the earth from all angles to break it all down to rubble, which was placed onto long toms to be sorted by hand or long-stick, the larger rocks tossed aside, the smaller sifted through. We had constructed a long tom, one about ten or so feet in length, for our own use at the claim. My father called it "the cascade for gold" on account a' the passage of water. It was a strange thing to watch men wash dirt, and stranger to take part. It was all such a giant mess, but the most efficient means.

Countless men hunched over pans in constant swirl.

Most I passed in town wore heavy boots and ragged apparel. I recognized some with the same pants my father wore, made by the man we met called Strauss, yet so many others wore holey clothes not meant for labor. Some rolled big rocks about.

I looked past the horde of men as I rode, for they was apt to ask for help. What they made of their work, I knew, they'd spend on games when the week was over. All cleaned up, they'd pass gold off to others under the light of large chandeliers and between decorated halls, while mirrors and extravagant glass reflected tired lives. But out here, in the middle of it, and in neighboring Middletown—so fitting a name—lay like drunkards the expired hats and holed boots and shirts torn through. Empty tins of oysters and sardines littered about, drained bottles, and all sorts of rubbish, not to mention broken tools left to rust.

Alongside me rode a man on a wagon, drawn by six oxen. His beard was as long and dirty as all the other miners, his face an unwashed brown. As he passed, I noticed he carried a load of salted meats, most likely headed to O'Connels' to restock, which was the beef market. One of the only three other kids in the diggins ran beside him, puddle-jumped in ruts the wheels slowly bounced over. He was maybe two years younger than me.

When had I stop jumpin in puddles? I wondered but couldn't remember.

I stayed a good ways away from the officer and his men. No more confrontation was needed, but I needed to see where they took my father. Could be hours he'd be there, could be days. The judge's return was my only hope. Not even that was certain.

The abandoned cabin was 'dilapidated,' a word my father sometimes used to describe what had happened to most of those who failed to get rich as promised. The structure leaned askew, half of it open or never completed. Served more as a lean-to than a place of shelter, its roof made of cloth that flapped in the wind. And that's where they was takin him.

'Haggard' was another word my father often used to describe men. 'Leathered' another, on account of weathered faces and all. I knew what he meant, and what I meant by dilapidated. Men aged hard in Hangtown, and so did the structures they built. Once gold was stripped from a place, it was off to another, as if no one took care of the past.

"What's key," my father had said when we first got here, "is to find bed-rock," with the soft dirt and silt layered on top over the years he referred to as the 'pay-dirt.' The diggins in this place was often six or seven feet deep, with the pay-dirt a couple feet atop the bed-rock. That's what I understood of it, anyway, with gravity pullin heavier material like gold ever-downward. Most of the diggins in Hangtown was surface diggins, why so many heads poked outta holes. But not 'dirt' by any means. The stuff was compacted and composed of gravel and stone and loose slate and clay alike. It took much effort to strip top-dirt to get to pay-dirt.

"Why's it called pay-dirt?" I'd asked him at the start.

"Cause the gold inside pays for digging it up and washing it out," he'd said.

Washed-out is how my father looked as he came to. From afar I could tell he asked questions to those who'd taken him into custody, same as they asked him, their prisoner. He saw me and nodded, flicked his head in a way that told me to head off, to leave him be. He and Lemi sat side-by-side in what little shade their new 'jail' offered. Hands tied behind backs, most likely bound to one of the beams to keep them there. Five men stood around then three took off. A bucket was placed in front of them, from which one man ladled unclean water.

The officer in charge saw me too and pointed. I looked in the direction he pointed, which was behind me, which either meant to go back the way I came or to head home, for he knew for certain where we lived from talkin with Cole Mullins or Slade or the third in their party.

I rode up to him anyway and soon he yelled, "You don't learn, do you?"

So, I said, "I need assurance my father and Lemi will be treated—"

"—Yes, fine, they will be treated as finely as we treat all prisoners under observation in Hangtown," he said by means of an interruption.

So, I said, "Someone's set to watch them both, all times."

And he said, "What are you getting at?"

So, I said, "What I'm gettin at is that those cowards who hired you, who started all this, could mosey on up here any time they please. What I'm gettin at is who's gonna offer protection for my father and Lemi should such a thing conspire."

"Read," my father said, just my name, his name, our family name.

"Your father is my prisoner, and so is this n———. Yes, I said it, and I'm not going to sugarcoat it for your innocent ears any longer. You're old enough to take care and fend for yourself, and old enough to hear the truth. This is how it has to be, 'least until the judge returns and we sort out this mess. Then we'll decide what needs to be done to your father."

"But—"

"I'm not finished," he said, another interruption. "I don't know when that will be, so don't ask because I know you're antsy to do so. The men you fear are not after you, and no longer after your father cause I have him here. He's safe, I promise. All they want is their property, and when they come for it, and they will, I will hand it back to them as previously agreed-upon."

"Previously agreed-upon by whom?" I said.

"By me," he said, "and them."

"That's not fair, nor—"

"Who says life's fair, kid? Go on home. You'll be safe there. If it makes you feel any better, I'll periodically check on you since you'll be alone."

"No, that don't make me feel any better."

"They will not mess with you, nor your father. Go to the store. Get some food and whatever else you might need for the next few days, in case it takes that long. Your father will be fed and watered 'least twice a day. He's not going to starve and you can come see him when it's not so bothersome as now. Two men will stand guard day and night."

The others looked uneasy, just learnin of their duties.

"Lemi—"

"Is rightfully the property of Cole Mullins, who, as you know, could use an extra hand, and, as I stated before, he has the proper paperwork."

"I'll be fine, Read," my father said, but I didn't believe him. How he said it was in a manner to send me off, same as the officer. "Tell Asa Cleavenger you need a bag of flour because we're almost out, or John Coffee if he's open, and whatever provisions you think you'll need. They know we're good for it. Panfry some pancakes. I know you hate them—just flour and water, is all—but sop them with beans or bacon grease. Keep occupied."

"You want me to work our claim," I said, not as a question.

I was sounding more and more like him each day.

"We could use the gold and might need some soon." He turned to the officer, not as if to bribe him—for what did it matter since he'd already taken what little we had left—but to ask, "Can he bring me something in the morning? Here, I mean."

"Matters," the officer said.

"Read, bring the journal," he said, meanin what we'd given Lemi.

I didn't want to say 'But that's all the proof we've got!' but almost blurted it out cause the thought was so absurd. Besides the maps we'd found, though not much could be made of them, all we had in terms of stakin our claim at truth was Lemi's story. Once that was gone, it was one man's word over another's, or one man's gold over another's depending on who could buy from the law more 'justice.'

"Not to hand over," my father added, "but to read it to him."

"I can read," the officer said, "some."

"But then keep it on your person, for when the judge comes."

"All right," I said, though all was anything but right.

"You'll send men periodically to check on him?" he asked the officer. "Those men shot up our cabin when we all could have been in there. I want assurance they won't do so again."

"I'll deputize two of these idiots now and have them set-up camp across from your place, if that pleases you. But I assure you the men who shot up your place have no reason to go after the boy now that everyone's accounted for."

I considered this, didn't much like it, and held out my free hand.

"My father's guns," I said, plural.

After a chuckle, he asked my father, "Can he handle a pistol?"

"He can," he said, without hesitation.

I couldn't, but what did it matter? The concern was not to leave either gun with the officer and his men. Not one could be trusted. I'd rather not leave my father unarmed, but his own arms was tied behind his back, and I'd check on him often per chance they let him go.

"Tell you what, Read," the officer said. He held my father's pistol by the barrel for me to take it by the handle. I could easily reach out and pull the trigger and end him, for it aimed at his chest, loaded. He waited till I let go of the extra reins and took it to say, "You can have the one, and if you shoot this outta the air," he said, and lifted a chunk of old wood the size of his hand from the ground, "you can have the other."

He threw the wood high in the air, off to the side and away from most people, and I pulled back the hammer, aimed, but let the wood fall to the ground in front of my father. Heads of all had followed its rainbow path from sky to ground, then looked at me.

"Waste of a round," I said, and reset the gun. I slid it in the knapsack and held out my hand again for the other. "Both guns," I said. "They're ours."

"You're a persistent sonofabitch, you know that?"

"I do," I said.

He thought it over. Every man with him had a weapon. He made a face that read 'what does it matter?' and handed over Lemi's revolver.

"Now get on out of here," the officer said.

"Go on, Read," my father said. "Work yourself hard."

There was more to say to the man who represented the law, and plenty more to say to both my father and Lemi—the man simply stared off and away as if this were normalcy—but unlike his unfortunate past, I kept my tongue. The revolver went in with the pistol.

If a boy could kill a man with only his eyes, that's how I looked at the officer as I circled round and headed off back to the claim with my father's horse in tow.

"Treat them well," I said over my shoulder.

13

ASA CLEAVENGER indeed offered credit for foodstuff, and I had enough in coin for a bread loaf from Samuel at the Bakery next to Scraton's Eureka Hotel, where men stumbled out either tired or drunk or both. No need to go to John Coffee's grocery. I only got what was needed then made my way back to the claim. One boy, two horses, three firearms.

Not much to do other than work and worry, so I did both for as long as the sun would allow. I picked the ground mostly to out frustrations, until the hate sweat outta me. I wasn't far from the water's edge, maybe thirty feet, so about four feet into the ground water welled at my boots. This new hole was next to another, so I knew I was close to pay-dirt and kept at it. Coulda finished out one of the other holes already started but wanted to start my own. There was a need to start and finish somethin on my own more than finish somethin already started.

I picked and shoveled myself deep, threw out the heaviest of rocks, some the size of heads, which I imagined they was, and filled buckets with the softer earth beneath. To climb out was slippery business, but I managed with footholds cut into the side of my grave.

"I could lie here," I said aloud, "and die, and no one would pay any mind."

A person could wander over, find me on my back, shot dead or perhaps self-overworked till expired, and cover me with the same as what I dug out.

Each bucket of pay-dirt was brought to the top-most portion of the long tom built two summers ago, and worked its way down, smoothed out by hand or by handle. The contraption resembled a ladder placed over flattened lengths of wood, the whole thing propped at an angle, maybe fifteen degrees, and lifted off the ground by short stilts. The canvas hose lay propped at the start of 'the cascade,' as my father called it, and since the long tom was lower in elevation than the source of the feeder end of the hose—which when ready I dipped into the stream—gravity itself pulled water through it and over the earth placed there.

Mud splotched all I wore from the dig, but to clean the pay-dirt in turn cleaned what I wore. Soon water reached the end and made the tiniest of brown falls. It was a lot of work for one man—or boy, in this case—to do lone, but it kept my mind busy enough not to drift too far back to town where I wanted to be. I tried to not think of my father and Lemi as prisoners.

Two men rode on horseback and stopped to watch my work, but even from afar I recognized them as the men assigned to protect our place, and thus me. They could raid the place and ride off, not to be seen again, but they seemed to accept their duty. Just, perhaps. They set-up a small camp and lit a fire, though it wouldn't grow dark for hours. They heated water for coffee and pitched a canvas tent, made it seem as if they'd only stay the night and be gone.

I kept an eye on em as they kept an eye on me.

They stayed to themselves as I worked.

Larger rocks and pebbles were inspected, tossed aside. All around, there was millions on the ground, a thick gravel, two years' worth tossed on either side of the trough. I stood in a valley between ranges much similar in shape to that of the Sierra Nevadas. More useless rocks than stars in the night sky, perhaps. The grittiest and heaviest of debris collected at each perpendicular board on the ladder. My father had taught me the term 'perpendicular.' This was where to find the gold. Using my fingers to brush through what collected, I found a tiny nugget and put it in a pouch. Then I found two more, much smaller but decent. They stood out like miniature suns reflected off the light of our own.

I worked my way down the long tom, one perpendicular at time, and by the time I reached the end had myself maybe a dozen and a half bits a' gold, maybe four or five dollars' worth. Most I ever found in one go. Hands numb and pruned and sore. But the work was far from over. Back to the top of the ladder again to filter out the smaller stuff, to wash away the dirt till it was no longer dirt. Not till all that remained was a fine sand too heavy to float downstream; tiny flakes of the yellow lay hidden within, of course, gold dust, just enough to be bothersome.

Each handful of sand went into a metal pan striped with a series of indentions hammered in from the underside. The secret of the pan was to swirl smoothly, to let the water carry off what wasn't heavy enough to sink to the bottom or be caught on the lips. The bigger pieces—and by 'bigger' I mean ones with enough stature to pick out by finger—went into another pouch. At this point, the swirl would get more and more precise till all the gilt was accounted for. Fools-gold, or pyrite, spilt over the side as well, which flaked easier than soft slate.

I spent a good three hours with the pan, hunched close to the ground, and went hard at it long into dusk, when their campfire glowed across the way.

Not too dark out, but more so when by oneself.

The men there glanced over, tipped hats, spat.

Inside, I spread out my labor on the table. A good days' work, all considered, perhaps ten dollars or more worth of gold, maybe as high as twelve. Eyes pulled to its candlelight gleam as if by magnet. Contracted men was paid five dollars a day for such labor, and typically pulled five dollars a day or slightly more from the ground or from the mines. The three of us coulda easily pulled twenty or thirty dollars' worth from our lot daily. But we had to move on soon, in a month or so, my father said, cause we'd dug out most our land clean, and lately, with exception to the last few days, found less and less. Soon it wouldn't be worth five dollars a day.

Other men once owned our claim, and it was strange to think of it. Back in late-'48 or early-'49, when the rush was most fierce and when we was still in Missouri and a larger family than two, prior owners had set their stake where we was. How it was done, then, to claim land, was as simple as a shovel or pick or wooden stake shoved in the ground. Whoever had first lived here had cut down all but a few nearby trees for lumber—an army of stump gravestones—and built the cabin. All we did was repair it, patch holes between logs to keep out the cold come winter. Not the most well-made of places, but a survivor of seasons.

My father had simply snatched it in their absence, for if a piece of land was abandoned over a stretch of days it was justifiable to claim it as one's own. This was the same reason we never left 'home' more than two days at a time, even on hunts, and if we did we'd leave candles to burn in our absence. My father took the cabin the first chance he got, and it's been ours ever since. Once the gold was gone, or at least less than five dollars-a-day fruitful, we'd either have to find a new place with a structure or build one or use tents.

After we first made it to the diggins, we'd set-up camp down-creek—at what he called a 'bad claim,' one on the opposite bend of a stream—and that served as a place-holder. We panned the creek some, found little. This was when my father first learned to prospect, and knew we was in the wrong place shortly after. We was about to move on but by luck he overheard those at this cabin was about to leave. My father knew gold remained in the ground, just harder to get. He'd heard the previous owners state, "Place ain't worth more than twenty or thirty dollars a day." Though that wasn't much compared to what they desired, it was well over what we ever found. Maybe my father knew they was about to leave all along, why we set-up our first camp close by.

I thought of him then as my stomach rumbled. Had he anticipated what had happened in town? Bet not, though he didn't seem too troubled. Would the officer make sure he and Lemi got food and water? I wondered these things, then set my mind to make enough pancakes to bring them some on the 'morrow, along with salted pork I'd procured at Asa Cleavenger's. My father was the one who shopped, so the cost of things was foreign to me. I hadn't asked for much, told the woman there our predicament, but would the gold I pulled today be sufficient? Other than the excitement of findin gold, its worth never mattered much to me.

A few years prior, the land in Hangtown was plentiful, with not much need to prospect. A small team of men could easily clear out several hundred to several thousand dollars of gold in a day, was rumored. The previous owners of our claim dug out a great deal while here, but the days of easy-pickin was long over. We dug deeper, worked harder, like all the rest. We took outta the ground what was left behind while others blasted mines.

"Why we here?" I'd asked my father one day.

"What do you mean?" he'd said.

"I mean, why'd we come west?"

He'd thought long and hard afore answering. Unlike so many in the diggins, he'd never gotten that mad look found in the eyes of most miners, that sparkle called greed. Frantic, most would work themselves thin, ribs exposed. All day, every day, but not the week-ends. My father was never like that and made sure neither was I, though we worked hard, which is why I asked him such a question.

"Your mother and I had a good life together," he'd said. He'd meant in Illinois. "But when she died, a part of *me* left with her. Suddenly life turned harder, especially raising a boy without his mother. I saw the same change in you, same as I saw in myself."

"I still think of her," I'd said. "Every day."

"Me too," he'd said.

"That why you drink so much?"

"One of the reasons," he'd said.

I'd known enough, then, at thirteen years of age, not to press the other reasons, though I knew one was to give him courage. The drink steadied his hands when they shook. Another reason, I'd guessed, was to help him sleep for he'd often watch the stars till they flickered out. I shouldn't have asked the question. Wasn't right.

"It was hurting us as a family, what remained of one,

anyway" he'd said. Whether he implied the drink was uncertain, but he'd ended our talk with, "And if we stayed there, with her ghost, or at least with the ghosts we created in ourselves, we'd only hurt more. Every day I went to her grave to talk to her, and on the last day you know what she said?" Before I could wrap my head around a way to answer such a question, he'd said in the same voice she'd given me, less-pronounced than my father, "She said 'Benjamin, you need to stop doin this, stop greivin. Start a new life, just you and the boy.' She didn't say those words, of course, but I felt them in my heart just the same. I was always 'the boy' for heavy talks. "The next day, I overheard men discussing plans to caravan a group of wagons west, for the 'rush."

And that's how we ended up in Hangtown of all places. We sold all we had wasn't needed, bought a wagon and oxen to pull and took with us only what was needed: clothes, provisions, Sasha and Nugget, the family bible. All else could be bought where we landed, which turned out to be true. Three men died in our party of twenty. Some sick of the coughin disease, some of worser things. I remember one concern among travelers was to happen upon Cherokee or what tribes frequented the plains, but those we came across was curious about our party more so than ever a threat. They rode with bows and arrows on their backs and not much on them but mud war-paint; they stayed a distance 'long as we stuck to the trail.

We'd taken more oxen than needed, ate some on the way as recommended by the hired guide. As a group, we went through a vast amount of flour and sugar and water and all other things we brought. And to lighten our loads we'd cast aside what was expired as we pressed on, whether spoilt or emptied. The sun-bleached earth, in places, contained half-buried skulls and weathered bones of previous groups' animals. Spent wood and broke-down wagons and whatnot had lain littered about, wheels buried what seemed two-feet deep. We'd even passed hollow carcasses of men and children, as if the salted earth refused to return them to dust.

No one ever took time to bury them, I thought then and now.

I then thought again of the hole I'd dug only moments ago, wide and long and deep enough to hold a coffin, how easily it would be for someone to forever put me to rest and cover me whole, and as I thought this horrid thought there came a presence in the dim of early-night like the first of so many stars. Soft orange surrounded a man on horseback as he took in a toke of smoke. Then the glow jutted to the side, thrown to fizzle out on the ground.

He rode by himself, far as I could tell, so quiet no one heard him, even me. The sight sent a shiver through me. Sometimes bad can be felt off a person.

I hadn't yet eaten, but already wanted to toss it up. The cabin was lit by three candles spread about, and I had a good fire stoked in the cook-stove to heat a meal. I'd planned for pancakes, but that would have to wait. A mix of flour and water sat in a bowl like glue.

The two men who was supposed to watch me failed at their task. Behind the man on the horse who approached, their own fire was all but coals, no flame. Silhouettes of men asleep or dead, and I feared this was the case.

Quickly I used a pry bar to lift one of the floorboards, one looser than the others. There was a small hole dug underneath, a place to put the gold. What I had collected wasn't much, but it went in that hole. My father had come up with the idea the night Cole Mullins and the other took what was saved. Before then we'd never thought to bury it like the dead.

Twenty or thirty more seconds and the man would call out, I knew, so I placed the pouch inside, then the journal, and reaffixed the wood, slid one of the table legs to cover it. I was better with the rifle, so I grabbed that from next to my bedroll and checked the chamber. Couldn't find either the revolver or the pistol and swore under my breath, looked out the window.

Horse hooves clopped closer and slowed. He was maybe ten or so feet from the door but said nothin. There came the soft hiss as he lit another smoke. I gave him a few more seconds. Far as I could tell, he simply sat on his horse and waited, but for what?

14

"I HEAR you out there," I said, rifle aimed at the middle of the door frame.

"I know you do," the man said, the voice of a stranger.

"My father, Benjamin Alexander Read, he'll be back in a matter of moments, but he's tired and will want to bed down for the night. Best come back—"

"He's tied to a post," the man said. "Not coming any time soon."

Caught in a lie.

The sound of leather as he adjusted on his saddle. The sound of a boot unwedged from a stirrup, then more tack as he dismounted. Then nothin, as if he hit the ground weightless.

"State your business," I said. "And afore you answer know you have a rifle set to end you should you step through that door without permission. I'm not a killin man, but take away my choice in the matter and I'll become one."

"Can I have permission, then?"

"No," I said.

The man laughed, said, "You're definitely your father's son."

"How do you know him?"

"Look, son."

"Only my father calls me son. Every man we know

knows this," I said. "Call me Read, same as him, and don't pretend you're a friend cause I never heard your voice prior to now."

"Read," he said, as if to taste the word on his snake tongue. "Look, you're a smart kid, so I'm not gonna sugarcoat it for you. I just want to talk, *de hombre a hombre*."

"I don't know what that means."

"Man to man, you and me."

"Are you Spanish? Mexican?"

"I was born in Arkansas," the man said, "so neither."

"Then speak the language we both comprehend," I said. "You have a gun, you set it inside the doorway where I can see. You do otherwise and I fire. After, I want to see your face. Anyone else with you out there? It's not right comin upon another's cabin at night."

"Fair enough, Read. I expect you to lower your weapon as well so we can talk in peace. No need killing each other over conversation. A man must deserve to be killed."

The way he said it made me uneasy. *Lower your own weapon,* he'd said. I hadn't thought then that he might already have a bead on me, whether through a hole or an empty knot between logs or from somewhere outside my vantage point by way of window. How quiet he was, he coulda set a better position without my knowledge.

"Don't deserve it, then," I said.

A click of metal nearly made me fire but didn't. I was apparently right that he had a gun drawn, the hammer relieving its threat. The way the light was, it was possible he could see *in* more so than I could see *out*, and for his own safety had the gun.

"Real easy like," I said.

The man sighed like the wind in a storm and filled the night with the sound of his weapon placed in its holster, then the loud sound of a belt. All I saw at first was his bony hand appear from the darkness. White as the dead.

He placed the entire holster, gun included, just inside the doorframe as told and slid it forward and into the light, as a courtesy. Death's hand disappeared just as quickly and in that flash I noticed the black or blue outline of an oak leaf on the meat between thumb and index—either drawn or tattooed—and peppered by powder burns, along with a few bad scars more pink than white from cuts or whatnot.

A heavy black club of a handle stuck outta the holster, as well as half the metal, similar in shade. Quite a big gun for such a small hand, but well-maintained and oiled, like the hand.

"And the other one," I said to the silence thereafter.

I didn't know if there was another, but it's what my father woulda said to eliminate any and all threat. My finger over the trigger, ready.

The man laughed again, drunken-like, and so I added, "As well as any other weapons you may have on your possession, knives included," and he said in response, "Fair enough," again, and then, "but I'm going to leave my rifle on the saddle if it fancies you."

"It does," I said. "It fancies me greatly."

I bettered my position inside the cabin and waited.

"Mind if I tie off my horse," he said. "She's known to wander."

His voice told me he was close enough to the hitch-rail by the door, and so I told him he was more than happy to, but also that he wouldn't be here for a long stay. The horse he rode seemed to not want to be tied, and he struggled with her and cussed.

"That's her name," he told me, "*Bitch*. I named her after my ex, who, like the horse, was known to wander. Someday she'll learn better."

Whether he meant the horse or his ex, I didn't know, nor did I want to.

Soon enough another holstered gun made its way inside

next to the other, a twin of the first. Dark as blast-powder. The man apparently wore two belts, which either meant he was odd, or he could shoot with either hand. But then he tossed in a third weapon, a sheathed bowie knife with a blade as long as my forearm, followed by a fourth, a hunting knife sharp enough to gut a deer; just the knife, which meant he most likely kept it on his ankle in a sheath he didn't bother to remove. The man thought himself funny, made a mess of noise.

"That all?" I said, but then he surprised me.

"Damn," he said, "you *are* a smart kid, aren't you?"

Leathery sounds.

The hand returned as he tossed in a *third* holstered gun, then a *fourth*, one on top the other, a big pile of weaponry he'd have to step over if he ever wanted inside. It took me several breaths to realize the two weapons as my father's pistol and Lemi's revolver.

I looked around the room, perplexed.

"You caught me," he said. "I may have been inside your cabin while you were busy, but only to prove a point. You turn your back a *moment* and the damn moment will take everything from you. Last free advice I'll ever offer. Never forget that, little Read. That's what the judge called you earlier, wadn't it? He told me as such. What, you thought he was a truth-teller? That I'm a myth? Don't worry, I was going to give them back, after we talked."

The sweat that ran down my face stung my eyes. It was a hot night, and I hadn't cooled from the earlier work, but what came outta me then was from his presence. The man emanated pure evil and I knew him to be Slade, whether or not that was his name.

"I know you?"

"I know *you*," he said.

He must have snuck in while I was hard at it, neck deep in the ground. But why give up the guns so freely if not still armed, if not backed by another with a weapon drawn. I looked around, saw nothing but black and the soft flicker of coals across the way.

Those two men are dead, I figured, or they woulda woken.

"You kill those men?"

"Who, Slumberin' Sam and Snorin' Sue?" he said, and let out a good-humored chuckle. "No, but even if they weren't sawin' logs, they'd not pay us much mind. Nothing can wake an overworked man. "The two Bobs, they are just civilians now anyway," he said, and tossed what I first thought was a coin through the open doorframe.

A badge clattered and came to rest a foot from my boots. I bent down to fetch it, never dropped the rifle from chest-level. Looked at it both in my hand and at the black rectangle from which the voice emerged. The word DEPUTY arched along the top over a worn star.

"I have the other," he said, "so I guess that makes us both Law now."

"So, let's speak Law," I said.

"I like you," he said, "but I take it the feeling's not mutual."

"What do you want?"

"Words are more powerful than rounds," he said. "I just want to talk."

I considered my options, which wasn't much, and said, "You never answered my question, the one about anyone else out there with you, 'sides those two civilians. Can I have your word it's just you and no others?"

"You can have my word, for what it's worth."

"What's it worth?"

"About as much as these."

My finger squeezed the trigger enough to be dangerous. I knew I was outta harm's way, 'less a round fired clean through the wood that separated me from him, or me from whomever. I imagined him—and others with Slade—

out there in the dark. Candlelight would pierce the night yellow-orange from the holes of rounds previously fired at our cabin. Suddenly I felt not so safe inside what always had, as if swallowed.

"Don't make me kill you," I said.

"Oh, right," he said. "You can't see what I'm holding."

"Which is what?"

"Don't be startled none, but I'm going to toss in something else I borrowed from you. My word is as good as these," he said, then, "and clover's my favorite; the black ones are terrible."

I didn't know what he meant till a small leather pouch was tossed inside, well up and over the pile of guns and knives. This act of his made me want to fire. With the rifle gripped in one hand, I grabbed for the pouch with the other and opened the bag. He'd eaten all but a half-dozen of my hub wafers, and for that too I wanted to shoot him.

"That all?" I said.

"That's everything, and I gave you my word already, good as those, so may I come inside so you don't accidentally fire that rifle?"

"Won't be no accident," I said.

"Boy, I like you," he said.

"Slow-like," I said, "cause *I* don't like *you* yet."

His hat preceded him, a tall thing as black and grimy as his long hair, which spurted out from under it. *A mop of worms*, I first thought, *lathered in grease.* A long chin shoddily shaven, perhaps with a knife blade, and a pointy nose broken once or twice. He was gaunt as gaunt gets, cheeks either cut with angles of dirt or pulled taught against his skull to create shadows. When he looked up, buried eyes revealed one as blue and the other as grayish brown.

"That a military uniform?" I asked.

The other deputy badge hung on one collar, upside-down as if in mockery of the law, and either by chance or by joke the shape of a smile and two slanted eyes stood out from dirt below the right breast pocket, crooked as his own smile, which he offered next as he stood upright. He was taller than me by a foot, not as short as I remembered, but that was always from afar.

"Asked you a question," I said.

"I fought in the *Intervención Estadounidense en México*," he said, "as they like to call it down in the south, or the Mexican War, as we like to call it far up as here. Killed maybe twenty Mexicans in my service to this country. Reason you and your father are here, I suspect, and the reason all the Mexicans here look at whiter folk as they do. You ever notice how they stare, like we took something from them? Well, I suppose we did. Same as you're staring at me now."

I thought of the Miwok slaughter and kept the rifle level.

"You kill all those injins," I said. I figured he wouldn't know them as Miwok, and so used the term I now thought of as derogatory.

"Mind if I sit," he said. He motioned for the table.

"Long as you don't mind this rifle pointed at you."

"I'd ask to refill my canteen, but I see your bucket's sprung a leak."

I wasn't dumb enough to turn and told him as much and that he and his friends owed us a new bucket, along with the two half-filled buckskin bags of gold he and Cole Mullins stole. I also told him he wasn't good at questions. He said they wasn't friends, but acquaintances.

"Your father's debt to Mullins is no longer my concern," he said.

"What debt?"

"I figured there's debt."

"*You* take it?" I said, and meant the gold, which he knew about, of course.

He motioned for the pile of weaponry at the door and said he already returned what he took, even the penny-candy, that he wasn't a stealin man, by any means, that people paid him for services, military or otherwise, and when they was rendered he collected, and vice versa.

"So why are you here?"

"I want to buy your claim."

"Not mine to sell," I said. "Not worth much anyway, now you best be off."

"I saw the way you worked, and the way your new friend worked the other day, how much the two of you found in a matter of hours. It's worth enough. I figure your father's not here to negotiate, might not be tomorrow, so it was worth asking next-of-kin—*you*—in case he's not around later to ask. I figure two half-filled bags of gold is good a price for this place."

I half-stepped forward, blinked.

He spat on the floor, and I bade him not to ever again.

"I apologize," he said, smudged it with his boot.

"Is that how he paid you? You figure I'm stupid enough to sell this place in trade for what that one-armed bastard stole from us?"

He shrugged in a way that meant he didn't give a hard turd one way or the other what I thought, or what I decided. It implied he'd get what he wanted one way or another.

"You want to buy our claim, for two half-filled bags of gold," I said, more ready to fire than I'd ever been ready to fire. "Exactly what was taken from us," I said.

"The offer stands, however you make it."

"Claim's not for sale."

"Everything's for sale, for a price."

"It's not for sale," I repeated. "And it's not mine to sell, anyway, it's my father's."

I wanted to ask about the maps, about the other two men who no longer existed in this world, but thought it best to stay silent and not feed him information.

We stared at each other a long while.

"Well, I guess that's that, then," he said, and stood.

"Where's Cole Mullins?" I asked. "And who was that other man with you the other day. The three of you shot up our place. I recognize you and Mullins but who was the other? Was that the Irishman, Richard Crone?"

"Bloody Dick," he said and smiled. "*Perdona mi idioma.*"

"Speak our tongue."

"Apologies for my choice of words. Nothing to fall apart over, Read. Wasn't me you saw. A friend of Cole's, I guess, maybe his second cousin. Seen the two playing cards often at the El Dorado, but my business there is for other … proclivities. I don't waste my money on cards, nor bad decisions. What I do know is someone other than me shot up your place. Why would I waste ammunition on wood?"

"Why don't you tell me who did then?"

"Because I have no reason to," he said and went to the door.

"There was a man inside they aimed to kill," I said, "a good man, and I reckon they'd not've hesitated to kill either me or my father had we been home."

"You weren't, though," he said. "Mullins only wanted his slave."

"Ain't no slaves in California. Law says so."

"If you say so," he said. "Have a good night, Read."

The man called Slade nodded, curtsied like a woman.

A strange man.

"Look," he said, "now, I'm going to take back my two guns before I leave, so don't shoot me in the back or nothing—they're named Left and Right, in case you're wondering—and my two knives—they aren't named. I'm leaving everything that's yours, the guns and the candies. That all right?"

I nodded and asked, "That all?"

"I guess so," he said, "if you're not willing to sell."

By a lack of words, I let him know we wasn't sellin anytime soon.

He bent down in a manner that was in no means a threat, much like his curtsey, and pushed aside the two holsters on top of the pile. He stuck the smallest knife into a strap on the side of his boot, retied the bigger one around his thigh like it was a part of him. With his back to me, he bent down again in a way so I could see his two belts and twin guns.

If he reached for either handle, I meant to fire, but he didn't, and I wondered two things: Would the two men in search of dreams across the way wake? And would they do anything even if they did? I figured no on both accounts. *The two Bobs*, he'd said.

His hands went to his sides to adjust his belts and I nearly shot him in the back, shot the doorframe instead, missed him by inches. His death woulda been an accident had I hit him. He flinched and cussed and perhaps thought it was a more purposeful shot, to warn him about the placement of his hands. I knew he had the ability to turn on a heel and gun me down in the time it took my heart to start its beat again, but he chose to say some words instead as he stared out into the night. He said a man should always look another in the eyes if he intended to kill, that death should never come as a surprise to anyone. He slowly turned and showed me what he had intended, to fix his britches, to notch each belt secure.

"And you should never have a look of surprise like that on your face after firing a gun at a man," he said. He winked and tipped his hat like a gentleman would. "It's a sign of weakness. So, I guess I lied," he said, "about the free advice. I seem to keep giving it."

"Pretend my wafers paid for it," I said. Apparently, my expression had changed for he responded with, "That's more like it. *That's* how you should look before you kill a man."

"That all?" I said, and it wasn't.

"They're going to hang your father and that colored feller at noon tomorrow if the judge don't come back, so if you want to put a stop to it, you have until then."

A part of me wanted to tell him to stop, but he made his way outside and was devoured by the black. Another part of me wanted to run to the loose board in the floor and show him the gold I'd hid, to offer it to him, with a promise of more if he'd help rescue my father and Lemi. Instead, I went to the door, perhaps in case he offered the same.

The soft glow of rolled tobacco hissed to life, and he let out a plume, threw the match to the ground beside him.

I finally lowered the rifle, pointed to the dirt.

He noticed this, and his demeanor changed, what little I could see of it.

"You came by to help," I said.

"That so?"

"You came here to buy the claim, you said, but that wasn't your purpose, was it? You knew I only had on me what I made today, which was decent but not much. 'Two half-filled bags of gold' you said, enough for me and my father to get by elsewhere a few months. That right? You have some kind of pull on your heart to set things right, and that's all you came up with, a way to give it all back, but for a price?"

Even as I said the words, I tried to figure it all out, but none of it made sense. The more I talked, the more he listened. Slade was a man who absorbed information, it seemed, a man who traded silence for others' words.

He untied his horse from the hitch-rail, turned her toward ours in the make-shift corral, and that's when I saw his collection. Ten or more scalps dangled from a length of rope on his horse's saddle; no head, just the black hair and flesh of the Miwok. I thought to ask about the head, but that would mean we'd been to where he'd been, had followed his path, saw what he did. He put his foot in a stirrup and brought his leg over, adjusted himself on top his ride, leaned forward, scratched the horse between her ears.

He tipped his hat to bid me farewell, but I kept at it.

"How you gettin paid for those scalps?"

His back was to me, but I felt his smile, knew he wouldn't answer. His business was his business, he'd say, though I knew the officer who'd taken my father and Lemi would be the one he'd seek for bounty, or maybe Sheriff Haswell, wherever he may be. Five dollars per, same as what a man made for a full days' work at a claim or mine. Wasn't right. Easier, by far, but not right. Innocent lives in exchange for money. At least fifty dollars' worth lay in wait on his ride. He spat, as if that was his answer.

Why had he come? I wondered, but then it hit me.

"You thought I'd sell you the claim in trade. My father and Lemi's lives for this place, in other words. You thought I'd hand it over to you if you promised to save them, maybe sneak in there tonight at that make-shift jail, take them by force or by sneakery. Why else would you tell me about the hangin next afternoon if only to rile me? Is that your intent? You think—"

"That all?" he said, with the same disrespect I'd given him. Apparently, he was done with my words.

I thought about it more, wondered if Cole Mullin's and his other friend were a part of the scheme I'd conjured, if there *was* one. Richard Crone, the Irishman, was he in it too?

"Would you," I said, "if the price was right?"

"I'll be honest with you," he said. "No reason not to be, ever."

The man called Slade gently shook the reins and click-clucked twice with his tongue. His palomino, from what I could make of her outline, made her way to the fence line. He and the horse admired ours; they'd come up to him and his horse outta curiosity. He reached inside a pouch on his saddle for treats, gave one first to his own horse as her head craned back, maybe carrots by the sound, then sidled up next to the fence to give one to Nugget, then one to Sasha.

He rubbed each their heads in turn.

"Which one's yours and which is your father's?"

"My father's is the one you just touched."

He admired them, whispered a few words only they could hear.

"I came out here tonight for two reasons," he said. "Neither was to bring you harm, and you have my word on that. Only to set things right."

I waited for his reasons as he pulled a long drag, filled his face with fire.

"But first a few more words of advice," he said and turned to face me, "seeing as you're on your way to becoming a man, and might be forced to become one sooner come tomorrow."

"Which is?"

"Learn to use a gun that can fire more than one round before having to reload, especially in a gunfight. See, if I was aiming to *kill* you, you'd have left me at the advantage."

He drew from his left as fast as my father could and aimed right at me but before I could react or piss myself he spun the weapon back in its holster, took another drag.

"Simple as that and you'd be dead before you landed."

I couldn't help but eye the spent rifle next to me, and the guns piled on the floor.

"And, unlike what you saw me foolishly do, you should *always* watch your back. I sat at your table for close to an hour without you knowing, while you were out working. Nice place, if I may say so, minus the holes. I cleaned each of those guns for you, those by your feet. They were well past needing maintenance. When I first got here, I thought you'd come on in during the middle of it all and want to spark up a conversation, but your mind must have been occupied, I can only imagine. Now, the guns aren't loaded anymore like your rifle, so reaching for them now would only be a waste of time. What you know, and with how much hatred you must be feeling right now after all that's happened, well, I don't blame you for wanting to try."

He was telling the truth, I knew.

"You'll only end up looking stupid," he said, not belittling, by any means, but the way a father might harp on a son, "wasting effort over empty chambers." He sighed again, loud this time. "I put the ammunition in the can next to your father's bedroll for safekeeping. As soon as I leave, you should reload, Read, per chance you are met by others less civil."

"What are the two reasons?" I asked, "Why you came here."

"The first was to tell you about your father, so you could say your respects face-to-face before he leaves this world. I know how much he means to you, and you to him. If the judge don't come back before they hang him, which I don't suspect he will, well, at least you'd each have the opportunity to say your goodbyes. Only one man's watching him now. I just came from there, so that's how I know. You can make of that information what you will."

"And the second?"

"The second will hurt some, and I must say I'm sorry in advance." He took a last pull from his tobacco, the longest pull, and tossed it aside.

I couldn't see his face, but knew those words hurt as they came out, or at least that he regretted to say them. "Your father did something," he said, "not too long ago. Not to me, but to another man. It's none of my business *what*, probably some drunken gambling debt."

He leaned toward the pouch on his saddle again, reached inside for another treat, something small, and had to fight off three eager mouths. He managed to get the carrot or whatever it was to Sasha, and then rubbed her between the ears as she chewed.

"She's a beautiful horse," he said.

It came out *she was a*, as if not the right tense.

"What'd my father do?" I asked, but he didn't answer. "*What* other man?"

But then I heard the soft-clop of feet of another horse as Slade rode off, his own ride nearly silent. One man simply appeared as the other disappeared. The approaching figure tipped his hat to Slade as they crossed paths, this much I could make from their silhouettes, but Slade didn't return the gesture, just exchanged some words and faded into the dark.

15

RICHARD CRONE, the Irishman. His nicknames alone could frighten, yet he appeared no older than a few years my senior, his build about the same as mine.

While I'd never met him before, the way he said hello gave away his heritage and I at once knew it to be him. And drunk, very so. He noisily unstrapped a lantern from his saddle, used his cigarette to light it, and was suddenly surrounded by a sphere of yellow.

"What do you want?" I asked. "I have no business with you, and my father's not here anyhow." I quickly regretted those words. *Alone*; that's what I told him. "Whatever business you have with my father, the two of you can discuss that after the sun rises, and when he's less *incapacitated*." Another word my father would use. "And here."

I grabbed for the rifle, held it loosely at my side. Only Slade and me knew it was as useless as a broom handle. The barrel pointed in his general direction.

The man wasn't much of an adult, not much older than me, really, maybe twenty years old at most, yet his mannerisms implied he was more incapacitated than my father, at least by way of drink. A mere boy. Many times, I'd seen my father as clobbered as one could get, yet this man-child, with his clean-shaven baby cheeks, was barely able to keep upon his mount.

Tipped his hat. Garbled words no man in his right mind could decipher.

"Yer right," he said. "My business is not wit'chu."

Richard Crone led his horse to the corral.

"That may be so," I said, "but, my father's not around at the moment, so you best be off. Come back tomorrow afternoon, or the day after next might be better. Whatever he might owe you can wait till then. Now, you have a good night. We clear?"

The words went either unheard or uncared for as he approached the fence line. When he stopped, he wobbled, as did the long shadow of him upon his horse. In the light of the lantern, I could make out more of his features: light hair, a slender face, longish nose.

It dawned on me then that I'd seen him before, at the Boomerang, or maybe the El Dorado Saloon. A card-player, known to run a game of three-card monte. Reputation is how I knew him before all this, and so I'd always imagined him as an older man, perhaps the same age as my father, who'd, of course, warned me of him plenty enough. "An ill-tempered quick-trigger," my father had said, though he'd never described his looks."

"Richard Crone," I said, mostly to confirm.

"Aye," he said.

He then drew from his right and put a bullet through Sasha's head, alighting the night. She stood tall on her haunches a moment in a flash of horror, then fell hard to her side. She continued to pant, so he put another into her with a flare from his barrel.

Nugget screamed off into the night, confused as I was.

The horse Richard Crone rode made as if to buck, but he somehow settled her to the ground with his hand on her mane. He dropped the lantern, which smashed on the ground. Fire spread below him, enough to spook his horse.

"Your father and I are even," he said and rode off.

16

NUGGET cried all night in the field, as did I into my bedroll. The men who was paid to watch over me arose to the noise of gunfire, got on their own horses and went on their way after some words with the young man. They may have feared the unstable Richard Crone the way I had after he put my father's horse down with raucous thunder.

What did my father do? What debt did he owe?

No one ever fears a boy the way one fears a man, and so I had wanted to ride after him, right after, guns ablazin at my side, wanted to drink hard like my father in case that should give me courage the way it would him, but Nugget had spooked bad and was otherwise uncatchable till she settled, which could be half the night or forever. She ran off the adrenaline—another word my father taught me. Like his liquid courage, it could fill a person, he'd taught me, or a beast, temporarily provide a man enough strength to lift a wagon with nothin but his hands. Never had my heart beat so violently in my chest. The adrenaline burned feverish.

You'll never sleep again, I told myself.

With three candles lit, I stayed up as long as I could, reloaded the rifle, as well as my father's pistol and Lemi's revolver. Slade was honest about his service to the weapons. Both was slick with oil. And I found the ammunition in the can, right where he'd said.

I prepared for war—from Mullins or Crone or others— or an ambush at the cabin like the Battle of the Alamo a dozen years prior in '36. I'd read about the thirteen-day siege of the mission near San Antonio de Béxar during the revolution in Texas, and now I couldn't help but wonder how long I might hold out holed up in such a way. The face of the mission, which was made of adobe, had been blowed apart, and here I was, lonesome, in a well-weathered wooden shack already full of holes.

Every sound of the night brought me to the window, barrel first. Around the sounds of Nugget came cries from fox and coyote as the warm of dawn approached. I imagined Nugget in the field, her snout over Sasha's. They'd been together for as long as I can remember. Sasha as old as me. As *young* as me.

My own cries stopped when I ran outta tears.

I imagined my father alive, and me the opposite—his hand on the shoulder of his dead boy, face sad and tired and full of tears, starin down on a face as young as the drunkard who'd killed his horse. I thought of what I wanted to do to all those who wronged us and found myself in a dark place. What had we ever done to deserve this fate? Life's purpose, I imagined: to be pushed to the point of exhaustion, forced to give up and exclaim, "I have seen the elephant!"

17

SLEEP took me in the early hours. I hadn't meant to slumber, for dreams could mean death, but I woke with my eyes crusted over, face puffy from the sobs of a child passed out from fatigue.

All in my head, I thought, but then sat up and remembered and took in all I could. Out the window, Nugget was no longer frantic, but stood guard over Sasha the way each would so the other could rest. The first time Nugget ever laid on her side, I thought she was dead, but my father had explained it in a way that made sense. "Protection," he'd said.

Nugget watched over now as Sasha forever-slept and would perhaps watch over her indefinitely if unprovoked.

My sad horse stood in a pool of black—a trick of the light of pre-dawn, the way darkness turns all that is dark the same color till the sun alters color back the way it's supposed to be. Red, I knew. So much red. Same color as my rage.

Maybe my father and Lemi slept like horses overnight, one up so the other could rest, though there wasn't much to do other than warn, for they was both tied, vulnerable.

Evil had wafted off Slade like heat, but for some reason I trusted him at his word. He reminded me of my father—the way he spoke to me more so than a man to a boy, the way he offered guidance. Despite the Miwok he'd killed, and my father's dead horse he'd allowed to be killed, it was Cole Mullins and this other he ran with, and this young man they called 'Irish Dick,' who had me worried.

A single man stood guard over my father and Lemi, Slade had said. But that appointed man would be up against two others should any of those horrid men try to take him by force. They could also simply pay the guard to look the other way, I knew, which was more likely.

And those paid men assigned to watch over *me?* They'd deserted as soon as the Irishman did his business, which left me curious about the arrested. Who kept *them* 'safe.'

To eat was the last thing I wanted, but I sat in front of the cabin and forced down hard bread and part of an apple. Stood watch over myself, for all it was worth. I ate around the bruise on the fruit and stared off into the field, lost for thought. Nugget stared off too, same direction but away from her companion; even dead, she still watched over her.

I put on my father's belt and firearm, secured Lemi's in the saddlebag next to the rifle. And I wore my father's hat, if only to help hide my age. It was time to grow up, to be a man, to take what my father always said children lacked: *responsibility*—another of the long words he had taught, both by name and by act.

As the sun fed the property its proper colors, I brought

my saddle to the horses and set it on a post, whistled for Nugget, then lost everything I ate. Sasha was a dark brown horse, which hid the wounds, but the amount of red that had spilt out was enough to fill buckets.

The bread came out hot, as well as what I ate of the apple, and suddenly I was reduced back to a boy: fifteen years old, same in years as Sasha was in hands. My father always said she was a fifteen-hand horse, measured by height. Maybe close to a thousand pounds, measured by girth. Now she was nothin but a heavy weight on the ground.

What to even do with her …

My father once told me he'd bought his horse for twenty dollars, though a horse cost more now, maybe a hun'ered. But a dead horse?

Their meat was common to eat overseas, five or six cents a pound, but all I ever seen of dead horse in the west was how they was left in the streets. If one expired in the middle of a wagon pull, it was common to unstrap the beast from its yoke and let it lie right there, in the way, at least till it rot enough or was taken by vultures. Moved easier in pieces than in bulk. And I figured that's how I'd have to leave Sasha.

A man could be hanged if he *stole* a horse, but what would the judge say about one *killed* outright? Or would he, if paid in coin or gold, see it as just?

My heart fell at the thought of tellin my father.

We didn't have enough to buy another horse, not at the moment, perhaps not for a while, and even so it would never be the same. The bond my father had—

"They're gonna hang your father," I said aloud as Slade's voice returned in my head, "and that colored feller … noon tomorrow."

High-noon was in six or so hours, I figured by the light.

"If you want to put a stop to it, you have till then."

Slade's words, as ugly as disease.

Put a stop to it how?

I wiped my eyes. A boy in tears was far from what was needed to save either of them. I went inside and followed my rejected breakfast with a swig of my father's whiskey, but that wanted outta me the moment I saw the mud and blood I'd tracked inside. Nearly lost it in the cabin but managed to run outside and purge into the long tom. Small chunks of what hadn't come out earlier lay in wait in the trough like nuggets of gold.

Back inside, the second swig of heat stayed down, made me dizzy, if only in my head, and the third as well. I poured an amount into our smallest wineskin to take to my father. He'd often tie the same one around his waist. I imagined he needed courage now more than ever.

Did either he or Lemi know their fate? Had they been told?

The officer and his men had promised to look after them both, but thoughts of brown creek water and moldy bread clouded my vision of their care-takin, so I figured not. I figured it was best to head into town, for noon could be discerned as a multitude of hours, and though I trusted Slade by his word, I didn't trust those other men. 'Lynch-mob mentality,' as my father called it, was a dangerous beast.

I thought of him all those years ago at the triple-hangin in '48, eyes glued like so many others to the three ropes and the men so quickly sentenced to their deaths. Or maybe it was five that was hanged, for no one seemed to have the story straight. A crowd had gathered, or so he'd told me, a hun'ered or more.

"What shall be done with them?" the judge had asked.

After a pause: "Hang them!" One man had yelled the sentence, my father'd told me, then the town joined in, his word spread as fast as the fire coursing through my body.

I wanted Richard Crone shot, same as Sasha. Shot in the head, then left to rot however way he fell, all the way down to his bones. I wanted Cole Mullins shot, same as the mere boy.

And for what it's worth, I wanted Slade to find the same fate as those two men; a sun-scorched skeleton embraced by a military jacket from a war fought so long ago, hat off to the side, hole punched right through it. Instead of coins, I'd place two licorice hub wafers over his empty sockets, or perhaps *in* them. They wouldn't pay no ferry man, no; he'd forever find himself in limbo, kept from crossin over to whatever might wait on the other side.

Hanged would suit them better … in place of Lemi and my father. And I'd be the one, this time, to get the crowd to chant when the question was posed, and the crowd would agree in a single voice made of many. The boxes under their feet would be kicked out from under em by the judge's men, or the horses or wagon they sat upon whipped.

Could I stand to watch them all die in such manner?

I thought so, but first I had to make my way into town.

It took the apple core and coarse words to coach Nugget away from the fallen horse. She had lost her trust with me for the moment, for what I had let happen, mayhap. Even with the bridle hid behind my back, she knew the intention. While I couldn't look another second at the gore, she stared right at it, but Sasha, in her final act, perhaps, was enough of a distraction for me to loop a lead rope around the pony. Nugget pulled, not hard, and finally let me have her.

I tied her to a fence post, loosely, in case she startled. The saddle took effort. She flinched at first, then settled as I told her all was okay, though all was not.

My father would have set me right if he was at my side. Every part of the set-up was either backward or opposite. "You're not well in the head," he'd say. And his words would ring true. The saddle horn pointed at her rear at first, before turned the right way, and the bridle, which I'd struggled with for some time was upside-down, with her ears tangled in leather where her snout should be and vice versa. The pony looked at me oddly.

"I know," I told her. "I know."

She snorted, as if she thought it funny.

I led her out the gate, not botherin to close it, and made my way into town.

<h2 style="text-align:center">18</h2>

ONLY one man remained in the make-shift jail: a beat-up version of my father. He'd been hit good across the jaw, bottom lip split. One of his eyes had swelt shut from another blow, the cheek that faced me dark like stubble, only purple underneath. He spat blood as I approached, and shook his head no. I went to him anyway, hopped off Nugget.

"What'd they do to you?" I asked.

He stared at the ground, said, "You should go."

But I stayed, said, "Who did this?"

And he said, "Same men who put us here."

So, I said, "Where's Lemi?"

Twin trails of dirt stretched into the distance, as if our new friend had been struck unconscious and dragged by his feet away from captivity. A few men stood afar, curious.

Had they witnessed what had happened?

"He's gone," he said, but he said it in a way that meant Lemi wasn't *gone* gone, simply taken elsewhere. "They brought the papers, put them in the officer's face. An argument ensued after the officer showed his piece," he said, spat again, "but ultimately he let him have him."

"Who, Papa? What happened?"

"No more of this 'papa' business," he said. "From now on, you call me Read and only Read. From now on, we call each other by that name, one and the same, same as everyone else does. You understand what I'm saying?"

"I don't," I said, but I did.

This was no time to act like a child; that's what his words

meant. Once a boy becomes a man, he shouldn't address his father again as 'papa' till that papa'd turned elderly. He meant it was time I finally became a man, for he had already started to turn papa-gray.

"*Read,*" he said.

If not for his arms tied behind his back, he'd slap me across the face if I didn't have an answer ready. But the look in his eyes provided the same stern message.

"Read," I said.

His name. Mine. *Ours.*

My father nodded, then I nodded, a delayed reflection of an older man and his younger self.

We shared unspoken word, and then I asked him again what happened, man to man.

De hombre a hombre, Slade had said in another tongue.

"Cole Mullins," my father said. "He and that other fellow he rides with—called him Richard, I think—rode in no more than three-quarters an hour ago, when it was still dark, and after a heated conversation they went on their way."

I wanted to tell him about Sasha, about the man who'd shot her.

But he continued: "They kicked the tar out of me before the one who was watching us knew what to make of it. They didn't touch Lemi, but the other man who runs with Cole spat in his face, told him he wasn't too fond of men like him and I said *I* wasn't fond of men like *him*. That's how I got the shiner. Punched me in the face."

My father, twice as unarmed as Cole Mullins, I thought.

"Heard him pull his gun," he continued, "but the deputy put a stop to it. The deputy called out for the officer, real loud, and he was apparently in earshot leaving one of the saloons. He came over, scattergun drawn, put it right into Cole's cheek, then teetered it to the other man, who was not much older than you."

"You see Slade?" I asked. "Did he come this way?"

"No, only Cole Mullins and the other."

Bloody Dick shot your horse dead, I wanted to say.

Instead, I brought the wineskin to his lips, let him take a pull. Neither of us thought of the whiskey burn on his split lip as it hit him. He grimaced, hissed inward through clenched teeth, but then asked for another and I delivered. I'd have taken another pull myself if not for the blood ring that circled the opening.

He cleared his throat, said, "Like I said, they argued, and Cole Mullins kept flashing the papers, said he was the rightful owner of the slave tied next to me, and the officer asked, 'How you expect me to tell one from the next, huh?' He said, 'Black is black and this one could belong to anyone.' When I corrected him, I received a slap across the face with the back of his hand holdin the pistol. Behind our backs, Lemi squeezed my hand, twice, as if to tell me something."

"What?"

"A warning, I think. I d'know."

"They're gonna hang you at noon today," I blurted.

"They … wait, what?"

"They're gonna to hang you at noon, later today, for killin that man at the creek, the one you shot in the head for what he done to Lemi," I said, and then the rest came out like rapid gunfire: "Those men was employed by Cole Mullins and the other and they think you killed that man outright. They don't care if it was *just*. No one sees it that way but us. Steal a man's horse and they hang you. Steal a man they think's a slave and it's considered just as bad. I don't know," I said, the last part too much like my father. "Grizzly got the other; we know that, and *they* know it too, but they know for absolute certain you shot—"

"How'd you come upon all this knowledge?"

I didn't want to tell him, for some reason, but had to.

"Slade came by the claim," I said, took a long breath.

"Richard Crone, too—the Irishman. Slade's the one who told me all this, that they're gonna hang you."

My father sat up, which seemed to take effort, said, "You recognized him: Slade. You're certain it was him and not another. And the Irishman."

"He introduced himself as such, and I recognized him. The other acknowledged when I called him Richard Crone. The two men the officer assigned to set-up camp across from us, watchmen for the night, they paid neither no mind. They slept through Slade as he came up on his horse, and later ignored Richard Crone and his ruckus, left when he did. Slade's the one who said they're gonna hang you today at noon."

"And you believe his word?"

"For what it's worth," I said, and thought of the wafers.

He seemed to consider all this.

"I see you're a deputy now," my father said with a bloody smile, all crooked like. He meant the badge on my hat. I'd forgotten I'd pinned it there until he pointed.

"Long story," I said.

Slade has one now too, worn flipped.

My father was about to ask about the ruckus, so I told him. Relayed all I could recall of our conversation, how he'd cleaned our guns and whatnot, then what came after.

"Sasha," my father said, just her name, and then he stared off.

Where's the officer now? Where're all the others?

The sky had turned a lighter shade of blue, miners already about, some on their way to stores recently opened to gather provisions, or to the Oasis Coffee Shop for the daily grind. Was it Sunday already, Saturday? All the days had jumbled, though I knew from the crowds and the attire it was the week-end. The Empire House was closed, as was Shepard's Ten Pin Alley, so it musta been Sunday. Didn't see Joseph Speck from the Methodist Episcopal, though.

Far off, the giant leaning oak haunted with its branches.

"Bloody Dick killed her," I said, mostly cause I wanted to say it aloud as I stared at the tree, to give what he done more weight than how I'd told my father how the situation transpired. Lemi was the story-teller, not me, but he was gone. "Richard Crone, I mean. Shot her in the head, same as you did to that man at the creek. She was strong, Papa, and it took two—"

He chose not to correct me about his name, maybe on account of the tears that soon needed to be wiped from my face with a sleeve.

"Slade's saddle was decorated with the Miwok scalps," I said to change the subject. "I think he and the officer in charge of this whole mess is in some kind of collaborition."

"Collabor*ation*," my father corrected.

He squinted, thought hard, and asked, "Either man do anything to you?"

"They showed no intent to kill me, and the second man just your horse. He said the two of you was even. It was he and Cole Mullins who stole our gold, not Slade."

"Slade tell you that too?"

"In so many words. I figure Cole Mullins and the other man owed him a debt of some kind, for his 'services'—Slade's word, not mine—and when they couldn't pay, got desperate. You know as well as I do there's been interest in our claim as of late."

A nod.

"You're a smart boy, Read, but why?"

There was gold to be worked, sure, but compared to other claims in the diggins, our place was considered 'meager,' unless Slade or even Cole Mullins knew something we didn't. Perhaps Cole Mullins' role in all this was as a prospector. After all, a man with one arm couldn't do much work with pick or spade, so that left only his mind, his ability to make sense of geography and rock and how the earth settled over time. Maybe he knew the history of our claim, what it once held. Perhaps there was more, lots more. We'd been told about a vein, but that had been chipped at over the years till gone. Why take interest in our claim now, after all this time?

And what did the Irishman have to do with any of it?

"What debt did you owe Richard Crone?" I asked.

My father looked down, ashamed.

"You're goin to tell me," I told him.

"I once told you I never understood gambling," he said, "but that's not entirely true. I understand gambling plenty, what it can do to a man; I just don't like it. Drank too much one night at the El Dorado, and the young Crone fellow came up to the bar, said he'd buy a round if I joined him for a game. I knew it was him. His reputation preceded him."

"Triple-card monte," I said.

"That's right," he said. "That, and then some rounds of poker. Dollar buy-in. The cards weren't in his favor. They were in mine, and though we didn't bet much, he said I cheated when I flipped over a flush to beat his set of threes. I didn't cheat. Even said the dealer was in on it or whatnot. I was up maybe twelve dollars when his temper detonated."

"You gambled our gold," I said, not a question.

"Only a dollars' worth, then it doubled, doubled again, and again, and——"

"So, what happened?"

"After he put up a fuss, I said, 'Don't want no trouble' and made to take back just the dollar I'd started with, said I didn't even want to join him in the first place, but he'd bought me a drink so it was only fair. But he threw his cards and said, 'Take the damn gold, ya cheatin' bastard!' He stood and drew a small knife but stormed off after we just stared at each other for a while, both drunk and tired, the dealer's eyes wide. And so, I did. I took what I'd won. This was a few months ago. Haven't seen him since."

I gave him a hard look.

"That's the entire story," he said.

"He killed your horse for eleven dollars?"

"For nothing, really, since I offered it back to him. He seemed to be a prideful man and pushed it back at me, said, 'Take your damn winnins,' and untranslatable Irish."

For whatever reason, I decided to keep a secret from my father, then. What I didn't tell him was that Slade had known exactly how much I'd worked outta the ground. Nor did I tell him the amount I'd buried under the pried baseboard, which was barely enough—if even—to pay back what I took on credit from the general store. A solid week of hard work to break even, I figured, which in turn reminded me of Sasha, who couldn't be buried, whose corpse would lay there, alongside my hard labors, for weeks on end. And this in turn made me wonder whether I'd find myself lonesome or with my father in the near future, or all three of us in partnership, Lemi included, should the judge return the next few hours and set things right. And this in turn made me think of the earth I'd have to slowly chip away.

"What are you thinking about?" he asked.

What if there's more beneath our cabin …

Over the two short years we had the cabin, we'd dug all around it, as others before us had, but claims was good for *all* land, which includes what may lie under any structure built upon it.

"Read?"

A vein beneath our very beds.

There was rumors of a man who'd ripped up the baseboards of his cabin during a fit of frustration, only to find a nugget the size of his fist, the gold revealed by his spilt drink. And according to the story, he'd found more in that hole, and by early morning he'd torn his home apart. Thousands upon thousands of dollars' worth of found gold and nowhere to store it, and so he bought a wagon and took all he had and left, perhaps headed back east to his family, for it was common. My father said rumors often opposed truth, but I always found rumors *shadow* truth. We'd never once thought to look under our cabin.

"Read," he said again.

"Slade offered to buy our lot," I told him, my mind all over the place. "For two half-filled bags of gold, exactly what Cole had paid him for his services, whatever that might've been. He didn't mention a dollar amount, just the bags, *our* bags, is my guess. I think he might have found out where that gold had come from and thought of a way to get it back to us, and to get something more in return. It was definitely Cole Mullins who stole from us, though, and him alone. Nothin else makes sense."

"Why, though?"

"You said there was once a small vein that ran through our property, which the previous owners and those before had picked clean."

"Your expression says you have a theory."

"When I first saw Slade approach on horseback, I hid all the gold we had, in the ground beneath the cabin. Pulled up a loose floorboard. I put gold *into* the ground. But what if there's more gold to be taken *outta* the ground?"

"Beneath the cabin."

19

I STAYED with my father the rest of the morn and watched as a jackrabbit hopped from one side of the town to the other while the sky turned smoky yellow. My stomach churned its knots at the thought of hot stew. Salted-dried meat and reheated beans and hard bread or cakes is all I ate 'long as I could remember, all *either* of us ate. My father's appetite wasn't as fierce; he only wanted the drink. In a matter of hours, he'd finished the wineskin—borderline drunk at eight or nine or whatever o'clock it may be, but that was all right.

Shoulda shot the damn rabbit.

No one came, not for a long while. People milled about in their routines, some stared, perhaps in awe over a father and his boy in such a situation. "Predicament," my father would call it. For all anyone cared, I coulda untied him. I'd suggested to undo his bind, but law is law, and whether or not we was in the right for the past we'd be in the wrong for the present if we did such a thing. My father said as much in so many words, even wriggled away.

"The judge will put a stop to this," he said when it grew quiet too long.

"But what if he don't come?"

"One shouldn't delve in what-ifs."

And one shouldn't live with—

I couldn't finish the thought.

Blood had crusted over his split lip, one eye swollen near-shut. They'd done a number on him, but when caught in a stare he smiled, said not to worry, though that's all I seemed capable of at the moment. The rifle lay at my side. In Nugget's saddlebag was the pistol and the revolver, both now cleaned and loaded. Both hungry, like my appetite.

More than once the idea crossed my mind to cut him free and get him the guns. The amount of booze that coursed through him by mid-morn coulda lain waste to any man who crossed our paths, but none of that was in the cards, as my *don't-understand-gamblin* father would say.

"No, Read," he said instead and that was that.

Together, we watched the horizon. Every head that rose from the wavy haze like a phoenix raised our hopes, then befell them: a traveler, a medicine man, a Miwok.

When a crowd started to gather, worry filled my father's good eye.

You're too old to cry, Read, I told myself.

"He'll come," he said.

"But what if he don't?" I said.

"Look," he said, though he could do only half of what he asked of me. "Read, if he don't, if life starts to spoil, it's going to spoil fast." He eyed the great white oak in the distance, where a majority of the people of town had congregated, as if for church services. Largest crowd I ever seen out front Elstner's hay and wood yard.

Sunday. Everyone dressed in their Sunday bests.

As I took in the crowd, I realized from where and whence they came; Methodist services were over, maybe an announcement made. All had come to see a man hang: my father.

"It's not yet even ten o'clock," I said, not that time mattered.

Reverend Hosford stood there among his congregation, gathered them round like sheep, even children: two girls in near-identical off-white dresses, a boy in clean attire.

The sun had a few hours on its course to noon.

No sign of the judge.

A lanky man with a beard the same size and color of his hat pointed up at the tree. Next to him, another swung a coil of thick rope, then tossed it up and over the largest branch. Already the man who caught it started in on a hangman's noose, hand-over-hand.

Spoilin' fast.

"Time to bring you to justice," a voice said from behind.

We both spun. The officer was suddenly there, along with two of his goons. He noticed the Deputy badge I had attired and laughed, said, "Well, who died and made you law?" And then he spat next to us, wiped his chin.

"You ain't law as much as I ain't law," I said.

"Oh, is that right?"

"Read," my father said.

"You're both named Read," the officer said and laughed, though he knew this.

"That's right," I said. I'd worn my father's hat all morning, with full intention to give it back, but that intention had come and gone and so when I stood it made me as tall as "The Law."

"Read," my father said again.

"Your man Richard Crone killed one'a our horses last night, you know that? And those men you assigned to watch over me, to keep *me* safe, you think they fulfilled their duty? You might want your pay back if you paid em." Even as the words left my mouth, I realized the two men who stood behind the officer may in fact have been those men. "You know as well as I do that to kill a man's horse is a hangin offense, so if anyone should hang today it's—"

"Who?" the officer said.

"Richard—"

"Who?" he said again before I could finish. "Now listen here, son," he said. "I'm sorry. *Read.* Only your father calls you son, right? Little Read, look, I don't believe I know who the hell you're going on about. Can either of you make sense of this gobble-de-goop?" he said, addressing the others. "What say you?"

"Nope."

"I don't believe so."

"Right," I said. "He don't *exist,* this Irish fellow, even though his hands are deep in your pockets. Elbow deep, I reckon."

He put his hand on the back of his rifle but that didn't scare me none. He knew I was right about the pockets.

"You in deep with Cole Mullins, too?"

"You're talking nonsense, boy."

"Read. And as far as the law is concerned, you got no *jurisdiction* to hang a man on rumor or lies 'either coward told you. Jurisdiction, my father taught me that word and you ain't got it. All you got is the ability to tie an innocent man up like you have and wait for—"

"*Read*," he said, his interruption spoken like a curse.

"—for the real law to—"

His backhand hit me hard and put me on the ground. I'd never been hit, not by no one. His gloved hand must have taken some of the sting, but it was hard and rough as a chunk of granite across my jaw, enough to make me spit blood next to the tobacco he then spat next to me.

My father made as if to stand, like a horse against a post to scratch an itch, but slipped and fell and made an agitated sound then spoke.

"Get your hands off my son," he said.

"Your son's in need of manners," the officer said. He spat again, the sound as ugly as what came outta him.

As I sat upright, the two men behind the officer shifted and stared at one another in a way that meant neither had ever seen a man hit a boy, or at least didn't approve. The officer held his hand out for me to take it. I wanted all my might to spit into it, but even through tears I knew it wasn't right. He'd strike me again, harder. My head rang like someone faraway at Baker & Keyser, the smiths, hammerin at horseshoes. Fire welled hot under my skin. I cried, but only because I had to from the sting. When I didn't take his hand, he set it back atop his rifle cause he had nowhere else to put it. He straightened the badge he wore as if to prove a point.

I am the law, he said without any words. *Says so right here.*

"Where's Lemi?" I said.

"Read," my father said.

"*Read, Read, Read*," the officer said, and shook his head. He made a tsk-tsk-tsk sound with his tongue against the back of his browned teeth. "What possible compassion could you possibly have left to give for that … that *n*——? That's the word you don't like, right?"

"Where'd you take him?"

"Not *take*. I *gave* him back, is all. We've already—"

"You handed him over to Cole Mullins."

"That's right. Far as paperwork's concerned, he's owner."

"Read," my father said, and I understood. *Inflection*, my father always told me, was a language within a language. A way to say a word different than it was originally intended. The way a father could say his son's name a number of ways to mean any number of things. This particular inflection meant to keep my mouth shut, so I listened proper.

The officer knelt down and offered his hand again.

I hesitated, then took it, and he lifted me to my feet.

He flicked the badge I wore, hard enough to *ping*.

"Deputy Read," he said and laughed.

I looked down as I dusted myself off and read the badge upside-down, same way Slade wore his, and when my eyes rose, I noticed neither man behind the officer had Deputy badges. Each of their shirts was torn, which meant they was indeed the two men assigned to watch over me, and that Slade had ripped the badges away, most likely without argument.

I'm gonna take these now, I imagined him sayin.

"Bob," the officer said. "If this little squirt of piss tries anything, so much as *flinches*, or even if he so much as says another *got*-damn word, you shoot him in the knee. You understand, or should I make myself more clear than that?"

As his answer, Deputy Bob drew his sidearm, cocked back the hammer.

"Good," the officer said. "And other-Bob?"

"Robert," the other-Bob said.

"Help me get Read, here—*Read Sr.*, that is—upright.

"Noon's hours away," I said, a terrible whine.

The officer rolled his eyes to the sun.

Bob took a step forward and squinted an ugly-browed eye to aim, but before he fired, the office raised a finger to the sky, and that was enough to prevent him from crippling me forever.

20

THE hangin tree loomed over the townsfolk like a giant's malformed hand punched out from the ground, arthritic branches curled with ugly knotted knuckles. A rope dangled from its largest finger and swayed with the wind. Then a second rope was thrown over, next to the first, and another noose made. Two horses drawn to hold the men.

I'd been pushed to the ground twice more in my efforts to say my piece. The man with the gun wouldn't put a round in me. Fire didn't live in those eyes. No man would shoot a boy my age, not with so many spectators shillyshallied about to witness some awful act.

Death fascinated man. All feared 'the great end' but none appeared too worried if Death decided to visit another outside one's own circle. I must admit that when my father first spoke of the three men hanged in '48, I was sad not to've been there, to've seen what he'd seen; now, I'm glad I wasn't. Rumors spread over time of more men hanged on the hangin tree, but those three were the only 'on record' and those 'not on record' perhaps ghost stories.

The officer and the man he'd called other-Bob half-dragged and half-walked my father into the direct center of the mass, and they spread the people apart like the story of Moses and the Red Sea. The waters of men and women and even children opened upon Lemi waiting there already. They shuffled my father next to him. Familiar eyes found me in the distance.

I took Nugget by the reins and walked her closer, till I couldn't see over the mess of people who'd swallowed them. Nugget hesitated, but I saddled and managed to lead her onto a small hill that overlooked the scene, perhaps fifty or sixty feet away, and even onto a slab of rock a few feet higher. She tested the earth, slid some, but I pushed her to climb, and she climbed. She trusted my decision to go up there like I trusted her not to fall.

Seventy-eight people had gathered, which included the officer, as well as Bob, the other-Bob, my father, and Lemi. All but a few wanted to watch. Cole Mullins was there, too, but no one else I knew by name, though I recognized faces.

When a man rode in from the west, my heart warmed, but it wasn't the judge; it was Slade. He pushed his horse like I had onto a hill she didn't want to climb on the opposite side, much farther away, saw me, tipped his hat, then focused his attention on the crowd, same as me. The collection of scalps was gone.

"Hang them," someone called out.

Sounded like Cole Mullins, and another repeated the sentiment.

Henry Thorp, I understood then. *The man next to him is Henry Thorp, from Lemi's writing—his previous 'owner.' And he no longer wants him as a slave, but dead.*

"Now hold on," the officer said. "Law is law, and just is just."

The way he said it made me want to fire upon him.

"These diggins is *Hang*-town!" another said, as two words. "Ain't no such place as *Just*-town. If Mullins, here, says this man and this dark fella murdered one'a his men, I'm apt to believe him. Mullins never done me wrong. He's a good man."

"He's a liar!" I said from my perch.

Heads turned to see who'd said it, then turned back.

"Read's boy," the officer said. He pointed at me and shook his head. He seemed to know his way around a mob, how to entice them. "He believes his father, this man we're set to hang in just a few moments, is outright *just* in killin' two men. Even says one of them wasn't in fact killed by his father at all, but by a bear. A grizzly bear."

Francis, and Dirty Jack. He won't even reference either by name.

"Let me guess," someone said, "that grizzly was wearing

some fancy dress." And then he curtsied like a woman would and got the crowd to laugh.

Even from afar I could tell Slade wore his crooked smile, not in spite of me, I knew, but in spite of the foolish man who'd danced and twirled in the dirt.

"That boy up there," the officer said, "would have you believe he and his father had *saved*, had in fact *freed* this slave. And before one of you calls out that slavery is frowned upon in our great State of Californie, Cole Mullins and Thorp here happen to be from the Carolinas, where ownership of slaves is legal and backed by law. They do not claim to be residents of this wonderful golden state but passing through on their temporary business of mining."

The map, I thought, then thought of the fallen Miwok.

"They have all the paperwork stating ownership."

He held up the writ, flashed it around.

"It says, and is signed by multiple parties and witnessed hereto, that Henry Thorp is the rightful owner of this property. Do I have this information correct, Mr. Thorp?"

"Man can't be property," I said, mostly to myself.

"Settlers in new territories," Thorp said, all business-like, "can determine, through popular sovereignty, whether or not one can allow for slavery within each territory."

A few grumbles from those in earshot, a few confused looks. Someone rambled on about the Wilmot Proviso, and slavery prohibited in any territory conquered by the Mexican War, and President James K. Polk's appropriation of funds to negotiate some treaty—an antislavery declaration that apparently "meant squat" so far out west.

"Manifest Destiny," said another.

"California's no longer a territory," I said when quiet.

"Doesn't matter," Thorp said. "I own it and can do as I please."

"Then why's he getting hanged too?" someone asked.

"A valid question," the officer said. "It appears Benjamin Alexander Read," he said, a finger in my father's face, "and his boy, came upon two men working for Cole Mullins and Henry Thorp, who happened to be looking after this property while they were away on business. I'm not sure what transpired, nor do I care about that business, but the two of them, now dead, decided to administer punishment to the—"

"Whipped him," I said, "for amusement!"

"—and was so rudely interrupted by this man and that child up there."

"Check the wounds on his back!" I said.

"Read's concept of *just* was to shoot one of those men in the forehead," he said. "Seen it myself. Shot him right through his damned skull and painted everything behind him red with all that ever flowed through him. The other man, well, he was found mauled, perhaps by bear, perhaps by mountain lion or bobcat, but what should be noted is that his remains, while not intact, was found with a round in his gut. Same type, I suppose, that killed *both* men. And seeing as Read Sr. is noted—by most I've asked—as a man of *principle*, it can be assumed this double-murder would not have transpired if not for the sake of this property, nor did this aberration put a stop to it. In fact, one might call him a *partner* of Mr. Read, of sorts, for soon after he became employed by and was seen working at their claim."

A got-damned liar!

"Mullins pay you to spread untruths?" I said, but no one listened.

"Hang them," Henry Thorp called out. "Hang them both."

"There should be a trial," said another.

"This ain' no place for trials an' you know it," said an older man. The weather-beaten miner hadn't dressed for Sunday services like most, and perhaps only owned the one outfit, for it was as brown as the rest of him, as though he'd swam in mud, hair and beard matted. "Punishment in this 'stablishment's swif-and-jus," he said. "Hang him and hang th'other."

Many spoke over each other.

I looked across the way, at Slade in his military uniform jacket, who seemed to take interest. His horse danced under him uneasily. He steadied her with a hand, the other on his longrifle. He adjusted his black hat, which matched the rest of him, and glanced over his shoulder, as though in wait for someone.

People below passed around the paperwork, some with nods, some unable to read but wanting a turn. No one argued for my father but me, nor for the man next to him.

"Should hang the boy too," Cole Mullins said.

"As guilty as his father," Thorp said.

The officer held up a hand to shush the crowd, and they soon shushed. The last words any of them said was "deserves them right," which then trailed off.

"We will not hang a child in this town," he said. "As an officer of the law, however, and with no Sheriff Haswell present, and having heard from all parties involved, I hereby sentence the formerly accused to be hanged by their necks until dead."

No, no, no rambled through my head, *this can't be right.*

"If the accused have any last words, say them now."

"Say somethin," I mumbled. "C'mon, Papa, say some-thin."

The wind blew, pushed dust like tumbleweed-fog across the town.

Lemi, he can't say nothin at all.

My father finally cleared his throat and said, "Make sure my boy's looked after in my absence. He's a strong young man who does me proud and deserves a good life. Deserves better than the lives you're so eager to take. Our claim's his now, his alone. He knows how to work it proper. The gold's his," and then to the rest of the gathering, he said, "and unless you want me haunting your souls forever, best leave him be."

"That all?" the officer said.

"No, that's not all. This man next to me is Lemi. I'm speaking for him now only because he can't speak for himself for the reason I'm about to tell you. He's a well-educated man, far more educated than anyone in this forsaken town, and he's a hard-working man. Doesn't deserve to be hanged as much as I don't deserve to be hanged."

Perhaps he was stalling. Perhaps he knew his fate.

"Those more deserving," he said, "as I told you before in private, are the two shooting daggers at me now, *those two ugly bastards.*" He motioned to Cole Mullins and Henry Thorp who in turn provided ugly faces. "Those two Carolinians don't deserve the gold they steal."

Cole Mullins threw his only arm at my father, struck him across the jaw.

Thorp pulled him back.

"That all?" the officer said to my father again.

"No," he said, and spat more blood. "This free man next to me, I speak for him now because he simply *can't*. The man I shot dead cut out his tongue for the sake of keeping him quiet about all the bad he knows of ol' one-arm here, and this other fellow I never met before."

Cole Mullins made as if to throw again, but decided not to, perhaps cause my father was twice as unarmed with both hands behind his back, or mayhap cause those who watched the last blow didn't much like what they saw.

Smiling, my father added, "The man I shot, his death was *just*, that much is true of this story you've shared with everyone. His life was put to an early end for a torturous, unrecoverable act, for taking this man's voice. The other I shot in the gut, an ugly wound, but it would have healed with attention, and I'd left him alive. That one was responsible, as my son says, of whipping this man next to me. I tended to Lemi's wounds myself. They were deep. We patched him up, then offered him equal work for equal pay. It was his decision to stay, not ours."

"Please tell me that's all," the officer said. "I'm tired of this nonsense."

"In fact, it's not," my father said.

All listened.

"I don't deserve this," he went on, "nor does *he*, so if you must hang a man today to appease this crowd, hang me, not him. My son has a journal, and although Lemi can't talk, he can write better than anyone here, and he's detailed his journey here. Offer him a fairer and more just trial than what you've offered me today. That is all I ask."

"No, papa," I said under a breath.

"Fair 'nough," the officer said. "String him up, boys."

"No!" I screamed.

The badge-less deputies stared at one another.

"I have one request," Cole Mullins said, "as a co-ac-cuser."

"Yeah, what?" the officer said, the words spat.

"Unbind him first," he said. "Make an example of him by makin it last." At least that's what I thought he said over the raucous of mixed conversation.

"And the other co-accuser?" the officer said. "Any special requests?"

Henry Thorp shook his head no.

The deputies untied my father, led him closer to the tree. He looked defeated and rightfully so. Suddenly I wanted to share one last drink, the two of us on stools in the Boomer-ang, each with a spirit. I imagined the bar-keep. I imagined whiskey, could taste it.

Too late to stop any of this now. Spoilt.

I touched the rifle, brought my hand back, then touched it again. I thought of takin aim at Cole Mullins, then, and quickly thought better of it. They'd string me up too, perhaps alongside my father. No, if I'd shoot anyone, it would be my father, to end him earlier so he wouldn't have to suffer. No man deserved this fate. I made sure the rifle was ready, though I wasn't.

Could I hit him from so far?

Wasn't far, but far for me. And I'd never fired from the back of Nugget. She'd toss me for sure, though the ground nor injury was none of my concern.

The first of the two horses was led to him.

I wiped my eyes, the scene a blur.

Slade had a trick up his sleeve. Mayhap he pondered what I pondered, thought of firin upon my father if I missed; or, more likely, if I couldn't bring myself to it. By the way he held his longrifle, I knew there was no way to stop the momentum of what had started. He shifted in his saddle, checked his weapon. But I couldn't help but think of Sasha, how Bloody Dick had put her down without hesitation. Two shots, one after the other. The first meant to kill her, the second to—

The man closest to my father, either Bob or other-Bob, leant his hands as a stirrup so my father could make his way onto the horse. No saddle, but bareback. Easier to slide off the back once they spooked her.

Slade looked my way. Our eyes met. He tapped his badge, which made me look down at mine, then he tipped his hat when we reconnected. Like Lemi, he spoke without words. Far behind him was a dust-plume, maybe that of two or three men ridin in hard.

The judge! Please be the judge!

I watched helplessly as the officer hopped onto the other horse meant for Lemi—not his own, and also not saddled—and made his way next to my father so they rode side-by-side. The noose would be more suited for the officer at this point, but he leaned down for the rope, which was handed to him from below. He lifted the noose over my father's head. Said some words I couldn't hear cause all who watched cheered support to kill my father.

The rope was thick, the knot brought down snug.

"Look away, Read!" my father said over the noise.

I did, but for a moment, to check on the dust.

Judge or not, whoever it was wouldn't make it in time. Slade looked over his shoulder too, then hefted his longrifle, cocked the hammer.

"Benjamin Alexander Read," the officer said, which regained my attention. "You shall hang by the neck until Death finds you. God rest your soul, and may you pray for forgiveness."

Those in front of the horses spread to either side. The entire semi-circle of congregation stepped back a few paces to provide room. The officer rode off a ways, which left my father and his horse lone under the hangin tree.

When I lifted my rifle, I caught a motion in my peripheral.

Slade shook his head at me in disapproval.

I lowered my weapon, for he was right. I couldn't be the one to do it. Tears mucked my vision. I'd draw attention to the son. Nothin good could come of me to fire upon my father but a ride to hell and lifelong memories and nightmares no one would ever want.

Look away, Read.

But I couldn't.

The officer aimed his rifle at the clouds and fired and the mustang reared and whinnied but didn't spook so he smacked the stock against her backend hard, and that got her to move. She bolted, my father's weight enough to keep him on long enough so when he was free, he simply swayed like the rope had on its own in the breeze earlier, then he fell into pendulum.

All who cheered for the spectacle turned silent.

My father panicked as any man would, his feet straight out. Then he kicked at the air, his hands at the rope round his neck, unable to find purchase, face instant-red. He swayed and kicked, wildly, swayed and kicked, until his legs faced the ground as the clock he mimicked wound down what was left of his life, toes a good two feet from the earth. Still, he fought. He was a strong man and pulled himself up by the rope enough to take a breath or two before the slip. Then another. Maybe the rope was greased, for he couldn't hold on long.

I hopped off Nugget, tossed the rifle to the ground.

Slade took careful aim but didn't fire. The sun above him gave him and his horse the smallest of shadows, as if on a slab of black slate. Still, he didn't fire.

I should have. I should have done it cause the coward won't.

The dust of horse hooves wasn't close enough to make any difference, and so I ran. I ran to the crowd. I ran to my father, heart beating in my chest, and I ran. My own footfalls the only sound until I got to him. Time slowed, and then sped up as a small voice called out the first name I ever called my papa, a childish word, and to hear a boy call out in such a way to his father and in such desperation turned the crowd sour.

Spoilt.

"He's just a boy," a woman cried.

"No one should ever experience such a thing," said another.

"This ain't right," said another.

"It's *just*, I say." The officer glanced around, took a few steps back from his position. He'd realized too late he'd been wrong, but what was there to do about it now? His deputies knew their faults, and they appeared equally disturbed and unsure what to do. Across from them, Cole Mullins and Henry Thorp watched in awe, and with smiles. Their expressions sealed permanently in my mind as I grabbed onto my father's legs and pushed up with all my might.

I looked for Lemi, but tied up he was soon trampled and lost in the chaos. Then he was back, at my side. He offered his shoulder and knelt, and we both pushed up as my father pushed down so he could manage another breath. His help provided the opportunity to go for my father's knife, which I wore on my belt, but as I loosed it and held it up for him to take by the hilt, the blade cut into me, tossed into the flurry. Cole Mullins had kicked Lemi in the back, which'd shook us both. The knife lost. A man fell upon Lemi, then, drug him away by his feet.

Adults slid arms around the children watching, to hold them back as my father's face turned darker shades, the sounds he made awful.

He was twice my weight. Took all my might to lift him even an inch. I wrapped myself around his thighs and pushed, up and up, and he tried to use me as leverage and pushed back, but it wasn't enough. He spun by rope, and I spun with him, feet in constant slip.

I gave it my all as the once-eager crowd dispersed. It was true: no one wanted to watch, not any longer. The woman was right. I was just a boy, not the man my father wanted me to be. And the other who'd called out was right, that no one should have to experience such a thing.

As my father and I continued to spin and dance under the oak, I caught Slade in the distance, whose rifle seemed to point right at us like the smallest of pupils.

No, no, no!

Not on purpose, we spun away from that fright, and my first thought was that my father would be shot in the back, killed with me clutched onto him, or maybe us both.

Slade's rifle-fire split the dry early-afternoon with thunder, some large caliber. I waited for the jolt of my father's swift death as I tried to look away from it all, but instead found the empty stare of Henry Thorp, whose chest blossomed open like a rose in sunlight as he flew back. He topped over dead, straight as a felled tree. Cole Mullins knelt next him, but there was no pulse to check but for the blood the dead man's heart continued to pump out. Cole Mullins dug through Thorp's pockets, took what he could, and fled. The second roar of thunder, which I hoped was aimed at Cole Mullins, sent my father's weight on top of me.

21

IN the wake of the storm, Judge Lynch and two others rode into the middle of town. One was the young man my father had hired to track him down. He'd been paid well, and he'd done his job, whether he'd gone to the diamond springs or beyond. A little late, but he'd done it. No matter, the judge had returned to sort out this mess, and he didn't look too happy about it. Behind them, ridin as slow as a horse can be rid' came Slade. He saw me, tipped his hat, winked. Even in the hot afternoon sun, he wore his all-black attire. He'd shot the rope.

My father had to dig his fingers deep into his neck to help loosen the noose's grip. The knot was tight from his own weight, slicked in grease to perhaps preserve it over time. Eventually, we worked the rope free and up and over his head.

He'd bruise, but he was alive; and although raspily, he breathed. The rope had cut into his skin some, enough to bleed, his neck red like a man had tried to strangle him. Perhaps one had.

The two deputies, Bob and other-Bob, had fled, though the officer who'd appointed them stood his ground. No longer on his horse, he towered over us, shadowed us from the sun. It took a moment to realize he'd drawn his sidearm and meant to fire.

"What the sam-hell's going on here?" the judge said.

Lemi sat next to my father and inspected him, unconcerned with the sidearm. He pointed at me and then gave a thumb-up and with his eyes asked if I was okay.

"I'm all right," I said.

In the dirt, Lemi answered the judge's question by writing a single word: JUST.

He hugged my father and me in a tight embrace, gun at his back.

The officer spat next to us, said, "You're far from all right," and over Lemi's shoulder moved his aim from me to my father. "The three of you are *far* from right."

I never understood the expression afore, though I'd heard it and said it, but the way in which he said it was enough for me to understand.

"I've seen the elephant," he said.

He meant he was *spent*, as tired and worn as any man could be. His body faced the judge, arm out to the side, gun pointed at us.

The officer hesitated, though he meant to kill us.

Judge Lynch's question had gone unanswered, verbally, and so he asked it again. He tossed in some curses, mentioned how he was on his way to seek justice for a foursome of murderers in the Hopkins' death and had to put that on hold for this. He asked how a petty theft coulda ended up in such calamity. No one had an answer, except Slade.

He'd caught up with the judge, dismounted.

With not so much as a word, he walked up to the officer the judge had originally appointed to look over the town in the Sheriff's absence, and then lifted a scattergun from beneath his longcoat. He ended the man's life in one fluid motion. No more than a few feet away. The shot went through the back of his chest. Only blood had time to shoot back.

Had he taken a moment longer, the officer would have ended us. Slade wiped his face, leaned over the body.

He pried off his own Deputy badge, tossed it over his shoulder to the judge like the flip of a coin, which the judge caught, then Slade removed the Officer badge from the dead man, flipped that one to me, which I caught.

"Everything's back in order," Slade said, "for those still here."

All the others had gone their separate ways.

"All this over a few bags of gold?" the judge said.

"More than gold," Slade said, then mounted his horse and left.

"Someone better explain all this to me," the judge said.

22

THE judge stayed in town two days longer. Come to find out, Slade had been hired as a bounty hunter of sorts. His job was to investigate the scalpins, for they wasn't all legal though lately "Someone's been offin' the injins," at least that's how Judge Lynch put it. My first thought was that Slade had been the one who had taken the scalps, that he and Cole Mullins had killed all those men and women and children at the camp up north.

Lemi looked after my father back at the cabin on the claim. My father tended to by him same as he was tended to by my father. He was happy to do it. The judge'd told me to meet him at sun-up the morn after the attempted hangin to explain our side of the story. "Your father's not well to talk," he'd said, "so you can on his behalf."

He'd also told me to bring all the evidence I had, which was plenty, and that there wasn't no need for no attorney. Slade had filled him in on what he knew, which was also plenty. We sat at a table at James Odle's City Hotel next to the "Thomas-Young" Round Tent, which only months ago went by "Ashton's" Round Tent. This was across the street and cater-cornered from the tree which had nearly taken my father as its fourth victim. In the distance, I could see its branches, one of few trees to offer shade, for all the others were pine and cut for lumber.

I brought the judge up to speed on all that'd happened after he left town. I told him about the two men we'd found at the water's edge, what they'd done to the muted man, and how we took him in after. It took a few tries to get the judge not to refer to Lemi by the word I didn't much like, and eventually he obliged, started to call him by his name. He laughed at the part about the grizzly and the cubs, though none of it was intended to be funny.

"Your father was in the right," he said. "Though he should have killed *both* men. I haven't had any run-ins with Francis, but Dirty Jack was nicknamed as such for a reason. You're lucky to be alive. He wouldn't hesitate killing a boy your age, after he had his way with you."

I didn't know what that second part meant but nodded.

When I showed him the map, he finally took real interest in the story, as if it held a secret of buried treasure. I showed him where we found the lot of dead Miwok, far past any water. I told him we'd gone miles into the mountains where a stream that fed it from the east had all but dried up. Told him all the details of the horror we found.

"Headless?" he said, astounded.

"Someone had cut off a man's head, yes," I said.

"Why'd you think it was Slade at the time?" he said.

"I seen the scalps myself, tied to his saddle."

The judge nodded, disgusted, but then waved me off and said, "Slade put a nail in my door sometime yesterday before I rode back into town, left me a bouquet of scalps—I guess you could say—to find dangling upon my return. Left a note with them too, signed it himself, though the man can't spell worth a damn. Same ugly script, like on this map."

"Cole Mullins wrote that," I said, and pointed to the

initials C.M. under the scribbled letters of HANGTOWN CRƎƎK, the E's drawn backward.

"The Same handwriting as all unlearned men," he said. "Look—"

He pulled the note from his pocket. A thumb-smudge of blood stood out on the bottom-left corner. He showed it to me, said Slade at least got his E's right. And his letters was all tiny lowercase and thrice as small as those on the map, and also written by a steady hand. Slade had shot Henry Thorp in the dead center of his chest from as far away as I had been on that hill. There was no way he could have done so with unsteady hands. And the rope—

The judge interrupted my thought, said that Slade had per chance expected a gunfight, though he luckily ended up as the only one who'd fired. This was his reason for the note, in case he didn't make it out alive. I'd hated this man called Slade until this moment. He'd risked his life for ours, but why? He didn't owe us, and we didn't owe him. *And*, the bastard'd led a man to kill my father's horse. Was this his way of atonement?

The judge cleared his throat, informed me he might stumble over misspelt words, for there was many. I moved in next to him and read as he read aloud:

J. LYNCH,

HOPE THIS DON' STAIN. THIS IS 12 SCALPS. BY THE TIME YOU FIND'EM AT YER DOR, THE READ BOY WILL BE OF INTREST. HE HAS A CRUDE MAP DRON BY C.M. (COLE), AND ONE DRON BY THE BOY OR HIS PA OR THE N—— (HE CAN READ N' RITE, MORE ON THIS LATER). SEEN THE MAPS MY-SELF, THO I FOUND THE CAMP LONG FORE THEM. MATCHES WHERE THESE SKINS N' HAIRS IS FROM. DRON WELL, THE 2ND. THE ASS YOU LEFT US AS LAW WAS BUYIN EM FROM COLE FOR AN

EVEN FIFTY DOLLARS. 13 DEAD, BY MY COUNT,
ALL INJINS. ONE FOUND W/O A HEAD. MIWOK OR
MAIDU, CAN'T TELL.
I BE-FRINDED A MAN BY THE NAME OF JOHN
THORP AFTER SEEIN EM W/ COLE AT THE ROUND
TENT, ALL SECRET-LIKE, AND HE SPOKE 'BOUT HIS
SLAVE OVER DRINKS ONE NITE AND WHAT HAP'D,
IN HIS WORDS, THO THEY WAS LIES. A TALL TALE.
I KNEW THEN NOT TO TRUST MULLINS OR THIS
MAN.

I thought that was the end of the note, but then the
judge flipped it over. "This all true so far," he said, "far as
you recollect?" and I told him every word so far was.

THEY HIRED ME TO FIND EM, SAME AS YOU
FOR ME TO FIND THE SCALPERS (MULLINS N' THORP,
FUNNY 'NOUGH). THEY PAID ME IN ADVANCE, AN
AMOUNT THEY SED THEY TOOK FROM READ SR.
N' HIS BOY. SO THEY SAYS. SOME DUST IN BAGS
MARKED B.A.R. CLOSE TO BEAR, WHICH IS FUNNY.
I RAN WITH EM FOR A WILE. DRUNK, BOTH TOLE
ME DIFFERNT COUNTS OF WHAT THEY DON UP
NORTH TO PURIFY THE LAND OR WHAT-NOT. AND
THEY SPOKE OF THE REWARD PER HEAD, HOW IT
BEAT DIG'N OR MINE'N.

At this point the words got smaller, so as to fit, and so
I leaned in close as the judge adjusted his glasses and leaned
in close, and together we read the last of it, he aloud:

UPON MY RE-TURN TO COLE'S CAMP IS WHEN I
SAW THE SCALPS, AND KNEW HE AND HIS MEN DID
WHAT THEY SED UP NORTH. THE READ BOY HAS
PAGES YOU SHOULD READ, WRIT BY THE N——

STAYIN W/ EM. A WELL-LEARNT MAN. THEY SHOT
UP THE READ'S PLACE. TRIED TO KILL ALL THREE,
THO THE FATHER N' BOY WERE GONE. I AIM TO
KILL JOHN THORP AND COLE MULLINS FOR THE
SLOTTER OF THE INJINS AND ALL OTHER HELL
SINCE YOU LEFT THIS TOWN W/O PROPER LAW.
THEY PLAN TO HANG READ. I WON'T LET THAT
HAPPEN. THE GOLD THEY PAID'S MINE, THO. JOB'S
A JOB. SAME AS JUST IS JUST.

We both leaned back, then I moved to the other side of
the table and then the judge asked what I expected: "How
much of that is true and how much is farce."

"None is farce," I said.

And he said, "That— that *dark-skinned* fellow's staying
at your claim?"

"He is, and for as long as he needs to."

"And he can read and write."

"He can, better than I ever seen."

I showed him the journal, then, what Lemi had written
the first time we'd given it to him, as well as what he'd written the other night. Lemi had stayed up after the thwarted
hangin of my father, under the flicker of candlelight. He
wrote twenty or more pages in his beautiful script recounting all that had happened, which included Cole Mullins and
John Thorp and another—most likely one of the Bobs or
the even the officer—when they shot up the cabin, and
about the "arrest" and all that transpired between then and
the lynch-mob. The judge read his story, old and new, as I
sat in silence. He cleared his throat once or twice.

"Far as I'm concerned," he said, "this is all behind us."

"Behind us?" I said.

And he said, "Behind us. I hired Slade to do a job and,
well, he did it. He put a stop to the injin killings, so local
Miwok and Maidu can rest easy. Some have taken to mining,

themselves, though they're not too good at it just yet." He sounded pleased in their safety, yet the last came out what my father would call offensive."

And I said, "Why do you not like them?"

And he said, "Them?"

And so, I folded my arms and said, "The Miwok. The Maidu."

But he didn't have an answer and flipped through the pages of the journal, shook his head, sighed. "This town needs reform."

"Hangtown," I said.

"A terrible thing to call it," he said. "There's a motion in place to change the name. Not from *Hangtown*, since that's not anywhere on record, but from *Dry Diggings*. This is a placer town and should be known for its deposits, not for its hangings. Do you know what 'placer' means, Read?"

It was the first time anyone had called me by my given name and not by 'boy' or 'son,' other than my father. Slade had done so as well, I guess.

"A placer's where you find gold," I said.

"A deposit of sand or gravel in bedrock. That's what this place is known for, and it shouldn't be known for the other … what almost happened to your father. Anyway, your story matches up with Slade's, and that's all I needed to hear. Head off home now, Read."

23

MY father slept for two days, and when he woke, he thursted and hungered like the almost-dead. Before that, Lemi wrote more, at night, mostly, but what he writ was his alone and none of anyone's business. He had to work through some things I could only imagine.

"You'll teach me?" I said to him before I went to bed.

He acknowledged with a nod, with a look that said, "But not today," and for the next however-many hours I listened to his pen-scratch, fell asleep to it. When I woke, he was at the stove: more damn pancakes. Food is food, though, so we ate heartily.

After, we both looked at the floor, knew what had to be done. Through the noise of planks ripped from beneath us, my father slept, turned over, slept more. We pried free half the wood that composed our floor. Hammered out the nails. Had us a pile of planks as tall as the table. We sat, the two of us, and stared at the mess we'd made. Not yet even noon.

We'd gone hard at it until we had a coffin-size hole.

"That's not for me, is it?" my father said. Scared us both.

He sat up from his long slumber and his knees popped like snapped twigs. But he knew what had to be done as well and smiled. Standing, he faltered, grabbed one of the shovels and sat back down. When he stood again, he used the shovel as a crutch.

"How long was I out?" he said.

"Two days," I said. "Three and we woulda buried you."

Lemi laughed, such a strange sound to make without his tongue.

All there was the hole, for we'd 'barrowed out all the dirt and made a mountainous pile next to the long tom to pan later. With each load, we'd first look out the window to assure no one watched, lest someone wonder. It was hard not to look at Sasha's body where she lay. Flies buzzed around her, sought the tears in her open eyes. But what to do with her?

"You need to eat," I said to my father, brought back in the moment, "and drink," I said, "but only water. We're out of whiskey."

"I don't need anything else," he said.

Way he said it, coulda meant either now or never again.

Then it was all three of us who stared down at the hole,

intimidated, perhaps. My father sat next to us at the table and ate the pancakes we'd left him. Three dozen or more gold nuggets lay scattered around the perimeter, what we'd found by hand. He then downed enough water from the bucket that it needed to be refilled, and he offered to go to the creek. He may have gone out simply to catch his breath, for we'd found quite a collection of gilted-quartz and the yellow metal in our earlier effort to hit bedrock beneath the cabin. He could have gone out, seen his horse, and needed a moment to right himself, for he'd only heard what I told him of the affair.

When he returned later, he had the filled bucket and a pick-axe. Strapped to his belt was a smaller one. And he said, "Well, let's get started," and so we did.

The vein we discovered stretched from the stove to the opposite corner.

24

DAYS later, we dug another hole. We needed a place to stash all we unearthed. We hid our haul each night with loose boards, covered with a loomed Maidu rug, and lastly my bedroll. The gold stayed there until we were done. I slept over fortunes, for what we found under our cabin would last three lifetimes, and so we split the gold three-way. Never fought over it. There was still plenty to be mined under the cabin, but we left our greed buried, eventually nailed the planks back down and, for many nights on end, sat at the table *transfixed* before sleep found us.

"We're all transfixed," my father had said, and without a definition, we all knew what he meant, that we were *done*.

Spell-bound, as if our eyes kept the floor held down.

Funny when you dig a hole, you're left with twice the dirt removed, at least it always seems that way. What loosened earth wouldn't fit back under our home, we left outside.

All three of us enjoyed the pan, and so we spent most days busy with less laborious work. Without much notice, we began to make not-too-drastic deposits in the bank, three separate accounts. There was enough under the cabin to drive a group of miners mad, but we kept our sanity close. We eventually covered the hole beneath my bedroll, left our tithes for the gods, one could say, and went back to work as expected from such a claim. We'd all seen what the elephant of the dry diggins could do to a man. None of us wanted that experience.

25

SLADE rode up weeks later, a horse in tow. First instinct was to fetch the rifle, same as my father's instinct was to grab for his guns. I knew Slade's speed at the draw, but with one hand on his reins and the other locked onto the lead rope behind him, he posed no threat.

How a man could wear an longcoat over a uniform in this heat was a question that couldn't be answered. He tipped his hat, knew we watched through the window.

"What do you make of it?" I said to the room, then Slade spoke.

"Read," he said.

I looked at my father, who shared the name.

After neither of us responded, Slade clarified, "*Benjamin Alexander* Read."

The man had saved my father's life, perhaps saved me, saved Lemi; still, he had to him a certain vibe that could raise the fine hairs on one's skin and prickle flesh. Not even his voice was pleasant, *not right*. The judge had trusted him, though, and that gave him clout.

He no longer wore the badge, but neither did I; mine

lost somewhere in the piles, perhaps somewhere under the house. That thought made me recall Slade watchin over me in my father's absence, made me wonder if he'd spent similar time watchin over us these last few days.

Had he seen what we done? He'd offered to buy the place, after all.

I followed my father out the door.

My father had put on his belt and cinched it, as if to show the man he'd fire if prodded to do so. The way he posed himself was a message, a lesson aimed at both me and Slade.

"I'm going to let go of these reins now," the man said.

"Why are you here?" I said, which got my father to put an arm in front of me and take a step forward, thus to push me back.

"And I mean to reach into my saddle bag," he said, "but only for a smoke. "Real slow like, no worries," he added. "Care for one?"

My father didn't respond, other than to take another step forward.

"Fair enough," Slade said. "But *I* do, and I aim to have one. I'm here because I owe you a horse, I reckon, and this one is good as any. Used to belong to the officer who tried hangin you. Haswell's nowhere to be found, so the judge has decided to appoint a new Sheriff, William Rogers. Bill already has a ride, so I figured you should have this one to save her from slaughter. Ever eat horse?" he said, his question left unanswered.

From his saddlebag he pulled out a carrot, snapped off a piece, and held it out behind him. "Her name's … well, I don't know her name, but she's yours now if you want her." He looked to the field, saw that Sasha's body had been taken care of by either man or nature.

My father didn't say anything, just listened.

And so, I listened.

"The Irishman's the one who killed your horse," Slade said, "though I feel a pang of regret having led him here, honestly, and I don't have too many *pangs* in my blood. Dick made it clear you done him something awful, and that he owed you as much. For all I knew at the time, you musta killed *his* horse, but now I know that's not the case. He said as much over a monte game the other night, drunker than a bottle."

He opened his pouch of tobacco, said, "You sure?"

Again, silence.

The man sat there and let us watch him roll up a smoke, as if we was supposed to accept that. His face puckered ugly as he inhaled and let out a billow that faded. He then slid off his mount and left her there as he took the reins of the horse he'd brought. He fed the nameless horse another carrot and led her to Nugget, who'd come to the fence out of curiosity. Slade hitched her there on one of the posts, finished his smoke as he offered my horse a treat.

"Well, I guess that's that," he said, and headed back. "Oh," he added, I owe you something too." Way he said it, I knew he meant me.

He untied a smaller pouch from his belt, tossed it toward us.

I imagined my father and I both followin its arch with our eyes, blinded temporarily by the sun, then each of us shot in the gut, yet neither of us took our eyes off the man and it landed with a sound of shattered glass. The pouch landed within reach, so I bent down to it, peeked inside at the assortment of colors.

"Clove's the best," he said, and hopped on his horse.

Slade sucked in the last of his smoke, tipped his hat.

As he circled round, my father finally spoke.

"The offer still on the table?"

What offer? I wondered, as Slade said those same words.

Lemi joined us outside.

"You offered my boy, not so long ago, two half-filled bags of gold dust," my father said, "for our claim. Same amount Cole Mullins first took from us, which he traded you for some service or another, which started this whole mess. If you're still offering, we might consider, so long as it's an agreed-upon understanding between the four of us."

I already knew my answer, and I knew Lemi's for he told me as much even without words. The diggins was the last place any of us wanted to live, not any longer. And now that the three of us was well off, we could go anywhere. What my father was about to trade the man was two half-filled bags, what was originally ours anyway, for the rest of the vein under the cabin.

A fortune.

"Now, why would I want to do such a thing?" Slade said.

Half a smile cut into his face, then, a horrid thing, like a crack in the earth left behind from some flood.

When he was gone, my father looked at me and asked, "You ready?"

And I was, and told him as much, saying, "Ready for what."

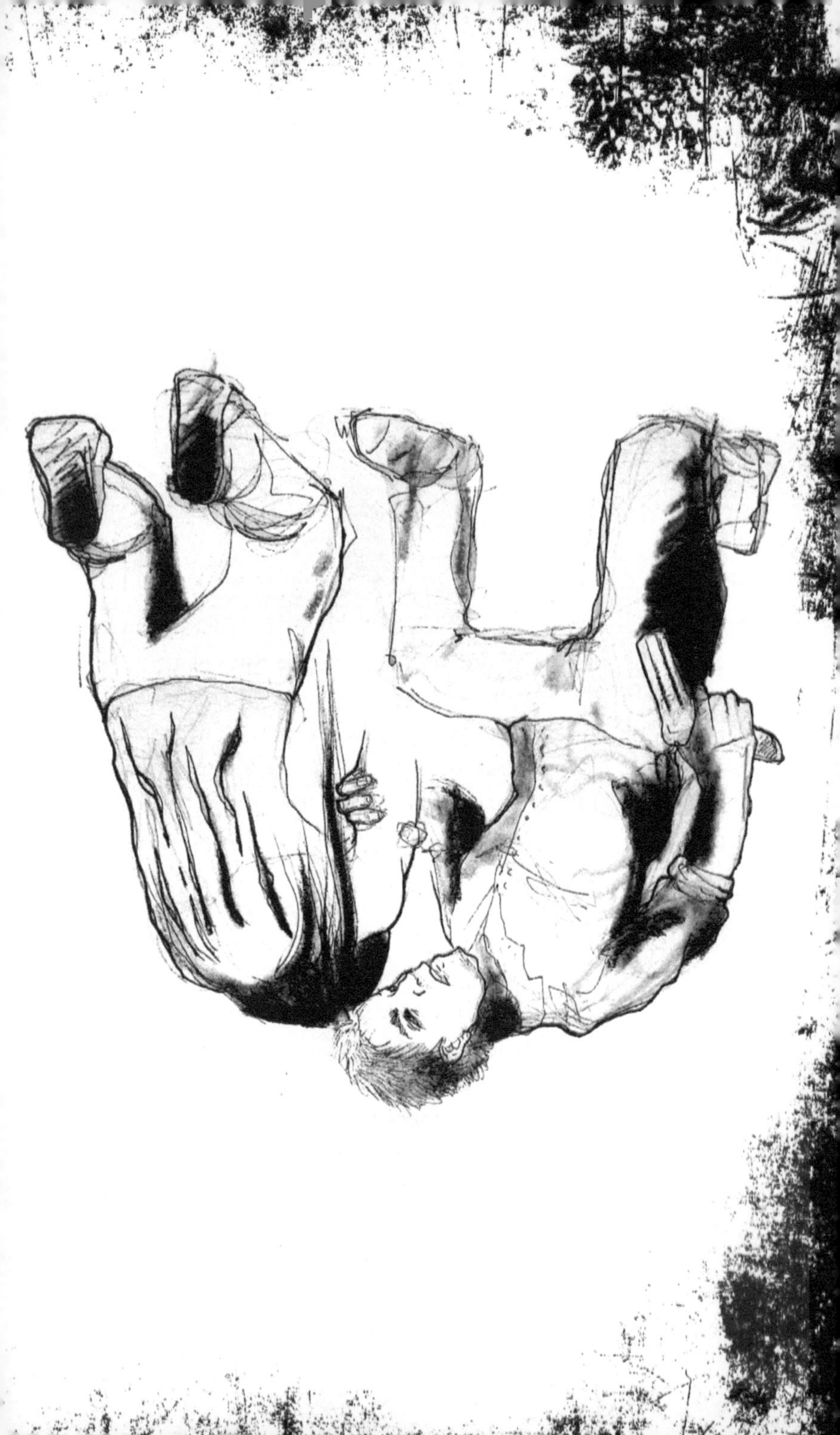

DIGGIN GHOSTS

In eighteen forty-eight a diggins was settled
    nuggets the size of fists
    plucked from dyin' creek-beds
    panned out seasonal streams
    yeller collected dust

For in this placer-town some men was hanged
    not once, not twice, thrice

In eighteen fifty-love their gilted restless ghosts
    haunted the mines by night
    drunk on the chilly air
    swam splashless 'long long-toms
    nightmare'd the lone sleepless

And in this unestablished place of sin
    Miwok and Maidu wept

In eighteen fifty-later a fourth was strung up high
    same evil oak tree branch
    damn harbinger of death
    both feet all a-dangle
    afore off'rin' to jump

And in this establishment past recurred
    'cause Lynch's law was just . . .

AUTUMN
1850

THE ELEPHANT

RICHARD

Crone witnessed the three hangings back in '49 and was convinced no man would ever hang again in the diggings, especially after a near-fourth. Crowds gathered for the lynchings, until realizing what hangings entailed, then dispersed. Once bodies stopped moving, interest fell, like the men. No one wanted to stick around for the sour fragrance of death.

Benjamin Alexander Read, the fourth man they'd tried at the rope, once took eleven dollars from him in a game of poker. Richard preferred monte, his slight-of-hand able to trick the slow eyes of drunkards, yet those in the saloon had talked him into a different game, which he'd lost. And so, he figured Read's horse—two bullets to take her down—would make them square, seeing as the amount he lost could've bought a decent horse.

If Read weren't such a seemingly honest man, weren't a *father*, he'd have plunged his knife deep into his gut and not later gone for the horse. The boy's why he hesitated with his blade. He'd seen little Read plenty of times in the El Dorado before it changed hands to the Elstners, always trying to un-drunk his father from the tables.

The acting sheriff interviewed Richard then, and again in the summer after getting involved in a game of monte with desperados later arrested for robbing a Frenchman named Prosper Cailloux. Richard had no fewer than three men shake him awake in the early morning. Men asking, "Where's the gold?" After showing the gold he won, fairly, they let him be, for he would've run if guilty; plus, his own story matched the bar-keep's recounting.

With Benjamin Alexander Read, he'd been approached for reputation. "Bloody Dick," some called him, a stupid *nom de plume*; sometimes simply "The Irishman" on account of his heritage. He hated the nicknames, but he'd poked more than a few who did him wrong. So what if he had a hot temper and a fast hand? Nothing he could do about either. No, with the Reads, it was Sheriff Rogers out for blood. He'd always had it in for him, even before the new title and badge, for Richard had sliced open the man's cousin's arm for accusing him of using waxed cards. The sheriff had nothing on him, just prodding for information.

"You shoot his horse?" the sheriff asked of the Reads. "A hangin' offense."

"They say I shot their horse?"

"Not outright, no, but they've got themselves a dead horse next to their claim, shot twice, and the only person home then was the Read boy, and he sure as hell didn't shoot his father's horse. A man says you was seen there the same night, that true?"

"What man?"

"A man," Sheriff Rogers said, "and I'll leave it at that."

"That so?"

"It is so. You shoot their horse?"

"What do the Reads say about the matter?"

"Only that someone came by and shot her dead, though they aren't willing to offer names. I seen the horse. Shot under the ear, again in the neck. Father's not saying anything, not the boy, neither, and the third in their party can't talk at all. But I asked around, and you was seen playing cards with Read, Sr. You pulled a knife on him, I heard."

"I play games with lots of men. I run a table at the El Dorado."

"Everyone knows that. And the knife?"

Richard Crone pulled the blade and showed it to the newly-appointed Sherriff, said, "Sure, this one. I was mad for losing a bad hand. Didn't use it on Read, though. Same blade I used on yer cousin, if I remember correctly. No one calls me a cheater and doesn't get opened. That why yer here, yer cousin?"

"One account says you lost a large sum in a hand of—"

"Who hasn't on this hell?"

The conversation went back and forth, but in the end, Sheriff Rogers rode away knowing as much as he'd known riding in: nothing. There was nothing. That was months ago, when water still flowed through the cursed town.

September the earth was parched, which meant more miners gambling their gold than digging it out from the ground, or panning piles previously dug, which meant miners would spend it on chance and liquor and women. Good for business and those who ran tables. More men inside than out by the time October rolled through, and that fed business into the winter months. Under the round tents and in the saloons and hotel establishments could be found heat and light, which attracted men as much as what they could expect or want to find inside.

Sporting types from all stretches of land came in from the cold, recognized by their fancy dress shirts clashing badly with the dirty ever-gambling miners. Fighting fixed boredom, fixed monotony. Shots fired out upon the slightest provocation, yet everyone had the hangings of '49 on the mind, and so threats were never much more than slung words or holes put into wood.

There was the Thomas-Young Round Tent, which not long before went by the name Taylor's, as well as Tom Ashton's across the way, the Adams Hotel, James Odle's City Hotel, with Scraton's Eureka Hotel splitting them. The El Dorado Saloon was always booming, though everyone called it the El Dorado, with the "Jackass" or "Hangtree" adjacent to it, formerly the Barkhurst's Placer Hotel, which was now run by the Herricks. Names and ownerships changed as rapidly as townsfolk, yet Elstner owned damn near everything on Main by the end of '50, including the saloon where Richard ran his table, as well as the hanging tree. The Chicago Dining Saloon on Maiden Lane was likewise popular, but nothing like the El Dorado. There, the whole town erupted before dusk and stayed lit—along with its people—through sunup.

Stores often stayed open past full dark.

Autumn seemed short-lived with winter rushing in early to accommodate the crowds, which is how Richard Crone found himself in the El Dorado slinging cards this chilly October night; Sunday morning, really, for it was approaching two o'clock when trouble met his table.

Whether by intoxication or fatigue, the solid ghost of a dead man approached his table: Manuel, the first of the hanged three of '49—one of the three responsible for Old Dry Diggings in California changing names to Hangtown. The same young man he'd watched hang until dead the previous winter now stood at his table. Rope marks and bruises encircled his neck.

Richard tried to say his name, but his breath caught short in his throat, dry as the creek. He'd watched this man's bowels give out, watched his feet dangle at the edge of a wagon as oxen slowly pulled away. Richard had swung in his own dizziness back then, mesmerized by the slow deaths of all three men, and had stilled only when the last of the hanged men stopped moving. All three had haunted his dreams for the last however-many years.

Ace of spades, Richard thought, *first of the money cards.*

He signaled the bar-keep, who only shook his head, too busy to give much notice. The Irishman wanted a drink more than ever, but that's not why he wanted the bar-keep's attention. Surely, he'd recognize the dead feller walking through the saloon, *smell* him. The bar-keep had gone to the hanging, same as everyone else. Yet he ignored Richard and the dead feller walking by him, turning back to the man he conversed with at the bar—a portly fellow with fair skin and rosy cheeks. *The American.* Another of the three hung in '49. Blood seeped out from his shirt as though from a flogging.

Richard Crone shook his head as his hands did so on their own. He blinked hard, twice, one for each of the dead in the room. The morning hours were rushing upon him quickly, was all, the whiskey twisting his sight. When he blinked a third time, the Spaniard in front of him was not Manuel at all, just some tan- or dirty-skinned man of no discernable origin with dark hair draping down to his shoulders. And at the bar, the bar-keep filled the glass of a white-skinned fellow, clothes untarnished. Spooked, is all. Tired.

"We playing this game or what?" asked the man next to him, a miner.

"Sorry," Richard said.

"*On joue à monte, ou quoi?*" said another in French.

A familiar face stared back at him with eyes of the dead: neck rotted, tongue swollen and protruded. This third ghost smelled of defecation and piss, which hit him swiftly, though no one else at the table seemed to notice the stench. The last of the three hanged in '49.

Richard Crone blinked again, and the Frenchman was another fellow entirely.

Poison in my drink, he thought, *for this can't be happening.*

"The hell," he said, the decay lingering.

Each of the three men at his table expected cards, and so Richard asked who was in and the Frenchman's dead-blue hand tossed in a few coins, said something else in his language. After pointing to the jack of diamonds with putrefied fingers, the money card this time around, Richard flipped them over, made them dance—trying not to think of the hanged men—and dropped one of the cards on the floor by mistake.

Not since he was a child had he lost a card, not even in a shuffle.

Intoxicated, no doubt, for his head spun as it had all those years ago, he spilled his drink in reaching down for the fallen soldier and a wave of whiskey flowed across the table, the drink fortunately flowing away from the deck. After righting himself after retrieving the card, he swore, causing all heads in the room to turn. The three ghosts were there amongst the crowd: two at his table, one at the bar. Their dead eyes glowed and burned into him.

"I'll get that, honey," said one of the whores. When not selling herself, she attended the tables, brought drinks and took away empty tumblers. She didn't seem to mind when a rotted hand brushed her arm. No, she smiled at the dead Frenchman, said maybe later she'd attend to him for she'd just been with a man and needed to freshen up. She smiled as well at the decomposed Spaniard. And in the time it took for the Irishman's heart to restart, for air to fill his lungs, she was gone, and so were the three ghosts of Hangtown.

"I seen the elephant," Richard said under his breath, a common phrase heard round the diggings when a soul had experienced far too much of the world at too significant a cost. Over the years, he'd seen many expired men give up the laborious search for gold.

Living men waited for the game to recommence.

"Apologies, fellers," Richard said." Too much of the drink, perhaps."

The three cards were inspected by everyone at the table, the jack tapped, then flipped over, quickly shuffled one over the other, over the other, over the other, and soon even *he* had lost the money card, thought maybe it was the left one, or maybe the middle when they slowed.

"*Au milieu*," said the Frenchman, pointing at the middle card.

Richard flipped it over, not too surprised to see the jack but mostly certain beforehand the leftmost card was the place he intended. Without word, he pushed back the pot.

"*Tu nous as tués*," the winner said.

"*Nos mataste*," said the other.

He'd heard enough French to know the difference between formal and informal, knew only that he'd been insulted by the Frenchman's words, and knew just enough

Spanish to know the Spaniard had used a word he'd didn't much care for by the way of its inflection, though he knew not what either man meant with their foreign words.

"You killed us!" the man at the bar called out, as if hearing his very thought. Richard knew that whiney voice, which had carried with him since '49: the hanged American.

"No," Richard Crone said. "You're not here."

But they were. His eyes moved from the cards to the bar, where the bloated man raised his glass in a cheer, and then to the dead men sitting across the table.

This can't be happening.

Manuel and … Bissi, that was his name, and the American. All three smiled wickedly, smelling of death and putridity that comes just before and long after a person dies, the smell of earth, decomposition, excrement, rot.

The Spaniard spoke next using words Richard had never heard before. He tossed a handful of coins onto the table and spat a mouthful of black onto the floor, the way blood looks under scant moonlight in the darkness of night. He started to argue as the Irishman stood there, staring down at anything but these rancid men.

No, Richard decided, no more cards, no more games. This was all from some fever, he told himself, for the sweat on his brow fell heavily and soaked into his attire as a cold rush swept down his spine, the dizziness overpowering.

"Are we playing or what?" a man said in broken English.

The use of familiar words pulled him out of the trance.

In front of him were three men wanting to play games of monte. Not one of them dead. They only resembled those from the past, Richard told himself. Haunted thoughts, is all. And the man talking to the bar-keep was just some whiter-than-white fellow in fancy dress drowning in drink.

Get a holda yerself. A few more rounds, then rest.

Three games came and went, and Richard won all three, of course. Then a fourth, and a fifth, his hands as sly as ever, which only made the others at the table anxious. He'd have to let them win a few, he realized, and tried in earnest, but both men were drunker than he and they each lost two additional games apiece. Frustrated hands pushed both coin and gold as wager.

"Let's call it a night," Richard said.

They wanted nothing of it, and for the next half-dozen games he intentionally slowed; any man capable of breathing could have followed the money card, especially since he made it turn up in the middle every damn time, but no, they chose poorly, as if they played with intent to lose.

The core gathering in the El Dorado watched their game, for he, the dealer, was up maybe a hundred dollars, and the next bet by the Spaniard was considerable.

"This is the last round, fellas," he told them. "Couldn't make it easier for you to win back what you're throwing my way." Richard kept his eyes on the cards, not wanting to look up for fear of death rejoining him at the table. "Last round," he said, "after this, *no más.*"

The Spaniard slid in three ounces of gold as the room hushed. Richard had no plans of taking that gold, for he could read drunkards as easily as cards and understood taking it would bring violence to the table. Three ounces of gold wasn't worth dying for, and this was the last of what this poor man had on him.

"If that's what you wish, you damn fool."

Cards danced a slow 1-2-3 waltz in front of him, 1-2-3, as a retch of bile worked him, a sour mix of hard spirits and tobacco. He forced it down, cleared his throat. The cards couldn't slow much more than he made them dance initially, 1-2-3, and once again he decided upon the middle in which to place the jack; *any* man not blinded by kerchief would know where to find the bastard. He even looked at the middle card as he waited for the Spaniard to decide.

The middle, amigo.

The El Dorado erupted in hollers as the young man pointed at the rightmost card, the eight of clubs, Richard knew, for he'd placed it there, as he had likewise placed the five of daggers as the leftmost and the damn horseman between them. The entire saloon knew where to find the jack.

"You're certain," Richard said, offering an out.

"*Sí*," the man said.

Everyone in the establishment held a collective breath amid mumbles, perhaps some wondering whether or not they were wrong in their own choosing. There were two dozen standing over the table as Richard let out a sigh and flipped over the middle card.

"*Señor*," he said, "you couldn't pick the shell with the pea."

"*La triche!*" the Frenchman next to him said.

Richard recognized the same words from long ago, understood the accusation without a need for translation. The Spaniard rattled off a string of Spanish, a few curses he recognized.

"An honest game," he said, but they wanted none of it.

"He says you cheated," said a man over his shoulder.

"I know what he said, and I did no such thing. I do not cheat, not ever."

"Says you waxed the cards."

"Now why in hell would I do that?"

"*Tricheur!*" the Frenchman said.

"*Engañar! El tramposo!*" said the Spaniard.

"I do not cheat," Richard said again, gritting his teeth. "Say those foreign words once more and I'll carve yer heart outta yer chest."

"*El tramposo, el tramposo!*"

"Call me a cheater again and I'll put my blade—"

"Cheater!" the dead man said, Manuel from long ago.

In a fluid motion Richard Crone's bowie knife was set loose from its sheath and plunged into the young man as if on its own accord, and what did it matter for the boy was already beyond life, hanged prior, and so he pushed until hilt met ribcage. Not blood but black sludge welled out from the man's chest, straight from his still heart. He thrust it in a second time, twisted the blade as the black bled to red, as if in his second murder the poor Spaniard had been brought back to life only to die again. The expression on his face was that of a boy, innocent.

"You will never tell me I lied again," Richard said.

Women screamed.

Chair legs screeched across wood.

A pistol drawn.

"*Qu'est-ce que c'est*," said the Frenchman, which needed no translation.

What is this, Richard thought, *yes, what in hell is all this?!*

A young man, perhaps as young as he, fell to the floor, dead almost instantly.

"I am not a cheater!" Richard said to the crowd.

He leaned over the fallen and frigidly pulled the bowie knife from the man's chest with a shaky hand, blood lashing across his face and marking him for murder. He tasted the man's death on his lips and spat it to the floor, wiped the blade with his handkerchief, re-sheathed his weapon. The only dead man in the room was the young Spaniard before him, toes up.

All three ghosts nowhere to be found.

Three ounces bet, one for each …

"You've just murdered an innocent man, Richard Crone," someone said in the crowd. "That's Miguel, who arrived in the diggings no more than a few days ago, and by no means guilty of any crime other than losing to your slight-of-hand."

In silence, the Irishman exited the saloon. He staggered home, drunk on both whiskey and what he'd done. Occasionally, he glanced over his shoulder, but no one followed.

Killed the already-dead, he convinced himself. *Already dead.*

"Can't kill a man's already gone," he said to the night.

A crescent moon smiled in the speckled sky as lunacy fed into him. He sang an Irish tune aloud, which echoed in the stillness. And by the time he made it to his cabin, he fell hard onto his bedroll and into a dreamless sleep that swallowed him whole.

Slapped awake, he opened his eyes to the light of morning, the night there and gone in a matter of one long slow blink of confusion.

"You are under arrest," a blurry man said as his hands were tied.

Sheriff "Billy" Rogers stood pointing a scattergun.

Two other men did the tying.

"Arrest for what?" Richard said, his dream of the three ghosts a smudge in his mind. "What I do? I'm not guilty of nothing. What time is it, I ask?"

The Sheriff eyed the sun, said, "Close to eight, I reckon, though I'm not sure that matters at this point. What matters is you killed a man 'bout six hours earlier, unprovoked. Stabbed him, no less. Witnessed by at least ten or more who named you. The kid you killed's the same age as you, maybe younger."

He'd often been called a kid, a 'mere boy' because of his features.

"I didn't kill no kid," he said, half-remembering.

Only killed what's already dead, a spirit, a spectre.

A fist busted him across the jaw, then, and he fell hard on his side and into the dirt. Boots kicked him in the gut, over and over again, until Richard pissed himself; that, or he'd done so in his sleep for all he could remember. Men smiled over him like the moon over their shoulders.

They dragged him all the way to Elstner's hay yard, threw him on the ground right under the hanging tree, and then it dawned on him what was about to transpire.

"*No-no-no*, I killed no man," he pleaded.

"You killed my brother, you sonofabitch."

A second punch to his face brought blackness and then light. Whoever hit him did so a third time, ringing his ears.

Sheriff Rogers spoke through the noise and the blindness, said, "The young man you killed over a game a' monte was recognized as this man's brother. I rode out personally to Chili Bar where he was said to be, brought him back to see who'd done it. You brought this upon yourself, Richard Crone. You're gonna hang. Blood's been on your hands for far too long."

"Bloody Irish Dick, he done it," another said. "I saw him."

"Not a hesitation of remorse."

"Stabbed him in the heart."

"Cheated the young man of his gold."

Three ounces, a fool's bet.

The voices came from all directions as his head spun in the dark like it had only hours ago. Then someone turned him toward the rising sun and the black turned to white, then dissolved from red into colors until the world returned properly. A trickle of blood tickled his upper lip from a single nostril and cool-slid down his chin.

"I am not a cheating man," Richard said, defeated. "I'm not a—"

True as that may be, he was held captive for all to see, tied to the trunk of the oak that had killed the three men from '49 who'd haunted him, and where a fourth, Benjamin Alexander Read, had almost died by rope. There he waited for most of the morning, slapped, spat upon, switched by stick, ridiculed in front of a crowd of two hundred angry men, women, and children. Some threw stones. Some threatened with knives, cut him, even.

Less than an hour later, per the sun, that number grew to a thousand in number, maybe two thousand, everyone armed with something aimed to hurt, anything from pick-handle to rifle to rock to spade. Richard Crone was beaten, bloodied, as his *nom de plume* implied.

"Bloody Irish Dick," said a boy no older than ten, "serves you right."

"What makes any of this right?" Richard called out to the mob.

"What makes you killin' that young man right?"

"Should stab *you* in the heart!"

"Bleed you right here."

He could barely stand by the time they untied him, and he was led to the same building where they'd detained the three desperados before they were sentenced to be hanged. The blood of those men still stained the floorboards brown, and his own blood now mixed in with theirs.

No way will this town hang another. Not me. Not anyone.

"Don't you all remember?" he said. "Can't you see their faces?"

"What faces?"

Within the multitude of miners and townsfolk, Richard searched for the Frenchman— Bissi, that was his name— and for Manuel, as well as the nameless American, but the three ghosts had left him back at the El Dorado, it seemed. No, they were buried long ago north of the diggings, their graves unmarked, bodies fed to the ground.

"I'm only guilty of killing a man already dead."

A farce of a preliminary examination then took place and was allowed to be gone through by a certain Justice of the Peace Humphreys, who Richard had never heard of until this moment, perhaps self-appointed, and a trial of sorts took place in front of the hang tree.

The evidence presented was brief.

"You are hereby ordered into the custody of Sheriff Rogers," the judge said, "with constables Alexander Hunter and John Clark."

"Please don't hang me," Richard Crone pleaded.

"Hang him!" someone called.

"Hang the bloody bastard!"

"String him up!"

"You are to be placed in the county jail at Coloma," the judge said over the noise of those so willing to end his life, and the words offered a glimmer of hope that rushed through him. The mob grew uneasy at those words, but the judge continued. "You are to be placed there until a proper trial can be held and presided over, where a jury of twelve—"

"Hang him!"

"We don't need no jury!"

A lariat fell over Richard's neck, cutting off his breath as he was pulled to the ground by rope, then lifted momentarily off his feet. Men dragged him by the neck, his feet trenching for purchase in the earth, until he came to rest once again beneath the giant oak responsible for the town's own *non de plume*. Oh, he hated Hangtown, and he hated this godforsaken dried-up worthless hell-hole of a diggings.

If only he'd stuck to riverboat gambling on the Mississippi, if only he'd avoided the temptation to travel out west for something as damning as gold and promised fortune.

Some of the faces he recognized, though most he didn't. Buck Harrigan was there, of course, as well as Wooley Kearny, and a man they both despised who went by nothing more than "Dutch Ben." Even through their hatred of that bear of a man, they must have hated Richard more at this moment, smiling even as the Dutchman lifted Richard onto his feet only to deal him a hard blow under the ear, felling him to the earth as if striking him with a sledge.

Hands slapped his face until he woke, body shaken like dirt through a grate.

"You want a fair trial?" someone said, "*this* is yer trial."

The judge had followed the gathering to the tree, as did Sheriff Rogers and the two newly appointed constables, but their voices, if they argued in his defense at all, would not be heard over the crowd, for by then hundreds of condemning voices spoke at once.

"Hang him!"

Elstner was there, the man who'd first employed him to run the table at his saloon, once saying, *You got lots of promise in cards, kid.* The man simply stood there now, arms folded, not saying a word, just shaking his head in disgust, perhaps ready to be rid of him.

A man he recognized approached, threw a deck of cards in his face, which rained down over his boots. One card drew his attention over the others, a man on a horse. If he had the chance to wager his life over a game of three-card monte, he'd choose that particular long-time friend as his money card. No matter who he played, odds would be in his favor 2-to-3. He'd tap the card, make them dance his three-beat waltz, and unless the judge and jury betting against him struck it lucky with their 1-in-3 chance of guessing right, he'd go free.

"You wish me dead?" he asked the crowd. "You want another hung?"

His audience cheered.

Richard Crone thought of the three in '49, how long they'd taken to simply die by the rope, none of their necks had snapped but their bodies were lynched and strangled slowly after pulled by oxen, the largest man for close to two minutes. He thought of the Read boy not long after, lifting his father by the legs, how that near-death had drawn out long until he was eventually saved and brought down. No, if his own death were upon him now, it would be swift.

Swift justice, is that not what these monsters want?

"Have patience, gentlemen," Richard said. "I will give you soon a fair lay out."

The appointed judge tried to hush the crowd, but they wouldn't be hushed, not one person. They continued calling out curses, one riling the next, riling the next, the lot stoked like a raging fire. Richard Crone imagined himself up on the tree's thickest arm, jumping high into the air and then out, falling a good six feet to deal Death's hand.

"If I'm to die today, let me jump from that oak," Richard said, pointing. "You want a fourth hung, then it will be *quick*, lest my neck not snap as it should."

"Then hang yer got-damned self!" exclaimed another.

All this over three ounces of gold.

Richard Crone ran to the tree and eagerly climbed, his fingers racking into its thick skin, unkempt fingernails filling with bark. He managed a foot or so, then slid, and had himself another good attempt when someone yanked hard on the rope tied loose round his neck, laying him flat out on his back, thus taking the air from his lungs in a moment of revelation.

Let me die this way.

"I have seen the elephant!" he cried, "Oh, I have *seen* the elephant!"

A Recounting by John Carr

I will give you an instance of my first experience, and what I saw before the bar of Judge Lynch's court. This was my first attendance at His Honor's court, but by no means the last. I was standing looking on at the games that were being dealt at the El Dorado Saloon.

In the game I was looking at there were three or four miners betting. It was the game of monte. One of the miners accused the dealer of drawing waxed cards on him; or, in other words, cheating him out of his dust. The gambler told him if he said so again he would cut the heart out of him. The miner repeated the words, when the gambler raised out of his seat, drew a large bowie knife out of his belt and plunged it twice into the man's heart; at the last plunge he turned the knife around in the man's body. Pulling the knife out of the body and wiping the blood off with his handkerchief, he coolly remarked: 'You will never tell me I lied again.'

The gambler was known as 'Bloody Dick,' or 'New Orleans Dick.' He was a New Orleans Irishman, and a hard case. Rumor said that this was the third man he had killed. I was within three or four feet of the man when he fell off his seat and expired. Word went immediately throughout the town that "Bloody Dick" had killed a man.

In the meantime, two men had seized him and taken his arms away, and in less than one minute he was surrounded by forty or fifty excited men, well-armed, with a full determination that he would not have a chance to kill anymore. It had been the custom among the gamblers, when one of the fraternity got into a scrape, to see him out. Ten or twelve drew their revolvers, but, seeing the angry crowd, they came to the conclusion they would let Dick take his chances.

In less than ten minutes, there was a crowd of at least five hundred men gathered in and around the saloon where the cutting took place. A motion was made by some of the crowd that he be hanged right away, but the crowd voted him a fair trial and a chance for his life. The crowd elected a middle-aged man to act as judge and another as marshal. The marshal summoned twelve men to serve as jurors, who were immediately sworn. The judge sat on a big pine log in the street. The witnesses were called and sworn. They were the men who were playing at the game when the man was killed. Other witnesses also testified to the facts in the case. The case was then given to the jury, who returned a verdict of 'guilty of murder in the first degree.'

The question was then put to the crowd: 'What shall be done with the prisoner?'

Someone moved that he be hanged. The motion was seconded, and the man who acted as judge put the motion to the crowd, and a unanimous shout went up from at least one thousand men, 'Hang Him!'

The prisoner, in the meantime, was present and using the most blasphemous language to the men engaged in his trial that ever polluted the ears of a civilized man. The prisoner was then placed in a wagon drawn by two mules, and escorted by at least one thousand men to the fatal tree, a little back of the town, where several men of his sort had already paid the penalty of their crimes by hanging from one of its limbs. It was a large oak tree. The wagon was driven under it, the rope tied around his neck and thrown over the limb, and hauled tight and made fast. He was in the meantime cursing the crowd, his god, and everything else, and spat in the faces of the men who were adjusting the rope.

When everything was ready, the mules started forward, leaving the body swinging between the earth and the limb to which he was hanging. Some of the guards stayed at the tree for nearly an hour, so as to be sure he was dead. The body was cut down, and buried a short distance from the tree on which he was executed.

That was a swift trial where justice was meted out with dispatch. No lawyers were present, no testimony objected to as incompetent, irrelevant, and immaterial. When witnesses were sworn to tell the truth, the whole truth, and nothing but the truth, they seldom if ever perjured themselves. No appeal was taken from Judge Lynch's Court to the Supreme Court. His decision was final.

"Dick" was well-known throughout the old mining camps, but honored Hangtown most generally with his presence.

After having committed this crime, he was taken into custody by Sheriff "Bill" Rogers, Alex Hunter, and John Clark, constables of the town who fought desperately to retain possession of their prisoner, but against the determined multitude they were powerless. He was taken from the place where the officers of the law had stationed him, into the street, and tried by a jury of citizens in the presence of excited thousands.

The verdict was "guilty," and as soon as it was pronounced, Dick was hurried along with the crowd to the plaza, where preparations were made for his execution. At this point, the mob were told that a sick man was in a house nearby, and that the uproar seriously troubled him. The crowd, at once, returned down Main Street and up Coloma Street to the oak tree where he was hanged. This was the last time that "Judge Lynch" exercised his power in old Hangtown.

Killing continued in this town, as elsewhere throughout the mining camps, but established law was now in force, and the perpetrators were saved from the mighty hands of the mob.

WINTER
1850

SLADE

THE bounty wasn't much for Cole Mullins, but Slade had followed his ever-fading ghost trails across California an entire season, mostly out of principle. What he did to the Reads was uncalled for and had ultimately chased the boy and his father out of Hangtown. What he did to the Miwok and that dark man was pure evil. No one who dealt such horrors deserved to live.

The coward was thought of as a lost cause by the judge, and seconded by Sheriff Rogers, and later forgotten by the one appointed after him, and the one after *him*. Law changed quick, and soon the bounty on Mullins' head released entirely. Summer came and went, followed by a faster-than-normal fall, and soon winter was upon Slade and still he hadn't found the one-armed bastard, despite having a hunch he was lurking around and gathering another crew.

Discovering where Mullins *had been* was the easy part, more so than the *where he was going* part. All he had to do was ask if anyone had seen a one-armed fellow, "cut off about here," Slade would say, touching his bicep, and people would either say they'd seen him or they hadn't.

"Know where he's headed?" he'd ask, but seldom anyone knew.

And so, the search went long.

IMMEDIATELY upon the attempted hanging of Benjamin Alexander Read, back in the high heat of summer, Slade had asked men of the town similar questions, and it took a few threats to make the correlation that Mullins might be headed to the diamond springs, a neighboring town; same place Lynch had rode in from that same damned day, no less. Took Slade three days after the incident with the Reads to determine the man's whereabouts, then rode to the springs hard.

The diggings there wasn't much, not compared to the

destruction done to Hangtown. A quarter as many structures constructed, a few dilapidated cabins. Men living out of tents.

Slade no longer wore the badge, but people respected him the same. Perhaps he struck fear into them with his attire, the oilslicker over his holey uniform from the war hiding secrets. The devil, maybe he wore the same outfit, collected similar bounties. He also had quite the collection of weaponry on hand, with both a longrifle and scattergun strapped to his horse, who he'd always called Bitch, and two sidearms holstered plainly in view and worn to intimidate.

"Look," he said to the miners in the springs, "I'm looking for a man who goes by Cole Mullins, maybe just Mullins or maybe just Cole. Has a warrant I plan to collect."

"You law?"

"I have reason to believe the stupid fellow's come through here," he said, "might still *be* here, but if *not* I need to know where he's going and I suspect you might tell me."

Didn't get much of a response.

"Warrant, you say? Let's see it."

The way each man looked at the paper after asking told him they were illiterate, and there wasn't a drawing of a face to go by. A few would flip to the other side, blank. Just scribbles on the front. Roger's handwriting was so bad he could barely make anything of it.

"Used to run with Henry Thorp, but that man's dead. Used to also run with two others, though I can't remember names, also dead. Guess you could say if you run with Cole Mullins, you're apt to get yourself dead. You seen him?"

He'd interviewed most of the springs this way, not a lot of men, offering that even if they ran with Mullins, it was none of his concern, for he was only interested in the partial man.

Wasn't until he offered a small reward when someone shared knowledge.

"I seen him."

"What he look like?"

"Just like you said, no arm."

"Which arm?"

"Left," the man said without hesitation, and that's how Slade knew this particular miner spoke the truth. "Had a nasty scar across his neck he said was from a bear cub."

"Bear cub."

"That's what I said, and what he said."

"He prospect here?" Slade asked. "I guess he's good for not much else, anything with a handle, really, given his handicap."

"Nah. Passing through, needed provisions."

"And where do you suppose he's headed with his provisions?"

The dirty miner shrugged, then looked up at Slade on his horse, said he'd seen him get wares from a trading post on the main thoroughfare, that the man there might know. Slade lost only a few coins in exchange for this information. This time of year, the diamond springs were drier than the diggings in Hangtown. A small sum of two bits alighted the man's eyes.

What he got from the man at the trading post proved more helpful.

"Heard you did business with Cole Mullins."

"If I did, I was unawares," the man at the post said. "What he look like?"

Slade hopped off his horse, then, bent one hand behind his back, pretended scratching his face and throat with the other, said he was an ugly half-man made uglier by wounds.

The change in expression told him enough.

"All I need to know is where he's headed."

"Sacramento, I think he said."

"Anyone with him?"

"He and another feller were on foot and talkin about

transport. The other had scars on his arms like the other's neck. No horses, neither of em. Strangest thing. Had on em a small, caged grizzly, so said the taller one, though not in their possession. Their wounds was too big to be from the cub, though, still seepin, so I imagine they took too long to shoot the mother."

There was a movement to hunt grizzly in all parts of California. The reward handsome, for the flesh from an adult could be sold to vendors, along with the fur, which could go for as high as ten or more dollars. He'd seen the El Dorado with bear meat on the menu once, two dollars a serving. Most grizzly cubs were shot when found, though there were rumors of some taken into captivity to be raised for sport. Bears fighting with mules and bulls and whatnot. Such a man had been run out of Hangtown not long ago; maybe this man was this other.

"How long ago they leave?"

"Yesterday morning. Not the first time I seen him here. Not the one-armed feller, but the other. I think his name might'a been William, could have gone by Bill, I don't know. Used to have a house where they hanged all those men, and he's come and gone 'least three times the last several months, like a rotation, maybe to and from Sacramento for business." The last part of the town's name came out more like 'minnow,' like the bait fish. "Stick around long enough and they might return to the springs like afore and find you."

Yesterday morning.

Which meant they had a full day's ride ahead of him. Less than that depending on what their cart carried, and whether pulled by horse or oxen. The skinny man didn't know.

"What was their business with you?" Slade asked.

"Sold me pelts, on occasion. But as you can see, I don't need more'a those. Anyone who decides to stay come winter round here's already accounted for the change in seasons.

And the Miwok trade for cheaper, their leathers scraped and sunned with better care."

This brought back thoughts of the massacred tribe far up north along the Weber, the dozen scalps Mullins and Thorp and their men had taken, and the beheaded chief or whoever he was, his head never found. He'd hated carrying around those scalps while on horseback, if only long enough to deliver them as evidence. He thought of the map, and the Reads.

Slade had shot Thorp through the heart himself, with Mullins scurrying off after the attempted hanging of Benjamin Alexander Read, and so they'd never collected bounty from the officer in charge, a man who he'd also shot through the chest. Could be they were exterminating Miwok not only for wrongful profit, but to thin competition in selling and trading furs.

"How much for that one," Slade said, pointing at the heavy pelt of a black bear. "I have nothing in trade but gold. Gave my last two coins to find my way here."

The man at the post looked him up and down, perhaps considering the old military uniform under the slicker, perhaps considering what the information he'd shared had been worth, along with the item itself, and laughed, saying, "Twenty dollars," a ridiculous amount. A skin of such quality could be bought for half that anywhere. Not much more would buy a decent horse.

Slade, offering not the slightest hesitation, reached for his saddlebag, then, pulled out a small buckskin bag that had maybe fifty dollars' worth of gold in it, tossed it to him.

"You serious?" the man said, peeking inside.

"Thank you for this and thank you for your time." Slade draped the bearskin over his saddle, hopped atop his ride. "If I don't find those men, I may come back here and wait like you said. Can I count on you tell me then if you see em?"

"I'll point them out myself and holler their names. What do I call you?"

Not answering, Slade rode back hard to Hangtown.

Sacramento was quite the distance and would take a few days to get there, a wagon or cart perhaps a week. And there was only one main path everyone took to and from the much bigger town, and so he stopped back at his cabin in the diggings to prepare for long travel.

Slade had the Read claim, which is what he now called home. They'd shown him the gold beneath the cabin, a vein that pumped enough blood for any man not to ever worry about bleeding out. Read and his boy and their new friend had unearthed plenty, he'd been told. The father, the boy, and the mute ex-slave, who went by Lemi, had split their earnings three-way, and had taken his original offer to buy the place: two half-filled bags of gold.

"You know that I know what's under your place," Slade had said, "and this gold dust, or what's left of it anyway, was yours to begin with, stolen by Cole Mullins and his men, though they used it to pay me for what they owed. Why would you accept such an offer?"

Benjamin Alexander Read had smiled, then, a genuine smile, said some nonsense about he and his boy and Lemi not ever needing to see the elephant of dry diggings, that any more than what they'd already pulled from under their cabin would corrupt their hearts. "We're not selling you our claim," Read had said, "we're *giving* it to you, and you're returning what's ours."

That's how Slade came upon his wealth, a majority of that in his first few days, until he paced himself, saying, "The gold's not going anywhere, lest someone pry up these boards while I'm gone," and "why do I need to rush and get all of it now?" And by October everyone spent their time in the saloons offloading what they didn't gamble away on women and drink.

In preparing for his long trip, he took his collection of gold and buried it, less the hundred or so he kept on his person, far up the hill where only he could find it, perhaps two thousand dollars' worth or more. He rolled over a rock that weighed more than him and dug a hole beneath, placed the bags inside, and rolled the rock back over it, covering any obviously-loosened dirt with fallen pine needles. He stayed there a long while, standing aside it. He smoked twice, the papers sticking to the sap on his fingers, and waited, but no one saw him other than bluejay and squirrel. He'd drawn on a deer at the sound of twigs snapping, scaring it off.

After he returned to the cabin, Slade nailed down the floorboards, just as the Reads had shown him, and covered it with a woven rug they'd also left, set the table over it. If anyone came while he was gone, they'd have to work for it; thousands more remained under there.

Sheriff Rogers, when asked, said he'd have a few men watch over the claim, in case Cole Mullins were still about, in case he and this other he'd uncovered in his questioning made any attempt at his life, not knowing he was gone. Left abandoned more than three days, the claim would be up for grabs, as was understood. "Whoever you get," Slade had said, "they can stay there, if they want, if that makes it easier." The sheriff agreed and hired a man for a fee and said he's stop by every other day to see that his man did as instructed.

Before heading out, Slade helped himself to the Assessment Role, a written account of all residents and shop-owners and businessmen alike in the diggings. Ever since the hangings, every man, woman, and child was accounted for: last name, first name or initial, then their business if they had one, whether that be hotel, store, grocery, bakery, tent, saloon, house, or other such dwelling. Miners and those not old enough were simply listed by name.

With his finger sliding down the page, Slade searched

for anyone by the name of William or Bill. He found a W H Duden, and a W Edgerly, and many other W's. As for men by the name of William there were plenty: surnames of Erwin, Luther, Larkham, Pankey, as well as a Wm Searls and Wm H. Smith, which he assumed were short-hand of William when put on paper, and lastly a William Tegan. There were plenty of other W's, but not one 'Bill' on record.

The last drew his attention, his sweaty finger smudging the ink, for next to the name was listed 'House.' For whatever reason, the name made him uneasy, as if drawn to it.

"You know William Tegan?" Slade asked the sheriff, but no, Sheriff Rogers hadn't, and neither had Slade, and after living over a year in the diggings, that seemed odd. They rode together to the Tegan residence, peered through windows, but found the place empty.

"He left three days ago, I reckon," said the neighbor.

"That right?" replied the sheriff, then to Slade, "I'll send a man with you."

Slade and a bearded fellow who went by Wakefield went as far as Sacramento and back, even stayed a few days, but there were no signs of Mullins or this William Tegan, nor any mention of either name, and so a week later Slade and his tagalong returned to the diamond springs. His friend at the trading post said neither had returned. Slade had expected to run into the back of the aforementioned wagon or coach along the way, but only rode past other travelers.

But that was back at the end of summer, and sometime toward the end of fall Sheriff Rogers called off the manhunt, an entire season wasted tracking down a man and another who both went through life ghostlike. No one knew of men selling bear cubs, nor bearskins, nor bear meat. No one had seen men scarred by claw. Tegan's house stayed abandoned the next month, and by mid-November had been leveled to its shoddy wood foundation.

Cole Mullins is long gone, he kept telling himself.

TO keep from going mad like that Richard Crone fellow, a man who'd truly seen the elephant of dry diggings, Slade slowed his work at mining, put away gold when he could, out of sight.

But the thought of Cole Mullins doing to him what he'd done to the Reads, even months later after long suspected gone, is why he eventually decided to return to his pursuit in the harsh December. Mullins knew, after all, what was buried beneath the claim, so what was to stop him from paying a visit in the middle of the night? Sleep and Slade had become enemies, one not wanting to be with the other, the smallest of noises from coon or owl or otherwise keeping him up at night with a gun pointed at the door.

A slit throat, he imagined, *a round in his head.*

He wouldn't have decided to go after Mullins again if not for a meal and conversation at the El Dorado, where bear once again appeared on the menu. He told himself "Why not?" and ordered what the menu described 'grizzly roast,' and got himself a slab of meat the size of his fist; only fifty cents more than a steak of beef, which went for a dollar-fifty, or a whole rabbit, for that matter. And for a dollar-twenty-five more he added two potatoes and greased baked beans. He ate well, paid in full up front, what most would consider a splurge.

"How often you have grizzly on the menu?" he asked his waiter.

"Not often, maybe once every three or so months. Is it good?"

"It is," he said. Similar to deer, only sweeter, and likewise naturally redder than beef, texture coarse-grained like pork, not a sliver of fat. "Who's your supplier?"

"Oh, I don't know. I can ask if you want."

Slade slid a hand into his pouch, pulled out an assortment of coins and found a half-dollar, which seemed to get the waiter's attention.

"Would you?" He pulled back the coin.

The young man nodded and disappeared into the kitchen as Slade smashed his potatoes into the juices, mopping up all he could. Depending on the kid's answer, this might be his last hearty meal for a good long while. "Long shot," he mumbled, mouth full. "Kid's just gonna come back and say 'I don't know' or 'the cook don't know.'" But he got that gut feeling again, same feeling he had seeing that last name on the Assessment Role.

"What you ordered," the waiter said upon return, "fifty cents more you could make it a square meal," he said, meaning by adding dessert. "Rice pudding and brandy peaches tonight. A half-dollar's a lot for words." His employer must have put him up to it. Smart.

"That so?"

"Want to make it a square meal?"

"That mean you're not gonna tell me where the meat's from?"

"No, you just look hungrier than most in here, and you have fifty cents."

Slade laughed, looking around the establishment. He was perhaps the only man hunched over his plate the way he was, arms to either side as if anyone eyed his plate he'd have words.

Good kid.

He reached into his pouch again, blindly grabbed another half-dollar, held both coins out to the young man and said, "Why not both?"

The kid's smile could fill joyous hearts.

"You sure?"

"Take the damn coins already."

"The bear was sold to us by Bill Tegan."

"That so?"

"Yes, sir," the kid said, then pointed at Slade's uniform. "You fight in the war? The one between us and Mexico?"

"Long time ago," Slade said. He rolled up his sleeve, showed the boy his line of parallel scars, one for each man he'd killed in the war, a reminder of what he'd done and what he'd be judged for upon his death. "Look, would you bring your boss out here? I just want to ask him a few more questions. You did well. Here," he said, paying him, and added a few more coins. "And bring me those brandy peaches or whatnot, they sound good. You did well."

The rice pudding went nicely with the meal, but the brandy only made him want more brandy, and so he ordered a glass, and as he finished the last an older man joined him at his table, sat across from him, thanked him for coming in tonight.

"So, this bear," Slade said, "delicious, by the way. I know a guy who runs a trading post in the diamond springs," he said, not quite a lie, "who's looking to find a supplier of skins, grizzly, to be precise. I'm wondering if you can put me touch with this William Tegan."

"Bill used to live here not too long ago, but not any longer," the man offered. "His place was torn down after he moved to build some new—"

"He still around?"

"Should be. Bought the meat from him this morning."

"You usually buy from him?"

"Off and on, last few years, though not so recently. He comes up to the diggings in the winters now, just before the bears hibernate, since by then they're fat and slow. I suspect he'll be out hunting again these next few days before it gets too cold. Told him we'd take another fifty pounds at most, so I'm sure he'll be selling to other places, is my bet. You enjoying your stay?"

"Very much so. You know where he is now?"

"Couldn't tell you."

"Won't, or can't?"

The man didn't know more, despite a sizable amount

offered, for William "Bill" Tegan had moved at some point in the last few months, sometimes stayed in a cabin up in the pines about fifteen or so miles east of the diggings. A considerable higher elevation of thick forest. He simply didn't know where, specifically, though would have told him if he knew.

Slade had traveled that same trail through the pines.

"Not a lot of bear here this time of year, so I'm sure that's where he hunts."

Slade stuck around for the next hour, thinking hard. A second round of brandy to go with the rice pudding and then whiskey to go with more whiskey, and suddenly he was thinking about the Reads and the Donners, then of Richard Crone hustling monte. Another dealer now stood where the Irishman once had but playing poker with four others. He thought of joining them for a hand or two but then thought better of it. He'd seen enough men lose all they owned over a single game of cards, and alcohol often made doing stupid things easier.

EVEN with winter approaching, and the first flakes of snow fluttering to the ground, Slade decided to head into the worst of it head-on, packing dry foods and skins of water, enough gold to get him by for at least a month, for if he didn't return by January, when snow started its heavy fall, he might not make it back to the diggings before riding on horseback became impossible.

Thoughts of the Donners constantly haunted his mind. Not four winters prior, in '46, their wagon train from the mid-west had come to a halt in the Sierra Nevadas because of snow. Slade had come from Missouri himself in '47, albeit summer, so he knew the terrain, and couldn't imagine making the trek through even half a foot of snow.

All through early-winter of '50 Slade had worked the

claim, at least up to this point, and had pulled out a few thousand's worth of the precious yellow. It was a long process, mostly because he had to slowly chip away at quartz and other rock to get to it, and there was only so much room in the holes he continuously opened and closed each day under the wood planks of the cabin floor. To do so without much notice was easy enough, simply closing the front door and shading the windows, but the threat of someone happening upon him digging under his floor was always there to slow him down. He'd occasionally break from his labor to peek out, to stretch his legs and walk around the claim and pan or cascade it down the long tom out front, enough so that those at the claims surrounding him wouldn't grow suspicious of the amount of time he spent indoors.

It was none of anyone's business what he did at his claim, but everyone in the diggings was always into each other's business.

Which is why he hid his wealth on top of the hill far from civilization. Each night around dusk he'd ride out for a smoke, well-armed, circle back a few times to assure himself no one followed, pushing Bitch to climb the slope. Most the trees had been cleared, but there was enough coverage to know if you were alone, enough options not to make a trail. As far as he could tell, no one followed. If anyone asked, this was where he went to collect thoughts.

He first went east, followed the trail up through the pines and into thicker snow, which fluttered down in wide flakes. Already a few inches covered the ground, and the farther he went that direction the thicker it became, as much as a foot of unmolested white to either side. The first to greet him was a white bear plodding his direction, enough of a scare for him to untie his longrifle and point it at the abomination, but he lowered it, for no bear stood on its hind legs so long.

"Tegan," Slade called out, but it apparently wasn't him.

They closed the distance between them, the white fur only a thin layer of snow collected on deerskins worn by the lone traveler.

Maidu, he thought, because of the wares.

The Indian knew enough common tongue to relay there was in fact a man up ahead who fit the description Slade gave him, along with a bigger fellow he kept calling "Bear Man." Although covered in snow, the Maidu not once shivered or showed signs of being cold, and went on his way, not accepting the sun-dried meat Slade offered in exchange for the information, but agreeing on the tobacco, which they smoked together.

"Bear Man not far," he said, then, "smoke," pointing at the sky, then he was gone.

Slade stopped to water his horse not long after and he took shelter under the canopy of trees. He leaned against a fallen trunk and had himself another smoke, staring up at a widow-maker not far away. Snowfall would surely bring it down soon, pray it never fell atop a person. He then sat on his haunches over the edge to rid himself of the previous night's meal. *A bear ridding himself of bear*, he thought and laughed, like the excrement of a cannibal, for he wore the black fur wrapped tightly around him as he did his business.

Pine needles will have to do, he thought, their touch like knife blades.

After remounting his ride, he decided to cover the bearskin with a blanket, and not the other way around, lest he get himself shot the next time he went on foot.

"Let's go, Bitch," he said. "I know, I know, need to find you a better name."

He trotted her through the snow, not too hard, thinking of his ex-wife and why he'd decided to name his horse after what he'd started calling her after she'd gone. The snowfall let up, then, like not even her ashes wanted to be with him any longer, for that's what he thought of the white falling all around him. Soon a plume of dark gray stood out against a lighter gray.

"You'd never leave me, would you?" he asked his horse, and as if in response she turned her head and made a face, wanting treats, which he gave her after hopping down.

Nowhere to tie her, so he hobbled her legs.

The cabin was still a good ways out. A trail led to it, but Slade chose instead to wrap leather high up over each boot, secured just below each knee with rope, and headed out through the deep snow. Both longrifle and scattergun slung across his back, he high-stepped through a less obvious path, one that not yet existed. Though his feet quickly chilled, the rest of him sweat heavily by his efforts, enough so that he eventually cast off the outer blanket, once again resembling a black bear, albeit one armed to the teeth.

He thought of the "Bear Man," William Tegan, and how he fit into all this. Could be a businessman, though keeping business with Cole Mullins meant his business with him was likely something fowl. Whether selling cubs or skins or meat didn't matter as much as the man's past, and what he'd done, one arm or not. Cole Mullins was no longer wanted by law, but in Slade's eyes always would be, and he'd spend every waking effort bringing him to justice. Yet he couldn't help but wonder if "Bear Man" would get in the way or step aside.

There was movement in the cabin; as he approached, he could discern two figures, one sizably larger than the other, nearly double. A clatter of dishware and utensils.

Snow fell again, and in a matter of so many minutes covered Slade in a thin layer of white, camouflaging him against his surroundings. He got as close as twenty or so yards, moving ever slowly, and made a cave of sorts around him behind the cover of a single tree as wide as he. Slade ducked into it, spread out his weaponry over one of the deerskins, checked his ammunition, readied each firearm.

The advantage he had, perhaps the only, was that neither man inside would know the bounty had been lifted from Mullins' head, for they'd been out of the diggings too long. And from out their window, all they'd see was the white of snow and brown of tree trunks.

"Mullins!" Slade called out, the sour name absorbed.

"The hell?" said a voice inside, one he recognized.

"Who knows you're here?" said the other.

"No one," Mullins said.

"*Someone* does."

Slade aimed the longrifle at the bottom-left corner of the window closest to the door, where he knew a head might peek out, though he didn't intend to shoot either man.

"Can't see a thing," one of them whispered.

"Quiet."

Even the softest of words carried over the dead silence of winter. Snow fell in clumps from the pines above, and the wind sang secrets; otherwise, not a sound but for Slade's heartbeat within his chest, within his ears. The afternoon stayed this way awhile.

"Who's asking, and what do you want?" said William Tegan.

"I only want Cole Mullins," Slade said, "and then I'll be on my way."

"What for?"

Same color as the snow, he let out a lie, stating, "The man you have in there, Cole Mullins, has a warrant out for his arrest for the attempted murder of Benjamin Alexander Read, as well as his boy, also named Read, and for—"

"I don't know Benjamin Alexander Read, nor his boy."

Both men peered out different corners of the window, Tegan on the left, Mullins on the right, and so Slade moved his aim toward the man he was here to collect. Each set of eyes looked desperately around for the source of the voice, which, as far as either was concerned, could be coming from any direction. They scanned the path in and out, then the white-blanket field.

"And for the possible mistreatment of an ex-slave once owned by Mullins' now-dead business partner, a ghost by the name of Henry Thorp, whom I personally shot through the chest. Don't make the same mistake and end up with the same fate as he."

Silent whispers as they let the information settle.

The larger of the two disappeared, then returned with the end of a rifle pointing out the window, which aimed anywhere and everywhere.

At least pretend to know my location, Slade thought.

The man's a hunter of other animals, he had to remind himself, not men.

If their roles were reversed, Slade would have pointed the damn thing straight out, holding it steady, not shaking in fear. And anyone approaching would come at them from the path, yet the man leveled the long barrel in a sweeping motion across his land.

"You best be on your way," William Tegan said.

"All I want is Cole Mullins, and *then* I'll be on my way."

"Cole Mullins ain't here," said Cole Mullins.

"I know your damned voice, you stupid invalid."

A shot fired, then, not from Tegan's rifle, but from a revolver out-of-sight behind Mullins' corner of the window. The shot hit a tree about fifty feet to Slade's right.

Could kill you right now, but what would that resolve?

"Close," Slade said, but I'm higher in that tree."

Two sets of eyes looked up the trunk, and it hurt to think men could be so gullible. Another shot rang out, this time from the rifle, which blasted a breath of fire from the tip of its barrel. The round buried into snow half a breath later not far from the first shot fired. They were trying to get him to shoot back, he knew, to give up his location.

Dumb as dirt, these men.

"Hope that wasn't you, Bill," Slade said, "who just fired upon law."

He wasn't law, not any longer, if ever he was, but what did that matter?

"Yes," Slade said, "I know both of you by name, cowering in there, though I only want Mullins, and unless you fire upon me again, I won't hold that last shot against you. I can look past the fact that you just fired upon an officer, which, by the way, grants the right for me and my men to rain hellfire upon you and your cabin. But neither of us want that, do we?"

Silence as they contemplated inside, perhaps discussing whether or not he was alone or had a posse with him.

"Look," Slade offered, "I've got a hundred dollars in gold on me, which I will be more than happy to offer you as a reward for handing over your one-armed friend."

"He's obviously lying," Mullins pleaded.

"I don't believe you," the man said, and fired again.

Slade, before deciding on this exact spot, had circled round the cabin, knew the only way in or out was through the front door, out the window, or up through the smoking chimney, and so he waited patiently for a better answer than that of wasted gunshots.

"I, along with four other men, are aiming at you this very moment, and upon my signal they will fire, ending both of you. Fire again and I will give that signal. Do you understand?"

"What assurances do I have?" the Bear Man asked.

"My word," Slade said.

"He don't got no other men out there," Mullins said, "and he don't got no gold, neither. The man's not right in the head, can't trust his word."

"How do you know?"

"One way to find out," Mullins said and fired his second shot.

The round buried into a sugar pine to Slade's left, close enough for bark shrapnel to hit the side of his cheek and flare him up inside. The silence that followed gave up his lie.

"See," Mullins said, "all alone."

The tip of William Tegan's rifle swung, came to rest so that Slade looked directly down its ugly black eye one blink too long. Slade ducked, hoped neither man saw motion within his cover, and swore to himself. He'd seen enough of the rifle to know it held two rounds, meaning Bear Man would need to reload if he fired again. Mullins' revolver most likely held five, so he was the biggest threat with three or as much as four remaining in the cylinder, though to hit him this far out with such a close-range weapon would require luck, and to reload with a single hand would take too long before he found himself dead.

Another rifle sounded and Slade found himself grazed, a round carving into his left shoulder, half an inch deep. He remained silent, even as the snow around him absorbed the red, blood spattered around him, the wound stinging something fierce.

Sonofabitch, he thought, but a graze.

And a lucky shot, he knew, for the next round from Mullins' revolver struck a tree in the distance, not even close, and one of them called to the other, "Where *is* he?"

Slade used the opportunity of Tegan reloading and Mullins' stray shot to pivot. He rose slowly, longrifle leveled above the snowline, aimed, and shot into the dark where Bear Man had stood moments before, then sank below his wall of snow. All in a moment. The big man cried out a wail that implied he'd perhaps been hit in the gut, a horrible place to be shot, for it meant a long death if not treated, and a long recovery if he were lucky enough to make it down the mountain and find himself a doctor.

"Mullins, you bastard, you got me shot!"

Cole Mullins fired twice more as the man next to him

screamed banshee-like; both shots and screams went wild. Mullins swore over the ruckus.

Down to one round; that's what he means by that ugly word.

William "Bill" Tegan let out another high-pitched cry of, "I'm spilling out, oh God, I'm spilling out. Damn you, Mullins, you did this to me, you, you did—"

"Shut your mouth, Bill, or my last shot will end you."

Bear Man must have reloaded for another shot rang out just after Cole Mullins leapt through the open window, splinter debris from the frame exploding at his feet. He landed hard on the ground where an arm should be, and with the other still holding the revolver struggled to regain his feet. Then a second rifle shot, and the cabin went silent.

Mullins took an instant to point his weapon and find aim at the white void in front of him, then ran awkwardly toward what Slade had determined was a stable for their horses.

Slade swung the strap of the longrifle over his back and likewise got to his feet, grabbed the scattergun instead, climbed hastily up and out of the snow in pursuit.

To run in snow was nothing easy, but that's what Slade did, one foot over the other. Finally seeing who was after him, Cole Mullins turned around long enough to fire his last shot, which buried in the ground twenty feet between them, and then holstered his useless gun and ran full-speed with a limping gait on the path leading to their stabled horses.

Only one way in or out, Slade knew, so he took his time, let his breathing catch up to his burning lungs as he made his way to Bitch hobbled not far from the trail. Two options: either farther up the mountain on this very trail, or back toward the diggings, for the path to the cabin with the Bear Man slowly dying inside—or already dead because of that last shot—ended at the stables. This meant Cole Mullins would be racing out of there soon, forced into making a decision which direction to go.

Slade removed the rope hobbling his horse and mounted her, casually tied the longrifle to the straps on the saddle. He waited for the inevitable to happen, checked that the scatter-gun was both loaded and not jammed with snow, and took in a long, deep breath, said, "Here we go."

Cole Mullins shot onto the trail on horseback as expected, snow flailing behind a clatter of hooves. Up the mountains would mean frozen death, Slade knew, and he smiled as the one-armed man headed not up the mountain but down, and coming directly at him.

Slade tipped his hat to the man as he passed, then kicked his own ride into a walk into a trot into a gallop and finally into a full-on run. Not long after, one horse caught up to the next and they were riding side-by-side, a dozen feet apart. Slade held his reins with his left, the wounded shoulder making him aware of the pain there, blood seeping through his shirt.

Nowhere to go but down, he thought, meaning the ground.

Cole Mullins kept onto his horse by means of his legs. mostly, with his one good arm holding reins out front with no other to hold the horn, and so that's where Slade aimed the scatter gun, at the arm, as he sidled in next to him; high enough above that arm so as not to hit the horse with the spray of pellets. Slade let out a breath, the barrel steady, fired, and Mullin's flew off his horse even as the creature kept running beneath him. His body tumbled a good thirty feet, scraping across snow and rocks. The horse kept on going, disappeared.

Slade pulled back on the reins and brought Bitch to a halt. She protested, wanting to race the other horse, but he circled her round, calmed her, then hopped off and clucked his tongue.

The deformed man had deformed further, his one good arm no longer good. It lay in ruin next to him, still attached, but by threads.

Like a pulled-apart woven basket.

He looked dead, but his chest rose and fell, perhaps knocked unconscious by the fall, and so Slade kept him alive longer by way of tourniquet, used his own belt and Mullins' spent revolver to twist the leaking faucet shut.

He stood above him awhile, had another smoke.

THE entire ride back to the old mining town, Slade thought of the Reads and what they'd gone through as father and son, and what that Lemi fellow had suffered before being freed from Mullins' and Thorp's men. All in all, he was happy the three had chosen to leave Hangtown. No family should ever have to live in such a horrid place. Once Slade had all he needed from the ground, he'd move on too, maybe even leave some of the gold behind like they had.

Cole Mullins followed in his wake, dragged by his feet by rope. Upon his back, the man carved their path through the snow amid horse print, light enough to glide. He left behind a rather large splotch of blood, as if the angry hand of God had come down from between the clouds and smashed him flat. Then the blood slowly thinned until barely there at all, more pink than red. He'd awakened not long after he was bound, but the gag kept him only to muffles.

Snow fell heavy. There were no other travelers.

For miles, Slade pulled his prisoner behind him, not too concerned about rocks or whatnot in the trail, or the noises he made, but once the snow cover changed from fluffy white to nearly transparent ice, he finally brought his horse to a stop, reconsidered his tow. They had another two or three miles to go, and that might end Mullins early.

The man cowered as Slade approached, as he should, then shivered, his skin as pink as the trail left behind him. Snow had collected on the man's poor excuse for facial hair, as well as on his eyebrows and mussed hair. Any longer in the cold and the frost might bite him severe.

"Whiskey?" Slade offered, kneeling next to him. He held out a wineskin full of spirit strong enough to warm the dead. He took a sip himself, let out a plume of breath, took another.

Cole Mullins eventually nodded, as if to say *I won't put up a fight.*

"Say a word and I'll break your mouth," Slade said.

The man nodded again, blinked heavily.

Slade pulled the gag free and tossed it to the side as Cole Mullins puffed his acrid breath like steam out the stack of a locomotive, eyes frantic. Between puffs he poured a small amount of the Irish liquor into Mullins' gullet, half of which was coughed out.

"You want to say a word, don't you? What word is that?"

"What do you want with me?"

"With you? Justice."

"I—"

But that was the last he said, the most selfish of all words, for Slade shoved the cloth back into his mouth until he gagged, which he figured is why it was called such, then let up a bit. He untied the man's feet, warned him only once not to run or kick or to try anything foolish.

"Can't be dragging you to hell," Slade said. "Get up," he added, then helped the man to his feet. Cole Mullins was a small man, but without most an arm, and now without some of the other, the man was light. Took not much effort to bring him to standing. Slade figured it would be difficult to run without the use of both arms, like running with them shackled. That's how this man looked, the one arm dangling, dripping at a slow rate from unmoving fingertips. No, he didn't need to worry about the hands, not at all. Slade figured he'd shot him about where he'd been shot before, opposite arm. Almost felt sorry for him. Almost.

He thought to ask him what he'd done in the past to lose the other arm, but found he didn't care, and instead said, "Try to head-butt me and I'll take one of your legs, got it? Try anything else and I'll take the other. So help me, I'll turn you into nothing more than a torso."

Mullins obeyed and let Slade re-tie the rope to the belt cinched around his waist. About twenty feet of rope separated him from the back of Bitch, and he was told to walk the rest of the way to the diggings, unless he wanted to be dragged face-first.

And that's how they traveled for the next two or three miles, a slow pace, but undisturbed. Every so often Slade glanced over his shoulder, but the man just walked as told.

HARD to determine what time it was when they made it back to Hangtown, for snow blew in all directions and the sky had mostly darkened to gray soot. The heart of winter meant it could be as early as five or six o'clock in the evening, everyone indoors. Not a soul stood outside, not even to drape drunken over shoulder from one saloon to the next.

Quiet as he'd ever seen the diggings.

Slade, a black bear turned white upon his mount, brought his prisoner down the main thoroughfare, not even stopping when Cole Mullins stumbled over some miner's pickaxe left out to rust in the cold, and so he dragged the man the rest of the way to the center of town. He found him nearly unconscious by the time they made it to Elstner's hay yard.

Even as they stopped, the man slid a few feet across ice. Slade hopped down, knelt over him as he'd done before, flipped him over, brushed the white off his face. He sat next to him awhile, rolled tobacco. He offered Cole Mullins a smoke, and on his back he nodded almost imperceptibly, and so Slade rolled two. Striking a match, he lit both and slid the second into Mullins' mouth, thinking how awkward it must be not to be able to hold the thing. The man had gone beyond cold, no longer shivered, no longer seemed concerned it was below freezing out.

"You know why I brought you here," Slade said.

Mullins chose not to answer, the ash of his cigarette growing long.

Slade finished his own, then stood, helped Cole Mullins to his feet. As if preparing him for Sunday services, he brushed the snow from his wares and straightened the man's outfit, which had mostly shred and had become cock-eyed. Looked as though he'd just climbed out of a grave. He thought then of the grave once dug for the original three who'd hanged, buried far up the creek, and then wondered where they'd buried the fourth, that bloody Irishman. Not that any of that mattered now. For all four of those deaths, and for Benjamin Alexander Read's attempted hanging, nearly the entire town had gathered to watch, to fuel the fire. But here, now, Slade found himself below the great oak once again, not a soul shouting for or against.

The dragging must have worked the tourniquets loose, for Mullins dripped steadily into the snow as he wavered unsteadily upright, his entire hand coated red, which created a small red crater below him that steamed heat.

A lone accusatory eye stared back at them both.

In the snow, they waited for a crowd, but not a man, woman, or child came, not at this hour, not for this partic-ular season. Be it spring or summer or fall, all would gather.

"Well," Slade said, "I guess that's it, unless you want to run."

Cole Mullins stood there, directly beneath the tree, what was left of his smoke still dangling and burning into his lip. Slade flicked it to the ground, said a few more words.

The man who wasn't law but out to seek justice on his own untied his prisoner's wrists, used the same end of rope to fashion an ill-knotted loop about his neck, the other end of which he untied from his horse and threw over the larg-est branch of the hanging tree before re-securing it to the back of the saddle.

"Goodbye, Cole Mullins," he said.

Slade hopped onto his horse, gave her a nudge with his boots and pushed her forward until the line grew taut, then pushed her more, felt weight lift. The rope creaked with strain, but he not once looked over his shoulder until he knew the man was a foot off the ground.

Still some fight left in him after all, he thought.

Cole Mullins, with Slade's belt and his own spent revolver tied onto the useless remaining arm to stave off his death, tried for the rope above his head. The shot arm was entirely dead, but the stump of the other, once amputated just below the bicep from some other gunshot wound, perhaps, attempted to grab the rope with its ghost arm and ghost hand and ghost fingers. The no-armed man spun and spun, legs kicking out, then after a minute or so stilled.

Slade turned back around, fed his horse part of carrot from his saddlebag, then another, and stayed there a good long while, collecting snow.

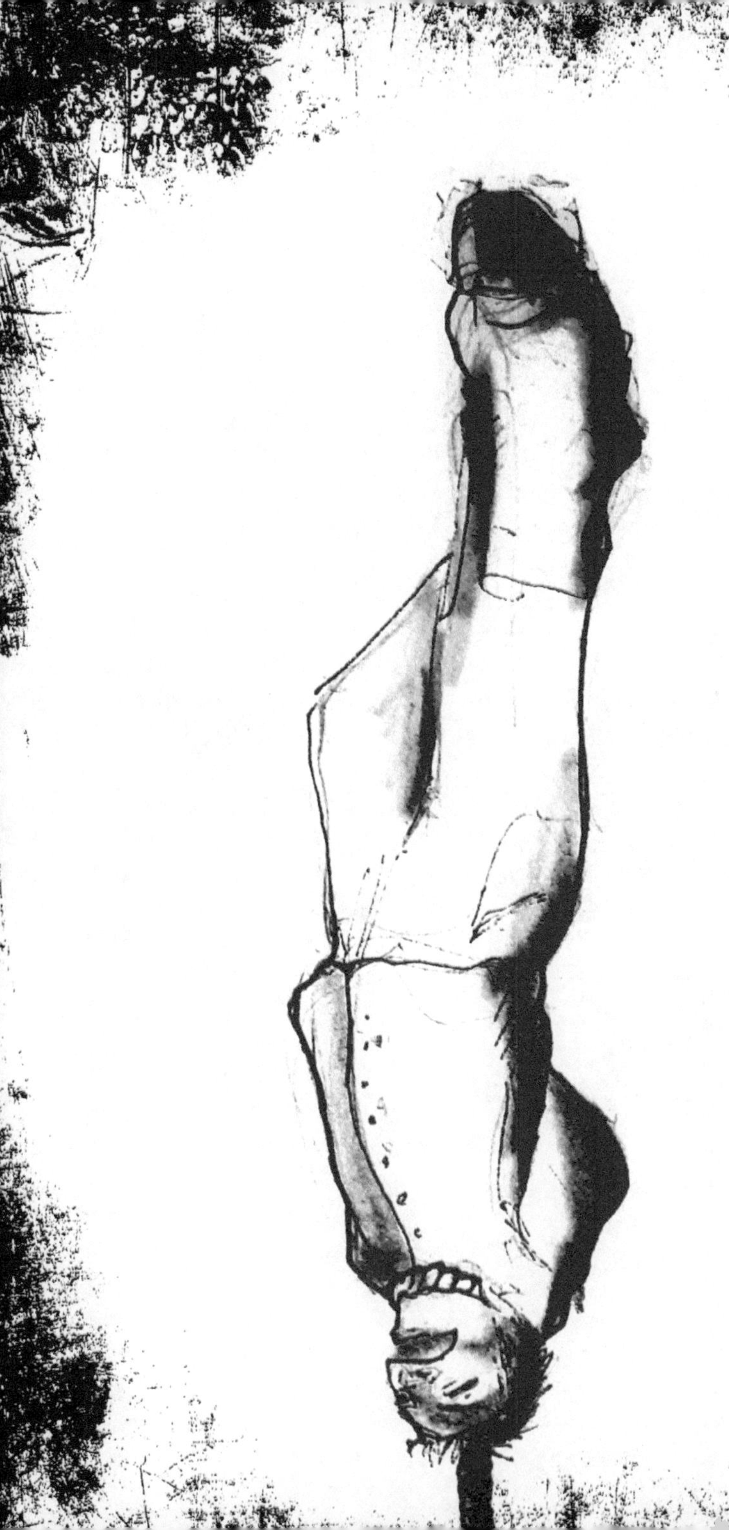

A FORGOTTEN DAY

THE HANGING TREE

HUATA has long since returned to ancient earth, the young Miwok girl's fragile and desecrated body found under a blanket of fallen leaves shortly after her murder, a ceremony held, and her bones buried thereafter beneath the oak that has protected this sacred ground for hundreds of years.

She rests where her innocence and life were stripped by a miner as hastily as gold from the land; her spirit entwined with the roots which feed into the tree that will continue to curse the old dry diggings for as long as even a part of it remains.

Despite all that's transpired, by mid-spring the small but abounding mining town will no longer go by such a name, nor by its moniker of Hangtown so as not to avert travelers. No town should ever have to go by such a designation, and so a year or so from now it will permanently change to Placerville by way of State Legislature, so-called after the placer deposits that once corrupted minds and drove men to administer punishments of crime by way of swift justice.

The girl's mother, praying words in an all-but-forgotten tongue, returns under the shade of its branches every so often. She is one of the last of her tribe and listens to her daughter's spirit on this day. No man shall ever hang again on this tree, she is told. Never recorded, the last hanged was he who had taken the girl, a fifth who died incapable of holding a rope.

An owl watches over the woman in the branches.

The young girl's father was slain years ago by the white man, his skull never reunited with his body and traded for coin, and she mourns him still. Most of her tribe, as well as those of the Maidu, are either gone or have meddled in the last of the mining to rid the land of its gilt.

A man by the name of Bruce Herrick joins the Miwok woman beneath the tree, for the oak is on his land, according to paper, and he no longer wants its burden.

Does paper not come from the tree? she wonders.

Previously a cook at the Placer Hotel, this man has since bought the property, having torn down the old structure once there to build the two-story brick building which has taken its place, an establishment once called the Jackass by the white man, or simply Hangtree, for on this very land three men once hanged, and then a fourth, and lastly a fifth, if you believe the spirits.

A barrowmaker by the name of John Mohler Studebaker stands behind him, a man responsible for carrying in most of the brick and mortar used in the construction, and behind him stands a constable by the name of George Ranney with a heavy axe slung over his shoulder.

"Time to cut down this godforsaken tree."

The Miwok woman knows not which of the three spoke the horrid words, for she has since turned her back to them, as she imagines the white man has done to her people for as long as she can remember. Her eyes are instead given to the owl sleeping in high branches, her ears to the wind rustling through the leaves, her mind connected with her daughter.

"Huata," she says, which means to carry seeds in a burden basket.

Herrick spare that tree;
Let not its branches fall;
Here let it always be
A warning to us all.

For it was back in forty nine
When our good town was young,
That three vile men for murder foul
Upon that tree were hung.

Therefore this tree must always stand!
For tis of great renown.
Then, Herrick, hold that axe in hand
And spare this relic of our town

For if you fell this noble oak
And its dear life thus strangle;
Upon the very next damned tree
Your worthless corpse with dangle!

– Joe Fischer [c. 1850s]

Allen, William Wallace, and Richard Benjamin Avery. *California Gold Book.* San Francisco and Chicago: Donohue & Henneberry, printers, 1893.

Borthwick, John David, George Cosgrave, and William Blackwood and Sons. *Three Years in California.* Edinburgh and London: William Blackwood and Sons, 1857.

Borthwick, John David, and Horace Kephart. *The Gold Hunters.* New York: Outing publishing company, 1917.

Braley, Arthur Wellington, Arthur Wison Tarbell, and Joe Mitchell Chapple. *National Magazine: An Illustrated American Monthly, Volume XXXVII.* Boston: Chapple Publishing Company, Ltd., 1913.

Brown, James Stephens, b. 1828. *California Gold: An Authentic History of the First Find, with the Names of Those Interested in the Discovery. Oakland,* Calif.: Pacific Press publishing company, 1894.

Buffum, E. Gould (Edward Gould), 1820-1867. *Six Months in the Gold Mines: From a Journal of Three Years' Residence in Upper And Lower California, 1847-8-9.* Philadelphia: Lea and Blanchard, 1850.

Carr, John, 1827-1896. *Pioneer Days in California.* Eureka, Cal.: Times publishing company, 1891.

Crosley-Griffin, Mary. *Hangtown: Tales of Old Placerville.* Universal City: Crosley Books, 1994.

Davis, Stephen Chapin, 1833-1856. *California Gold Rush Merchant: The Journal of Stephen Chapin Davis.* San Marino, Calif.: Huntington Library, 1956.

Farnham, Thomas Jefferson, 1804-1848, Thomas Jefferson Farnham, Van Dien & Macdonald, and Nafis & Cornish. *Life, Adventures, and Travels in California: to Which Are Added the Conquest of California, Travels in Oregon, and History of the Gold Regions*. Pictorial ed New York: Nafis & Cornish, 1849.

Haskins, Charles Warren. *The Argonauts of California: Being the Reminiscences of Scenes and Incidents That Occurred in California in Early Mining Days*. New York: Fords, Howard & Hulbert, 1890.

Hyer, Joel R, and Clifford E Trafzer. *Exterminate Them: Written Accounts of the Murder, Rape, and Slavery of Native Americans During the California Gold Rush*, 1848-1868. East Lansing: Michigan State University Press, 1999.

Jerrett, Herman Daniel. *California's El Dorado Yesterday and Today*. Sacramento, Calif: Press of Jo Anderson, 1915.

Leeper, David Rohrer, 1832-1900. *The Argonauts of 'forty-nine: Some Recollections of the Plains and the Diggings*. South Bend. Ind.: J.B. Stoll & company, printers, 1894.

Levy, JoAnn, 1941-. *They Saw the Elephant: Women in the California Gold Rush*. Hamden, Ct.: Archon Books, 1990.

Margo, Elisabeth. *Women of the Gold Rush*. New York: Indian Head Books, 1992. Previously titled *Taming the Forty-Niner*, 1955.

Oakland Museum of California, et al. *Silver & Gold: Cased Images of the California Gold Rush*. Iowa City, IA: University of Iowa Press for the Oakland Museum of California, 1998.

Paul, Rodman W. (Rodman Wilson), 1912-. *California Gold*. Cambridge: Harvard Univ, Press, 1947.

Parke, Charles Ross, 1823-1860, and James Edward Davis. *Dreams to Dust: a Diary of the California Gold Rush, 1849-1850*. Lincoln: University of Nebraska Press, 1989.

Parsons, George Frederic, 1840-1893. *The Life and Adventures of James W. Marshall: The Discoverer of Gold in California*. Sacramento: J. W. Marshall and W. Burke, 1870.

Peters, Charles, b. 1825. *The Autobiography of Charles Peters: In 1915 the Oldest Pioneer Living in California, Who Mined in the Days of '49 ... Also Historical Happenings, Interesting Incidents and Illustrations of the Old Mining Towns in the Good Luck Era, the Placer Mining Days of the '50s*. Sacramento, Cal.: The La Grave co, 1915.

Read, George Willis, 1819-1880, and Georgia Willis Read. *A Pioneer of 1850, George Willis Read, 1819-1880: The Record of a Journey Overland from Independence, Missouri to Hangtown (Placerville), California, in the Spring of 1850, with a Letter From the Diggings in October of the Same Year and an Account of a Journey from New York to California, via Panama, in 1862, Capture by the Confederate Raider Alabama, Etc., and a Visit to the Nevada Silver Mining District in 1863*. Boston: Little, Brown, and company, 1927.

Rolle, Andrew F. *California: a History*. New York: Crowell, 1963.

Schlappi, Jane, and Marilyn Ferguson. *A Walking Tour of Historic Placerville, 1848-1874*. Placerville: Heritage Association of El Dorado, 1973.

Seidman, Laurence Ivan, 1925-. *The Fools of '49: The California Gold Rush, 1848-1856*. New York: Knopf: distributed by Random House, 1976.

Sioli, Paolo. *Historical Souvenir of El Dorado County California: with Illustrations and Biographical Sketches of Its Prominent Men & Pioneers*. Oakland, Cal.: Paolo Siolo, Publishers, 1883.

Williams, Annie Keeler, 1869-, and George W. Keeler. *Early California Gold Rush Days*. Sunland, Calif.: A.K. Williams, 1948.

Winkler, Jack R. *Old Hangtown: A History of Placerville, California from 1848 through 1856*. Placerville: JRW Press, 2000

NEWSPAPER ARTICLES USED IN RESEARCH

Daily Alta California ("New Diggings at Placerville"), Apr. 18th, 1850

Daily Alta California ("Sacramento Intelligence" [From the *Times*, Aug. 19]), Aug. 22nd, 1850

Marysville Daily Herald ("Mining Intelligence"), Oct. 8th, 1850

Daily Alta California ("Mr. Wilson's Correspondence"), Oct. 9th, 1850

Sacramento Transcript ("Rogues in the Mines"), Oct. 30th, 1850

Daily Alta California ("Judge Lynch"), Oct. 13th, 1850

Sacramento Transcript ("Interesting from the Diggings"), Dec. 16th, 1850

Sacramento Transcript ("Rich Diggings Discovered"), Apr. 30th, 1851

Sacramento Daily Union ("Indian Murder in El Dorado County!"), May 13, 1851

Sacramento Transcript ("Hurrah for Placerville Again") May 14th, 1851

Daily Alta California ("Sacramento News" [per Gregory's Express]), Jun. 8th, 1852

The Placerville Herald ("The Miner's Ten Commandments"), c.1853

Georgetown News ("Midnight Meditations" [To the Bard of Lindenwood These Lines Are Inscribed]), Sep. 5th, 1855

Sacramento Daily Union ("California Indian Chiefs"), Jan. 31st 1857

Los Angeles Star ("Public Meeting—Address by Gov. Weller"), Sep. 26th, 1857

Stockton Independent ("Frazer River a Humbug"), Jul. 10th, 1858

Daily Alta California ("Reminiscenses of the California Gold Mines in 1848"), Jul. 18th, 1858

Sacramento Daily Union ("Political Meeting at Placerville"), Aug. 18th, 1862

Sacramento Daily Union ("Letter from Placerville" [Occasional Correspondence of the Record-Union]: Early History of Hangtown; The Vigilantes at Work; Old Times; Personal Recollections; Distinguished Citizens), Mar. 6th, 1875

Sacramento Daily Union ("Early Days"), Apr. 21st, 1880

Sacramento Daily Union ("The True Story of 'Hangtown'"), Apr. 24th, 1880

Santa Cruz Weekly Sentinel ("How It Was That Placerville Came to Be Known as Hangtown"), May 8th, 1880

Sacramento Daily Union ("Hangtown"), May 10th, 1880

Daily Alta California ("Pictures of Pioneer Life"), Aug. 23rd, 1885

Sacramento Daily Union ("The First Hotel"), May 26th, 1888

Sacramento Daily Union ("Hangtown History Again Recounted"),
May 28th, 1922

The Mountain Democrat ("A History of Old Hangtown Written in the Year
1862"), Sep. 4th, 1925

The Mountain Democrat ("'Hangtown' as Camp's Nick-Name Traced to 2
Different Lynchings: One Authority States Word Originated in Execu-
tion of Cabin Robbers; Another Connects Death of 'Irish Dick' with
Origin"), Feb 28th, 1930

Calexico Chronicle ("Facts about Counties in California"), Jan. 10th, 1931

The Mountain Democrat ("Placerville, Past and Present" [A Pioneer's
Daughter]), Jan. 3rd, 1935; reprinted from Pony Express Courier

The Mountain Democrat ("Inn Burned: Tree Shown in Picture of Old Hotel
May Be Historic"), Jul. 30th, 1936

Geyserville Press ("Historical Sidelights of California Cities"), Dec. 3rd, 1943

The Placerville Times ("A Bit of Hangtown History"), Aug. 20th, 1947

The Prospector ("1850 Print Gives Name of First Hotel"), Jan. 1950

Healdsburg Tribune ("California Stagecoach Days"), Feb. 8th, 1973

Sierra Heritage ("They Cut Down the 'Old Hang Tree'"), Sep. 1986

The Mountain Democrat ("Hangman's Tree"), Aug. 7th, 1992

The Mountain Democrat ("Why Do You Think It's Called Hangtown?"), Feb. 21st, 1994

The Mountain Democrat ("Waterin' Hole with a Past: Hangman's Tree Specializes in All Sorts of Spirits"), Jul. 24th, 1995

The Mountain Democrat ("The Hangman's Tree in Hangtown, Part 1: The Hangings"), Jan 15th, 1999; "Part 2: California's Forced to Take Law in Its Own Hands," Jan. 22nd, 1999; "Part 3: Hangman's Tree Passes Its 150th Birthday Under a Cloud"), Jan 25th, 1999

The Mountain Democrat ("Hangtown Revisited: Franklin Street Account"), Nov. 30th, 2001

The Mountain Democrat ("Placerville and Vicinity, Part 17: The Sporting Men of Hangtown"), Jan. 11th, 2002)

The Mountain Democrat ("'Irish Dick' Gets Launched into Eternity at End of Hangman's Tree Noose"), Jun 20th, 2002

RELICS COURTESY OF THE EL DORADO HISTORICAL MUSEUM

California Historical Society Quarterly, Vol. 7 (c/o the CA. Historical Society)

"Hangtown," a research paper by Marc Johnson, Nov. 1986 (c/o the Mountain-Tallman Museum)

Minutes of the Court of Sessions for Jan. 14th, 1853 (c/o the Huntington Library)

SPECIAL THANKS

A final shoutout to the El Dorado Historical Museum for granting access to valuable records and relics about the history of Hangtown, California (now called Placerville), such as a photocopy of the letter from J. Studebaker Johnson (of automobile fame), who spent time in the diggings.

Dear Sirs,

I thought you might be interested in keeping the enclosed. It was given to me by my grandfather many years ago. The name was John M. Studebaker, who passed away in 1908.

– J.S. Johnson

The enclosed included a poem, "The Hang Town Tree, 1853," (used at the end of this novel), which was also accompanied by a typed note from John Mohler Studebaker that reads:

Joe Fisher. An old South Bender, author of the above, who crossed the plains with me in 1853. I helped to cut this tree and carried brick and mortar to build a building for Bruce Herrick.

Let us not judge them too harshly for those were the rough days of the great gold rush.

ABOUT THE AUTHOR

Michael Bailey is a recipient of the Bram Stoker Award (and nine-time nominee), a multiple recipient of the Benjamin Franklin Award, a five-time Shirley Jackson Award nominee, and has an insane number of other accolades.

Born in Hangtown, California, he has since authored novels, novellas, novelettes, and fiction & poetry collections. Recent work includes *Agatha's Barn*, a tie-in novella to Josh Malerman's *Carpenter's Farm*, a collaborative novella with Erinn L. Kemper called *The Call of the Void*, and *Sifting the Ashes*, a collaborative poetry collection with Marge Simon.

He runs the small press Written Backwards and has edited and published numerous anthologies, such as *The Library of the Dead*, the *Chiral Mad* series, *Miscreations: Gods, Monstrosities & Other Horrors*, and *You, Human*.

Currently living in Costa Rica, he is rebuilding his life after surviving one of the most catastrophic wildfires in California history, which is explored in his memoir *Seven Minutes*. Find him online at nettirw.com, or @nettirw in most places.

For a full list of published books by the author, see the bibliography that follows.

NOVELS

Palindrome Hannah

Phoenix Rose

Psychotropic Dragon

NOVELLAS

Agatha's Barn

The Call of the Void
(with Erinn L. Kemper)

NOVELETTES

Our Children, Our Teachers

COLLECTIONS

Scales and Petals

Inkblots and Blood Spots

Oversight

The Impossible Weight of Life

Sifting the Ashes
(poetry with Marge Simon)

NONFICTION

Righting Writing

ANTHOLOGIES

Pellucid Lunacy

Chiral Mad

Chiral Mad 2

Qualia Nous

The Library of the Dead

Chiral Mad 3

You, Human

Adam's Ladder
(with Darren Speegle)

Chiral Mad 4: An Anthology of Collaborations
(with Lucy A. Snyder)

Miscreations: Gods, Monstrosities & Other Horrors
(with Doug Murano)

Prisms
(with Darren Speegle)

Chiral Mad 5

www.ingramcontent.com/pod-product-compliance
Lightning Source LLC
Chambersburg PA
CBHW020058310726

48970CB00002B/373